THE WEDDING

THE WEDDING

Yann Queffélec

Translated by
Linda Coverdale

An Alison Press Book
Secker & Warburg · London

First published in England 1988 by
The Alison Press/Martin Secker & Warburg Limited
54 Poland Street, London w1v 3df

British Library Cataloguing in Publication Data
Queffélec, Yann
    The wedding
    I. Title   II. Les noces barbares, *English*
    843'.914 [F]   PQ2677.U3/

ISBN 0 436 39490 1

Printed and bound in Great Britain
by St. Edmundsbury Press,
Bury St. Edmunds,
Suffolk

For Françoise Verny

For Marie-Rose and for Edgar

Part One

Chapter One

The water was getting cold. Stepping out of the bath Nicole reached for a towel and dried herself slowly. The smell of freshly baked bread, mingling with the sweet scents of the countryside, put her in a languid mood. Furtively, she tried on her mother's black shoes, and pulled a face. They were a bit too big, but made her look taller. Then she caught sight of herself in the oval mirror, cloudy with steam, and smiled. She was thirteen years old, almost fourteen, but she looked eighteen with a prematurely ripe body, red lips, almond-shaped blue eyes and a fiery mass of reddish-blonde hair tumbling about her shoulders. She spent an hour every day trying to bring the flames under control.

The door slammed downstairs: Mama had just gone out. She and Papa would be busy at the bakery until nearly midnight. Nicole felt a twinge of guilt as she thought of the trick she was playing on them—and on a Sunday, too! She would definitely go to confession tomorrow. But what to confess? She had hardly lied at all. She really *was* going to spend the night with Nanette, her grown-up cousin, who was very much on her own now that Bernard had left her.

Of course, she was going to meet someone first . . .

She had lied to Nanette, too. But not really badly! She had mentioned a little family get-together at the house of some Parisians, a birthday party to which Will—the American from Arzac—had also been invited. He was going to drop her at Nanette's well before midnight.

3

Nicole stretched luxuriously. It was nice thinking about Will with his dancing green eyes flecked with gold. It was nice to be getting ready to go out. She let her imagination zoom. Will at the Bastille Day dance, inviting her on to the dance-floor under the brightly coloured lanterns for the most beautiful tango in the world. Will on the dunes and their first kiss. She remembered the rustle of the wind through the pines behind them, the mild night decked out in stars and the lights twinkling down by the sea.

The trouble she had gone to, trying to look her best! The night before, using the heat as an excuse, she had slept in the attic on a mattress. In fact, she had wanted to get started early on her preparations. She checked her lipstick. It was one of Mama's old ones fished out of the wastepaper basket. A lucky find! At school, if you wanted a little colour for your mouth, you had to press your moistened lips against the dahlias on the wallpaper. Sleepless with anticipation, dreaming about Will's enchanting green eyes, she prepared herself carefully, sweetened her breath with a liquorice pastille, dilated the pupils of her eyes with lemon juice and brushed her teeth with powdered charcoal. Nanette had recommended this. Finally, she starched and ironed the flounces of her white muslin dress with its square neckline.

She had met Will two months ago at the Fairway, a waterfront bar that had dancing in the afternoons. It was Midsummer Day and her parents thought she had gone to the beach. 'I'm an American serviceman, a pilot, may I sit down?' He had very black hair, combed straight back without a parting. She ordered a fizzy lemonade, he asked for a beer. He smiled and stared at her, ignoring Marie-Jo who left in a huff. 'You're very pretty,' he said, 'we can be friends if you like.'

Dazzled by his green eyes, she mumbled: 'It's late, I have to go home.' Will had driven her halfway back to the bakery in his Jeep. It was not until the next day that he kissed her.

The following week, he came to the shop and introduced himself to her parents. Every other day he wanted to pick up a hundred loaves of bread for the base at Arzac on the coast. Every other day he arrived, just before closing time, and was impeccably polite and radiant. He behaved as if loading bread into his Jeep was his greatest pleasure. He chatted to Madame Blanchard, teased Nicole in a friendly way, went to the bakery to say hello to her father and, as time passed, he began staying to dinner. Nicole was allowed to accompany him back to the main road, at the top of their street. From there you could see the lighthouse beams when the sun went down. Her parents never dreamt that this pleasant young man, who was at least twenty years old and treated Nicole like a sister, would cover their little girl—who was still only a child to them—with passionate kisses.

He called her Love, he called her Amour, he called her Lovamour, entwining their names in hearts drawn on the sand. Gazing into her eyes he said: 'Don't be afraid, come close to me.'

Nicole, frightened by his big hands, said: 'No, Will, I swore not to until I marry.'

One evening he was on edge, almost nasty. When this made her more nervous than usual he said: 'It's finished, Lovamour, I'm going back to America on Monday morning.'

'But that's in two days!'

'I want to get married, Lovamour, I want to marry you.'

'I'm too young,' she lied, 'I'm only fifteen.'

'It doesn't matter. I'll come back later to get you.'

Nicole had cried all night. It was too awful, Will, whom she would love for ever was leaving. The American base was being shut down, how stupid! Of course he had promised to marry her . . . The next day, he came to say goodbye to the Blanchards with his arms piled high with flowers and bottles of sparkling wine. 'I want to speak to Madame and to Monsieur as well.' Covered with flour,

5

the baker came to the room at the back of the shop. 'I want to say something, but it's difficult in French.' He had a ranch in Michigan, not too far from Lake Michigan itself, it was hard work, some seasons the crops were poor or the animals fell ill or insects got into the corn, but anyway he had finished with the Air Force, he was going home. The thing was that he wanted to get married. He was hoping that some time in the future he would be able to marry Nicole. Her parents looked at each other in astonishment, wondering whether to laugh or cry. Nicole had turned the colour of the pimentos drying on the wall. Madame Blanchard thought to herself: She's very young, almost a child, but an American . . . and a rich one. We'll have to think about it! Her father, after a deep sigh, had expressed her thoughts: 'Well now, we'll see how things go . . . We'll just have to see how things go.'

Her mother opened a packet of lady-fingers. Will and her parents raised their glasses of wine to each other. Nicole was allowed to have the watered-down dregs, and then a fizzy lemonade.

After dinner, the young couple went to look at the light-houses for the last time. Nicole knew them all. 'That's Saint-Nicolas . . . and the red light in the distance is Cordouan. Over there, that twinkling light is a buoy marking a wreck.' That night her mind was not on the lights, and the big hands were groping for her body: she had to fight against those fingers and all those kisses which made her head spin.

'Tomorrow'll be our last evening, Lovamour. There's a party at the base. D'you want to come?'

'I don't know, Will. I'll have to ask my mother.'

'No, whatever you do, don't talk to her. I'll pick you up here at nine o'clock. Next year, the two of us'll get married at my ranch . . .'

Why did Mama keep her scent locked up? It was aggravating! There was nothing on the shelf but the family bottle

6

of egg-shampoo, vanilla-scented talcum powder, brilliantine, caustic soda, and her father's aftershave: oil of jasmine diluted with alcohol. It was quite strong, but on her skin, perhaps . . . she rubbed a few drops behind her ears, then wound up sprinkling it all over her body, her feet and her cotton handkerchief. Then she filled the half-empty bottle with tap-water and was aghast to see that the aftershave floated to the top.

The clock downstairs struck a quarter past eight: she had no time to dawdle, but lightheartedly went on doing so, however, lingering over the selection of her undies from a whole drawerful, all very dainty and quite proper. Then it was time to put on the dress, and she almost lost her nerve: it was close-fitting and a little too tight round the waist. Apart from that, the effect was charming. Will would be proud of her as he introduced her to his friends. She would borrow one of Mama's handbags on the sly— it would make her look more refined.

Nicole did not see anyone as she went out through the courtyard, hurrying past the apparently empty bakery. The sun was still high over the horizon in a blazing blue sky. She crossed the ploughed fields, keeping close to the hedge to avoid the prying eyes of Simone and Marie-Jo. Those two had been eating their hearts out ever since she had begun parading round the beach with the American pilot. When she mentioned marriage, they were green with envy! 'I'll write to you from Michigan,' she had promised.

Her heart pounding, Nicole paused in the shade before reaching the crossroads. Taking the lipstick out of Mama's handbag, she checked her make-up once more. The pocket-mirror slipped from her fingers and shattered.

Will was already waiting for her in his Jeep, watching her arrive with a cunning look on his face. He did not say a word about her dress, or pay her a single compliment. Nicole noticed a bottle between his knees.

Accelerating like a maniac, he cried: 'It's party time tonight!' He drove at breakneck speed along the bumpy road, aiming for the puddles, sideswiping the pines, cutting across the dunes and laughing his head off.

'Will, you've been drinking!' Nicole was horrified. The engine shrieked and the wheels splashed mud. The jolts were going to ruin her pretty dress and make her sick. She clung to her seat and begged, 'Don't go so fast, Will, you're going too fast!'

'No, darling, faster and faster!' he answered, pointing to the black clouds looming in the west, and grabbing the bottle to take another swig.

When they arrived, a few stray drops from a distant thunderstorm spattered on to the dry earth. A grinning orderly raised the barrier for them, then went back to catching raindrops on his tongue, tilting his face towards the sky.

The ranch and El Dorado were a myth. William Schneider was a night-watchman at a car park in the Bronx. He had a police record for petty theft and his wife scrubbed floors. Their son Terry was two years old.

Behind its barbed-wire fence, the camp at Arzac consisted of some huts facing the sea, a radio antenna, and a pole flying the American flag. A hen-house was tucked under a cliff and muffled clucking was sometimes heard. There was no one in sight: most of the occupants had left for home the day before. A few men had stayed behind to settle the last accounts with French suppliers.

'Here we are . . .'

They went into a room overlooking the sea. The walls and floor were of raw wood, and the wind rattled the corrugated iron roof. At the far end, draped in front of a gas stove propped up on logs, some bathing suits and shorts were drying on a line. Beer crates flanked a grey metal locker. Beneath a bare lightbulb hanging from the ceiling, beer bottles cluttered a Formica table striped with burns from cigarette butts. There were ammunition cases for chairs. The sea could be heard pounding on the cliff.

8

Will had just turned on a gramophone, the arm set to release the plaintive voice of Frank Sinatra.

His green eyes fed greedily on Nicole, gleaming with such naked desire that she kept her arms crossed over her breasts. He let out a wolf-whistle as the last rays of the sunset broke through the storm-clouds, shining over the window-sill to light Nicole's hair with a violet glow.

'Sit down, darling, don't be scared.'

In a daze, she hesitated in front of the ammunition case, thinking of her crumpled dress.

'Sit on the bed. You must sit on the bed, darling. Are you thirsty?'

'No thank you Will . . . What about your friends? Where are they?' Sitting on the very edge of the mattress, she was thrown into a panic by the pictures of naked women tacked up all over the wall.

'My friends are coming, darling, we're having a party! They'll all be here.' Will had taken a bottle of whisky from the locker and was gulping it down noisily.

'Oh no, Will, please don't drink any more!'

'I'll drink if I want to and you will too, darling, you'll drink with me.' He laughed obscenely and began swivelling his hips. 'And afterwards, we're going to fuck. Scared?' He had grabbed her roughly and was sputtering into her face, showing the whites of his eyes. 'Drink!' he shouted.

Catching hold of her suddenly by the scruff of the neck, he tried to tip the bottle into her mouth. She struggled so violently from rage and fear that her dress was drenched in alcohol. She ran screaming towards the door and was just turning the knob when he grabbed her hair, pulled her backwards and sent her flying on to the bed. The dress slipped up round her navel. She shrieked even louder, and he slapped her. 'You're gonna shut up and drink.' He poured whisky all over her, from head to toe. Choking, she tried to claw her way off the bed. 'You'd better stop screaming, or else . . .' He flicked his cigarette-lighter. With bulging eyes Nicole watched the flame's reflection glitter on her whisky-sodden hair. Will sneered at her. His free hand wandered over her terrified body. 'You've wet your pants, darling,' he murmured in a sugary voice, winking at her. 'I'll take them back to New York . . . as a souvenir.' His green eyes grew cold and leaden. 'Take them off!'

She was paralysed with shame.

'Off!' he thundered, ripping out a hank of her hair and setting it on fire.

He smiled smugly, breathing heavily while he watched the little girl obey him. Picking up the panties, which had fallen between the black shoes, he waved them like a scalp towards the light, then stuffed them carelessly into his trunk. 'Now we can fuck, darling! My wife always wants to fuck.'

He fetched another bottle of whisky from the locker and pulled the cork out with his teeth. She tried to run, but staggered in her terror and fell, scraping her knees. He sent her spinning with his foot, then dropped to all fours crouching over her and panting. Bruising her tightly closed lips, he forced her to drink, knocking the mouth of the bottle against her teeth and clowning around whenever she gagged.

'No, Will, no,' she managed to moan once more, but those were the last words she spoke that night. Will unbuttoned his flies and tore into her with a single thrust, deaf to her sobs and cries of pain. Unable to come, he cursed and beat her. Nicole lay whimpering beneath him, slack and almost unconscious, her body and mouth bleeding. He dragged her to the bed, his trousers down around his ankles—'Little French darling'—he went over to the door and shouted into the gathering darkness: 'Come on, guys, she's ready!' Then he trampled at his trousers furiously to get them off, knocked back another gulp of whisky and returned to his prey on the bed.

A door slammed outside. Aldo and Sam had been drinking in the neighbouring block, waiting for Will's signal.

From time to time they had peered in through the window.

Aldo was a pot-bellied hulk of Chilean origin: the sandy-haired youngster named Sam was a minister's son.

'My friends,' announced Will. 'Party time, darling.'

He stood her up on her feet, but she collapsed with a moan. Sam held her up with one arm round her waist while he grubbed around under her dress with the other, laughing crudely. Will grabbed the embroidered flounces and pulled them up savagely, snapping the belt and tearing off the buttons. Only the sleeves and the collar were still in place. 'Just like a football game,' he sneered, and after ripping off the dress with a stupid snarl, as if he were skinning a rabbit, began to laugh hysterically.

Then everything was quiet for a moment. The three men leered at their naked and trembling victim as if she was a hard-won prize. The unhooked bra hung from a torn strap. One of Mama's shoes had ended up under the bed. Nicole huddled there in tears, trying to cover herself with her arms.

'Lovely,' said Aldo hoarsely, as his big hairy hand slid the scrap of bra down her bruised arm to get a better view. 'Lovely.' He unbuckled his belt. 'There,' he told Sam pointing at the table.

He raped her among the playing cards and cigarette butts, towering over her as she lay across the table. When she instinctively fought back, thrashing her head from side to side and trying to bite, he got excited: 'Yeah, come on, girl, come on!' Every time she opened her mouth, Will poured whisky into it. From time to time he tore out locks of her hair to watch them burn.

They took turns violating her, fighting over the privilege of butchering her virginity. Aldo sodomized her, pulling her hair about like the mane of a stubborn mare. On his gleaming, sweaty chest sprouted a forest of hair where a gold crucifix swung like a pendulum between his nipples, flinging large drops of sweat down on the unconscious girl.

Sam was left as voyeur. At first, as soon as the other two had taken a break to drink and catch their breath, he rushed in frantically, but he soon got over-excited, he had to settle for gaping at the horrendous assaults of the Chilean, who amused himself, still standing over her, by picking up the table where he had her pinned down and walking round the room. Will, who was more jittery, poured beer over Nicole and suggested that the two of them should take her: 'like a sandwich.'

'Go to sleep, baby,' said Aldo finally, 'We're tired.'

Grabbing Nicole round the waist, he threw her across the room on to the camp bed. Then he gathered up the scattered cards and came back to sit at the table, adjusting his trousers wearily.

Will had collapsed in a corner among the empty bottles. He was about to pass out when a rooster crowed, shattering the night. 'That shit bird,' he muttered, tapping his forehead as he disappeared outside, stark naked.

He was back in a minute with the poor bird which flapped its clipped wings in outrage, beating the air with its claws and spitting out its cock-a-doodle-doo in spite of the fist wrapped round its neck. 'No,' said Aldo when Will made as if to perch the bird on Nicole, who lay unmoving across the bed. Turning away, Will calmly strangled it, watching the pink tongue vibrate and the light in the eye fade under the cockscomb at half-mast. He waited until a red flood welled up in the wide-open beak before relaxing his grip. Armed with a saucepan, he went back outside, returning this time with some eggs. With his thumb he cracked one in the air over Nicole so that it landed between her breasts. Then he rustled up an omelette he shared with Aldo, eating in silence from a frying pan without a handle. The Chilean mopped up the grease with his fingers.

By the early morning light, all violence had vanished, leaving only a vague stupor uniting the three men and their victim. The sea was quiet. The gramophone crackled faintly as the record spun round and round. A sour, morning-after stench hung in the air. Time stood still and each one of them seemed sunk into the torpors preceding birth, memory or madness. Aldo was sprawled over the table, one arm dangling. Will had collapsed on the floor near Sam, who was curled up like a dog.

One shoe still on her foot, her mouth and eyes half open, Nicole stared unseeingly at the rusted metal roof.

After a while Sam came over to fondle her. 'Blood,' he murmured in a dull voice, and again: 'Blood!' He seemed ecstatic, turning his hand over and over under the light as if the blood from the rape were pure gold. He kissed his fingers, nodded his head blissfully, said 'Blood' once more, then decided to paint himself like an Indian with this providential elixir. Catching sight of the pair of panties in the tin trunk, he pulled them over his head as a cap, and like a Sioux driven crazy by the beat of a tom-tom, began parading round the table chanting: 'Whisky ... Beer ... Sandwich ... Blood ...' in a nasal twang. Every time Sam said 'Blood,' Aldo said: 'Coca-Cola hoo hoo,' under his breath. Will brought out his harmonica to accompany them.

A grim little dawn was creeping over the walls when Sam's nerve gave out. He grabbed the neck of a scotch bottle and clobbered the still-glowing lightbulb with a backhanded swipe. There was a brief explosion and sparks streaked to the floor.

'It's not true,' Sam began to snivel, holding his head in his hands, 'no, no,' and he moved restlessly about the room, throwing on clothes at random from those strewn on the floor. He went outside, still repeating: 'No, no, not true, no ...' Will mimicked the whine of his lament on the harmonica.

Sam came back with a bowl of fresh water, a towel, and a thermos of coffee. Timidly he began to wash the child, who took the towel from him and held it over her body. She accepted the coffee, tried to drink, but began vomiting

13

in tiny bitter spasms that did not relieve the knot in her stomach. Sam collected Nicole's things, the handbag, the missing shoe, the panties off his head, and helped the girl cover herself with her dress—its torn flounces and missing buttons meant that he had to fasten it by knotting the material together.

'I'll take you back, come on . . .'

With a haggard look she burst into dry sobs, moving her lips soundlessly. Staggering, she collapsed against Sam, who hugged her with frantic puritanism. He was stone cold sober now. They were about to leave when they heard a loud grunt behind them.

'She's mine,' muttered Will, lowering his head like a bull about to charge. He smacked Sam with the dead rooster, then finished him off with a knee to the groin. Closing in on Nicole, he slammed her harshly against the wall. The green eyes looked as dead as mud. 'Money,' he babbled, grabbing her handbag, 'money for you, my little slut!' Out of her purse fell a photograph of Nicole in a bathing suit. It was inscribed: 'To Will—Yours for ever.'

She left on foot in a fine drizzle, saw no one at the gate, and started plodding across the dunes in a fog. It's not far, it's just over there. A stretch of sand, a bit of road, and that's it. A lock of damp hair hung down over her nose. She was shivering and bleeding as she tramped along without feeling anything at all. The black shoes were definitely difficult to walk in. Arriving at Nanette's, she thought that she was tired and that a piping hot croissant would be nice. She went through the quiet little garden and round the corner of the house, found the key in its niche, opened the door, took off her shoes and groped her way upstairs. A glassy daylight bathed her room. She put her purse down on the fluffy eiderdown of the big bed, then looked around automatically. That was when she saw herself in the wardrobe mirror. There was blood all down her legs, her dress was in shreds, her hair in matted clumps, her mouth swollen, her eyes crazed with horror. As memory flooded back in short bursts, she tottered towards the staircase, tripped over a step, and began shaking the banister howling: 'Nanette, Nanette, Nanette, Nanette, Nanette . . .'

Chapter Two

Ludovic was a long-limbed little boy with an emaciated face. He had sloping shoulders, muscular arms and light brown hair cut very short by Madame Blanchard, who was afraid of lice. His eyes were inordinately green. His glances darted about like those of a beast at bay.

In the seven years he had been living on the coast, Ludovic had never seen the sea. He listened to it. What he saw from his attic window, however, was the courtyard, the bakery, and beyond them the monotonous pine trees, shrouded in morning fog. The sound of the sea could be heard roaring or murmuring day and night. In bad weather it was so loud that it even drowned out the baker's snoring. The child would gladly have gone to look at the sea but the door was kept locked.

When Monsieur Blanchard crossed the courtyard, carrying the steaming round loaves from the bakery to the shop, the smell of hot bread wafted up to Ludovic. Each morning, on the floor under the dormer window—even in his hair—he harvested a fine white powder with a fleeting taste.

Downstairs the shop-bell never stopped ringing. At night, breaking the silence, he would hear the music of soup spoons at the supper table, and all too often the shrill cries of the women punctuated by the baker's furious outbursts.

His meals were brought up to him once a day late in the afternoon. Clear soup with tapioca, turnips, and the grey mullet Monsieur Blanchard caught in the harbour, at the end of a pier where the housewives dumped their slops. He never got bread, not even stale crusts. Nicole had withheld her milk: the baker withheld his bread.

Madame Blanchard and her daughter took it in turn to deal with him. One with grey hair, one with hair the colour of bread. They did not talk to him so he never talked. But voices could be heard through the attic floor, words were roughed out in his memory as time passed and the muddled signs and sounds eventually became familiar. When the door closed, Ludovic threw himself on his food and ate with his fingers.

Monsieur Blanchard never came up to the attic. One morning when he was leaving the bakery, his eyes met those of the youngster lying in wait for the smell of hot bread. The man spat and shook his head with rage. That same night there was pandemonium downstairs. The father and mother cursed their daughter, and she cursed God. Suddenly the door burst open, revealing the two furious women, the mother dragging her daughter by the hair: 'You're going to put this on him, slut! That's what he deserves, your Yank!'

'Never!' sobbed Nicole.

'Then drop dead!' screeched her mother, shoving her out of the room. And it was she who savagely undressed Ludo then decked him out in a torn dress with dirty flounces that hung down round his calves.

He never wore anything but girl's clothes, apart from some men's underpants in coarse blue cotton that had been taken in at the waist. The rubber sandals on his naked feet would not fasten anymore. He had a daily jug of water for washing and a small dressing-table with a basin mounted on pivots, which he managed to force off its track. A shard of mirror remained on one of the panels. He twisted his face round in front of it, never seeing more than a little bit at a time. The green eyes fascinated him. Then one day the baker's wife finished off the scrap of mirror with a poker.

He relieved himself in a box of sand, and sometimes next to it, as a form of protest. Madame Blanchard would say: 'If that isn't disgusting!' before twisting his ear and forcing him to kiss the filth. The guilty boy begged for forgiveness on his knees.

In the winter he slept in the bottom of the wardrobe muffled up in a military overcoat beneath the clothes on hangers. In the evening his shadow walked round with him. He drove himself crazy trying to catch it. In pleasant weather he spread out some flour sacks on the floor and lay near the open window, listening to the sea, sniffing the smell of the night air, hearing the night itself then falling asleep rolled up in the flannel cover from an ironing-board, unconsciously putting his second finger on his anus. He was not afraid of the dark, but the slightest thing disturbed his sleep. A trickle of saliva at the corner of his mouth made him cry. If his hand brushed his arm, he let out screams of horror, immediately hearing a flurry of blows coming from the ceiling below. Hunger turned his imagination over to the idle fancies of insomnia. Sometimes in his sleep he ground his teeth so loudly that Monsieur Blanchard thought his walls were being devoured by weevils.

Ludovic preferred to whisper rather than talk, because the normal tone of his voice frightened him. But at night, other people's voices pounded in his head, the words rattling around like hailstones:

The kid has to learn, he has to go to school . . . you can't just let him rot in the attic . . . he's not really an idiot . . . Mama said he was born all by himself . . . I could take him back with me for a few days, if you like . . . what business is it of your mother's, it's not his fault . . . you just have to let time go by . . . don't you think he's sweet . . . you'll end up getting fond of him, just wait . . .

One night he attacked the door and kicked it to pieces.

The elder Blanchards had considerable trouble subduing this somnambulistic rebel who seemed impervious to beatings. The next day, the child watched in fascination as the master of the house repaired the door without saying a single word.

Cousin Nanette tried to persuade her aunt to send him to live with her as a boarder. Nanette had a house and some land outside the village. She was allowed to visit Ludo once a week, to talk to him and make him talk, to teach him how to count on his fingers and to ask if Mama Nicole was nice to him or if he liked to have his face washed (you dirty piggy!) and she told him proper little stories about Baby Jesus, the Gauls, the kings of France and the various guilds, asking suddenly if he remembered all the good times they had had together not so long ago. Ludo never answered.

After Nanette had gone, the baker's wife confiscated the little cars and other presents she brought—so he would not choke on them, Madame Blanchard said.

To fill his empty days he took advantage of all the broken-down treasures surrounding him—a rickety armchair, baskets with holes in them, a sewing machine and a gas mask that he smashed up just a little bit more with almost sensual pleasure. When he was sad he plucked out his eyebrows.

Up among the roof-beams he had made a cave of sackcloth conducive to forgetfulness. A rope provided access. He spent entire afternoons settled comfortably up there, oblivious of the passing of time, fiddling away at sunproofing his darkness.

For company he watched spiders spin their webs to trap flying prey fooled by the back-lighting. He liked to spy on the spiders as they rushed in for the kill. The agony of their victims showed by only a slight flutter of wings. One August evening, he heard noises in the gaping fireplace, stuck his hand up the chimney without thinking, and began to scream: a barn-owl had grabbed his wrist with its beak and claws. Terrified by his cries, it flew up among the rafters. Ludo gazed at his arm and saw a star-shaped wound. Above his head perched a bird the colour of shadows and as silent as the moon.

Fever laid the child low for an entire week, giving him nightmares in which the soldier's overcoat came rumbling out of the wardrobe at him with wide-open arms. He had no appetite for mullet any more. He wore himself out from daybreak on, staring at the half-closed eyes of the owl, which seemed to turn to stone at the first ray of light. It hunted at night, returning in the morning with scraps of mice whose grinning teeth Ludo examined while the bird was away. After a month of taciturn harmony between child and animal, the barn owl disappeared.

Ludo knew the view and the sounds by heart, the roof of the bakery, the road leading past the bakery to the ploughed fields, the barking of dogs, the precise colour of the pines as they varied from month to month, the restless sky smelling of resin or a pungent odour like burning. When there were storms, a stream rushed through the courtyard. He had the impression, quite often, that the door was about to open, that there was someone behind it keeping an eye on him through gaps in the wood. Then he forgot about it.

He lived without electric light, at the mercy of the sun, which did not last long enough in winter. In summer the heat from the roof exhausted him, but he loved the blue sky, the countryside in flower, the magic of long, sweet evenings, the red splash of the Virginia creeper on the walls of the bakery, and the iridescent banquet of constellations at night.

Madame Blanchard put him to work when he was five years old.

She would burst in on him early in the morning with a basin of potatoes to peel or with some peas to shell. On rainy days, loads of wet washing were brought in for him to hang out to dry on a line that cut his territory in two. Lost in his own thoughts, he clipped on the clothes pegs and watched the rose-coloured corsets of his torturer drip on to old newspapers. He knew everyone's under-clothes at a glance, dressed himself up in them and sucked on them like nipples. When the weather was fine he was thrilled to see them flapping in the wind down in the courtyard, like old friends waving to him from afar.

One wintry evening he noticed a light gleaming through the floor. He scraped the dust from between the boards with his comb, put his eye to the gap, and was surprised to discover the redhead downstairs, her hands joined at the side of a bed with the coverlet turned down. He blinked his eyes when he realized that she was not wearing anything at all, then looked at her more closely. From that moment on, Ludo spied on his mother and was furious when she moved to a blind-spot. He was mournful as he looked at the softness of her naked body.

God knows, she had tried to miscarry him. All the charms and all the old wives' tales: nettle vinegar, onion peelings, the taproots of black radishes on a moonless night. She had even cut herself on a soup spoon trying to give herself an abortion. 'Hold your arms up,' said her mother, 'keep them up, let the baby strangle itself on the cord.' She raised her arms as high as possible, a hundred times a day and a hundred times a night, her hands clenched round the bed-posts to hasten the hanging. Her nightmares were haunted by little pink gallows.

'Her fingers are still ink-stained from school,' her father grumbled, 'and here she is pregnant with a good-for-nothing in her belly. The mayor and all the village are busy snickering that it only goes to show she was asking for it. And soon it's the bun in her oven they'll be craning their necks to see! And with the ink still wet on her fingers!'

21

'Let him peg out,' raged the mother, 'he's got to die! God Almighty won't let this happen. That we should be the laughing-stock of the neighbourhood . . . that the bread I mark with the sign of the cross every day should be unclean and tainted with sins, the sins of my own daughter! Soon the neighbours will know she's in the family way and they'll point the finger of scorn at my house.'

Nicole did not go back to school at the beginning of term. 'She's helping me in the shop at the moment . . .' said her mother. But she did not help her even for a month. She stayed upstairs, embittered by the customers' roving eyes already searching under her smock for the tell-tale swelling. Alone in her room, she pressed down hard on her abdomen with the bull's sinew her mother had fetched from the attic to make her confess—'Go on, say it, slut! Tell your mother you're a slut!' It was like a second rape on top of the first one, this time with a whip. Forcing herself to fast, she had lost weight at first, and thanked God, thinking she was saved. Then one day she began to vomit. The child was there after all. Waste away as she might, the child was blossoming. It was maddening, this body inside her own, these two hearts walled in together, this blind duel within her very blood. She cursed the intruder, cursed herself, beat her distended skin, wept over her beautiful breasts turned into milk-jugs . . . Until the very end she spent her nights swearing, with five-kilo weights on her stomach, or mummified in wet crêpe bandages pulled so tight that she felt faint.

He was born one Sunday evening at the end of March, after the angelus bell: it had just stopped raining. The baker's wife cursed Nicole as she delivered him, cut the cord with a straight razor, and went to inform Monsieur Blanchard, who had gone fishing in the harbour.

'It's a boy, René, you must go and see about the registration.'

The baker spat into the water. 'Go yourself, she's your daughter!'

22

'Not me, not ever. I see people in the shop every day, even the mayor . . . and there's got to be a Christian name.'

Her husband raised his eyes. A sand barge was drawing alongside right in front of him, the wash eddying towards the bank as the stern was manoeuvred close to the quay. The poop loomed up with its name like a coded epigraph: LUDOVIC BDX 4377. The captain had told him about a German king named Ludwig who was slightly mad, and although the captain did not like krauts, he was partial to loonies since he was a little cracked himself. Nice name, Ludwig, but Ludovic sounded more French.

So the bastard was named Ludovic.

He heard footsteps and voices in the distance. Pricking up his ears, the child put down the fish-head he had almost finished polishing with his thumb-nail, the only nail he had not bitten to the quick. He went to his look-out. From his aerial cabin he had a clear view of the entrance to the attic, thanks to spy-holes torn in the sackcloth. The key turned. Nicole appeared first, followed by Nanette, who hung her wet cape on a clothes horse.

'It's coming down in buckets! Where can he possibly have hidden himself this time?'

'Up there, as usual,' sighed Nicole apathetically.

'He's a real monkey,' marvelled Nanette in a whisper. 'Just like Brieuc. We always had to pretend to find him.' Then in a louder voice, as if to no one in particular she said: 'He's too young to be climbing like that. You have to be quite agile, and awfully strong.'

Ludo dropped a mullet head, scraped and polished to the bone, through a tear in the cloth. He had about ten of them in his aerie, and pretended to bite his fingers with their tiny sharp teeth.

'Look at this! A fish-mouth,' remarked Nanette casually as she picked it up. 'Now it's raining fish. But it's Ludo I came to see. Unless some wicked witch has changed my Ludovic into a mullet. You never . . .'

23

'What's the point,' cut in Nicole bitterly. 'You know very well he's up there.' Picking up a broom that was leaning against the wardrobe, she started poking the cloth where the shadow of a huddled body could be seen.

'That's enough now! Come down and say hello to Nanette.'

'Leave him alone. If he wants to come down, he'll come down on his own.'

Without glancing at his visitors, Ludo dropped a bit of rope and slid down it to the floor.

'He's always showing off, that one. Go on, run a comb through your hair, and wash your hands before you say hello.'

'Wait a minute,' cried Nanette, kissing him tenderly, 'I'll take care of you. Still dressed like a scarecrow! You could at least put trousers on him.'

Nicole's face froze. 'Mama says no. She says he's too messy.'

'But I've told you and your mother a hundred times that I'm quite willing to pay for his things myself.' Nanette was getting more and more angry as she stroked Ludo's face: he huddled against her, intrigued by the gold locket she wore on a ribbon round her neck. 'And just look at this bird's-nest! You'd think his hair was cut with a penknife. Same thing with his shoes. In the middle of winter he's running around barefoot like a waif. And it's not warm up here, either.'

'So what? He doesn't feel the cold.'

'And you don't give a damn! Remember that there's still some of *you* in him . . . I don't know what to do. The child has to go to school and to Sunday school. You can't just let him rot in the attic. My coming once a week isn't nearly enough!'

'Mama says he's not right in the head. He throws fish-heads down into the courtyard when someone goes by. He puts armchairs in front of the door and pushes to try and keep us out. And sometimes he even goes on the floor.'

'He's unhappy, that's all it is! But he's not an idiot—definitely not. Just look at those lively eyes he's got. I'd be glad to take him back to live with me.'

'Mama says that's not possible. We're responsible if there's any more trouble. We've got quite enough to worry about as it is.'

Nanette let go of Ludo, who went to the far end of the room, turned his back to them and began scraping the wall with an old nail.

'That suits your mother splendidly, it would suit her even better if I stayed away. It's no coincidence that she's never around when I come visiting. I'd like to tell her again exactly what I think about all this.'

Now Nicole had the awkward look of someone who lets a third person attack a member of the family with impunity. 'Well,' she said, shifting her feet, 'I've got to go back downstairs, my father's waiting for me to help with the next batch of loaves. Come and say goodbye to me before you leave, and don't forget to lock the door.'

'Of course I won't forget. But what about him. Aren't you going to say goodbye to him?'

'Oh yeah! You're right,' sniggered Nicole, 'but it's different with him . . .' Then she turned on her heel and left without another word.

Nanette opened the wardrobe then held her nose. 'I've told you a thousand times to air this out during the day.' The sound of the nail scratching on the wall grew shriller. 'Mustn't keep these fish-heads, they stink. I brought you some chocolate, you like chocolate don't you? But don't go eating the whole bar at once like you did last time.'

She had opened the dormer window as far as it would go: gusts of wind mixed with rain swept through the stuffy attic. 'You know, you and your nail are giving me a headache. And just look at the dust you're making.' Since there wasn't a decent chair, she had sat down on a big greyish stump that must once have been used for chopping firewood.

'So it's another of those days when you don't want to talk. You remember what I said last time? I promised that when you talked properly, we'd go to the zoo. You'd see elephants, giraffes, ostriches, and if you're very good, I'll buy you an ice-cream.'

Nanette was a small, colourless, person, about thirty years old, with features lined by bitterness that got worse every year. She had lost a three-year-old son, Brieuc, from a virus she had picked up during her pregnancy in the colonies. She had had to have two blood transfusions since then.

'Well, since you won't talk, I'll read to you. But you've got to be good and stop all that scratching.'

The noise of the nail stopped. Presenting the shaved nape of his neck to Nanette as he faced the wall, Ludo looked as though he had been sent to stand in the corner.

'You can look over this way, Ludokins, it won't hurt you. And please smile, you never smile at poor Nanette. Bet you've even forgotten how much is two and two.'

'Four,' faltered a wavering voice.

'Well done! You see, you're not so stupid! And how old are you? Forgotten that already? The age of discretion . . .'

'Seven,' stammered the child.

'Seven what? Seven years! You're seven years old. A year is three hundred and sixty-five days . . . Would you like me to read the same story as last time? Remember? Or don't you want to tell Nanette you remember?'

Ludo had begun slowly scraping on the wall again.

Mama says he fell out all by himself and now he's a bit crazy . . . what difference could it make to your mother nothing's going to happen . . . the last time he was little and anyway it wasn't his fault.

'If you don't remember it doesn't matter. And stop digging around in your nostrils with your fingers. You'll end with a nose like a potato.'

26

Nanette had pulled a yellowing copy of *The Little Prince* out of her handbag; a king of diamonds marked the place. Following the words with her finger, she began to read exaggerating the punctuation, like a village schoolteacher emphasising the subtleties of a favourite passage.

"So you, too, come from the sky! Which is your planet?"
   At that moment I caught a gleam of light in the impenetrable mystery of his presence and I demanded, abruptly:
   "Do you come from another planet?"
   But he did not reply. He tossed his head gently, without taking his eyes from my plane:
   "It is true that on that thing you can't have come from very far away . . ."
   And he sank into a reverie, which lasted a long time. Then, taking my sheep out of his pocket, he buried himself in the contemplation of his treasure.
   You can imagine how my curiosity was aroused by this half-confidence about the "other planets." I made a great effort, therefore, to find out more on this subject.
   "My little man, where do you come from? What is this 'where I live,' of which you speak? Where do you want to take your sheep?"

'You remember about sheep? They're out in the fields. You see them coming up the road at night, with the dog barking at them.' Nanette went back to her book.

After a reflective silence he answered:
   "The thing that is so good about the case you have given me is that at night he can use it as his house."

'What's a case?' asked Ludo. Trying to look casual, he had come closer to her and was craning his neck to get a good look at the illustrations:
'Well . . . a case is like a box. It's a bit like the wardrobe, in fact, only smaller.'

27

Ludo looked at the wardrobe. In the pockets of the clothes hanging there he had found handkerchiefs and hair-slides, which were now hidden away in a niche between the roof and the wall. Then he spotted the wide-open door to the atttic on his right, and the dark cage of the staircase.

'And what's a sheep?'

'But I just told you! They're in the fields. They're the animals that come home in the evening on the road past the bakery.'

A few quiet steps had taken him to the wardrobe, which he touched cautiously.

'That's right,' said Nanette fondly, 'It's a kind of case, that's quite right.'

"And if you are good I will give you a string, too, so that you can tie him during the day; and a post to tie him to."

She had not noticed that Ludo had come back to her after a cat-like detour past the open door. Frowning, leaning his back against the partition between the dressing-table and the sewing-machine, he seemed all ears. One fist was hidden-beneath his dress.

'What's a post?'

'A post? That's for tethering sheep. It's a piece of wood you stick in the ground. It's got a bit of rope on it, too. It's splendid that you're asking questions. You'll see, you'll be as clever as the others, you poor little darling.'

In his sweaty left hand, Ludo was clutching the attic key he had just stolen.

"But if you don't tie him," I said, "he will wander off somewhere and get lost."

My friend broke into another peal of laughter:

"But where do you think he would go?"

"Anywhere. Straight ahead of him."

Then the little prince said, earnestly:

"That doesn't matter. Where I live, everything is so small!"

And, with perhaps a hint of sadness, he added:

'Straight ahead of him, nobody can go very far . . .'

'This book is really nice, isn't it, Ludokins? You know, I've read it, I don't know, perhaps, a hundred times: I really have! And each time it makes me think of Brieuc. I told you about Brieuc. I showed you his photo. He's my little boy. He went away too, off to another planet. I remember him every time.'

'Why did he go off?'

'He was a little prince like you. One day we'll go and see him up there. But he didn't throw fish out of windows, he didn't tease anybody, and he relieved himself without making a mess.'

Ludo scowled. He gave his head sulky little taps against the partition while Nanette, who had put away the book, shook out her damp cape before slipping it round her shoulders.

'Well, I've got to run. I'd love to stay longer, but your grandmother doesn't care for that. Let's see! How about you escorting me to the door today?'

Nanette had hugged the child close to her and was planting big kisses under his ear, rocking him cheek to cheek. To help hide her own feelings she kept telling him that he really did not smell too good, he was the sweetest little piggy-wiggy and that the next time she came he would not escape without a dab of eau de Cologne.

Just as she was about to leave, distressed by the big shining eyes staring at her, Ludo suddenly blushed deeply, held out his closed fist and dropped the stolen key at her feet.

From time to time Nicole would sneak up to the attic to see her son, without a word and without a sign of either love or dislike. She avoided his green eyes and watched

29

him on the sly, standing in the doorway, ready to leave. Ludo grovelled in front of her as soon as she appeared. Now and then he boldly lifted his eyes to hers, but Nicole turned away.

One afternoon the child's face was blotchy and he scratched at it nervously. He seemed uncomfortable and was breathing noisily. Nicole waited for a few minutes and then, unable to bear it any longer, went downstairs to wake her mother from her nap.

'The doctor?—what next! Why were you up there anyway? He can have pimples all over without giving me back a decent, respectable daughter. I sacrificed everything for you, gave you everything you wanted—and you end up with a bastard and disgrace us all! Go and help your father in the bakery instead of bothering me.'

She buried her head in the pillow. Nicole listened to the rain beating on the window-panes. Three days of rain. Three days now, and they were all drowning in boredom. Her thoughts elsewhere, she went downstairs and crossed the courtyard bareheaded, jumping determinedly from puddle to puddle. Once outside the bakery she turned round and went back to the house. In the pantry under the staircase she found some sausages, an apple and a stuffed tomato which she carried upstairs to the attic without looking at Ludo. He took the shrivelled apple and breathed in a strong bitter-sweet smell like the one that sometimes floated in the air when it was very hot. He did not touch the sausages or the stuffed tomato. That evening, Madame Blanchard almost skidded on them when she came in, and cursed her daughter from the top of the stairs: 'Thief! Good-for-nothing! Snake in the grass'—adding that under her roof, at least, bastards did not get fattened up! If that's what Nicole had in mind then she could go out begging or whoring! She carried off Ludo's dinner so he went to bed on an empty stomach, holding the apple close to his nose. Towards midnight, when he was drowsy, he bit into it with a strange, vivid, happiness and devoured it.

He had no memory of having once lived on the floor below, or of having had a hard time between his mother and his grandmother, who made him drink from bottles that were either too hot or too cold—if he died of it that would have been perfect. He did not remember being beaten, lugged about, gagged in his cradle—'Now we can have some peace and quiet!' He had no memory of hearing Nicole shriek, during a nightmare about the rape, that she was going to throw that miserable creature into the fire! Or of having barely escaped death in the bakery that night. Monsieur Blanchard had had to grab his daughter round the waist and tear the child from her arms to keep her from putting him into the oven. He himself had incinerated all Nicole's dolls and all her toys in it on learning of her pregnancy—'You slut! You can play at being a mummy now in real life!'

After this scene Nanette had taken Ludo to her house in the secret hope that she would be allowed to keep him. 'You can be sure we're not going to come asking for him,' Madame Blanchard had said. 'But don't let anyone see him and don't ever bring him round here.' They moved him at night.

He was a timid child then, almost mute, silent when questioned and withdrawing completely if pressed. He was three years old. He could stay in one corner all day long with his mouth hanging open. Sometimes he tried climbing on to shelves or up curtains. When approached, he would raise his elbow before his eyes like a shield, as if to ward off a slap. Nanette spent months humanizing him, consoling him and letting him sleep in her bed when he was frightened. She brought Brieuc's toys up from the cellar, the toys she had not been able to bear to give away. Ludo's speech and posture improved, and he learned how to smile.

A year later, for the first time since the departure of her son, Nicole turned up unannounced at Nanette's for dinner. 'Father drove me over. He had a job to do at the farm.' Ludo sulked at first, then drew closer to the beautiful visitor, who looked him up and down with a strange expression and then ignored him for the rest of the evening. He exerted himself to attract her attentions, he waved his drawings in front of her, he made his spinning top hum at her feet, but to no avail: she went away without having acknowledged his existence.

That night, shivering in his pyjamas and bedroom slippers, Ludo was picked up by the police almost a kilometre from Nanette's house. They took him, naturally enough to the bakery, his original home. Madame Blanchard almost exploded in front of the chuckling sergeant, furious that her niece, who thought she was so clever, had let the little creep make them all look ridiculous.

'Here's your bastard!' she shouted at her daughter, awakened by the noise. 'You deal with him!'

It was three in the morning. Nicole's eyes were glazed and empty. 'Come on,' she said to Ludo, casually. He followed her up the stairs. He had not gone up more than three steps when she swung round and pushed him violently backwards: his head struck the tiles, and he fainted.

That was when they decided to lock him in the attic. They did not want to add murder to rape.

One morning, around midday, Ludo could not believe his eyes. His mother was trying to smile. It was like a ray of sunlight at the end of a tunnel. More astonished than delighted he hardly recognized her in a sky-blue tailored suit, her hair loose and fluffy, her eyes flecked with gold, tall in her high heels.

'Good morning, Ludovic . . . say good morning to me.'

He did not answer, savouring this perfumed vision like a ripe fruit.

'So, can't you say good morning?'

'Good morning,' he murmured.

'Not very chatty are you. And you were screaming again last night.'

She gave another smile and her bright face melted into sweetness: but the shining eyes stayed cold, like two small

32

pebbles, and the harsh tone of her voice belied her expression.

'Today you're coming downstairs to eat. There's visitors. You say good morning nicely and stay quiet in your corner. You washed already?'

She sniffed the air in his direction and made a face. 'Go and wash and do it properly or you'll be sorry. Then you'll get dressed.'

While he was washing she averted her eyes and emptied a bag of boy's clothing on to the floor: a pair of grey trousers, a checked short-sleeved shirt, short socks and cheap shoes.

'Hurry up, please!'

He picked up the clothes and hid behind the armchair for privacy, avoiding the eyes that made his heart beat so fast. He took off his dress, slipped the trousers and shirt on the wrong way round. He was used to buttons down the back and Nicole lost her temper: 'You really are crazy, my mother's right. All this stuff fastens in front. Come over here.'

Turning her head away to avoid the sight and smell of him, just as ill at ease as he was with the situation, she helped her son get properly dressed. She refused to touch the fly zipper, and he broke it trying to get it closed.

The stairs terrified Ludo. He did not want to venture down them, they made his head throb:

Mama says he's cracked . . . Mama says he fell all by himself . . .

Finally he went down backwards, looking up as if he were climbing.

In the dining-room at the back of the shop he got his first close look at Monsieur Blanchard. His hair was carefully combed, the locks on the side brought up over the top of the skull and slicked down with brilliantine. A pink furrow across his forehead showed where his beret usually sat. Ludo thought him very dashing in his black three-button suit. Madame Blanchard was quite festive with her permanently waved hair and a flowery dress. She was arranging chairs round the table while she wondered out loud if anything was missing from the place-settings. Two silent strangers were leaning against the wall. One was a man on the far side of forty, in a grey suit with a thin white pin-stripe, nervously crushing his hat against his stomach. He had silvery hair and was missing two fingers from his left hand. Leaning against him, standing with his toes turned out, was a big boy of about ten years old chewing a wad of gum and looking at Ludo with unfriendly eyes. He was carrying a bow and arrow and wore a black belt with a skull for a buckle, and a Buffalo Bill type fringed jacket.

'Well Ludovic,' announced Nicole in an embarrassed voice, 'this man here, Monsieur Micho's his name, has agreed to be a sort of father to you.'

'That's not true,' interrupted the fat boy, 'he's not his father, he's mine.'

'Be quiet, Tatav, or go and play in the courtyard,' the man with the missing fingers said placidly.

Nicole seemed to relax a little.

'And he's Gustave. He'll be sort of like your big brother. You'll have to be very nice to him.'

As this remark was not addressed to him, Gustave showed Ludo an enormous tongue coated salmon-pink with chewing gum.

'Don't want a brother. He's not his father and why's he named like a sand barge? At school they say his father was a kraut . . .'

'Time to start thinking about apéritifs,' grunted Monsieur Blanchard. 'Pour them out, Mama!' Then, in a quieter voice: 'What about it, Micho? D'you feel like talking now or after a little pick-me-up?'

Madame Blanchard let out a shriek: 'My dress is covered with ink stains!'

'Oh that's just one of Tatav's jokes,' Micho reassured

34

her. 'It's nothing, it goes right away. He's a great joker is Tatav. Right, Tatav?'

He cleared his throat and sighed, looking ill at ease. 'Well, got to get my feet wet sooner or later, so I'll take the plunge. Tough luck if I sink like a stone.' He now slipped on a pair of white gloves he had pulled from his pocket. 'Because of my lost fingers,' he explained, 'and with all that dirt and grease, when you're a mechanic there's no way to keep your hands clean. So here goes . . . I'm not so young anymore, but like they say, I've got some money put by. And as for him, Ludovic I mean . . . like the sand barge, that's funny! Well, it's okay with me.'

To the astonishment of the baker's wife, he placed his gloved hand on Ludo's shoulder.

'That's all I've got to say . . . Oh, and also that I'm happy to be getting married to Mademoiselle Nicole.'

His voice was low, but hummed along like an old, well-oiled motor.

'Did I ever misjudge you, Micho!' cried Monsieur Blanchard. 'That was some speech. Ah, I always knew it would work out between you and my daughter.'

They polished off the two bottles of sparkling wine Micho had brought with him. Nicole raised her glass but only pretended to drink. It was Vouvray, a wine of evil memory, the mere sight of which still turned her stomach, and her soul, after eight years.

Flanked at the table by Tatav and Micho, Ludo recognized the taste of bread he had discovered with pleasure long ago at Nanette's house. He also remembered how to use his knife and fork, but almost choked when he felt the bubbles from the fizzy lemonade in his mouth. Tatav silently broke wind with pestilential effect, then stared at Ludo and announced: 'It wasn't me who farted!'

The dinner lasted for five hours because of the shellfish. Ludo did not eat any. He only sucked the downy seaweed covering the shells. The faster the wine flowed, the more Monsieur Blanchard went on about the crabs being so plump because of being so fresh, and the more Micho tried to outdo him by insisting that it was hard to find crabs so plump, even when they were fresh.

'Don't like 'em,' groused Tatav, 'I'd rather have sausages and eggs fried with onions. And the barge boy stinks.'

'Come on, Tatav, be nice.'

Madame Blanchard gazed at her sleeve in consternation. Most of the stains had disappeared, but rings were beginning to show up.

The conversation flowed on . . . 'Yes, the crabs were superplump, but careful now, even in season you get surprises, you sometimes see crabs going off in mid-June. Of course, in this heat, the wine could not really be up to snuff, the ice-box was overworked. Overworked but still working. After all, Peilhac had not slipped back into the Dark Ages. Speaking of which, there were two blacks in the beachfront hotel, no not in the kitchen, but part of the clientele if you please. A married couple, or so they said, who had come all that way for some relaxation . . .'

Nicole did not contribute anything to the chatter. She was marrying an older man, but he was the richest for some miles around. He was in love with her. He would not bother her. She would be free, free at last, she would change villages and be able to go out once again and have fun. She had been hiding for eight years now!

'You have any idea who Micho is?' her father had asked. She had said yes.

'He's willing to marry you and take on the simpleton.'

Micho had arrived one evening, very proud and very sheepish: her parents had left them together.

'It's hard to have a boy the way things are—he ought to have a home.'

She had said yes.

'It's no life for you both, being alone. Tatav and I, back there at The Hedges, the two of us just rattle around. The house needs a woman's touch.'

36

She had said yes.

'Since he's here, the boy needs an education, he should live like a normal boy, with real parents and a real home.'

The engagement dinner and the formal request for her hand in marriage had been arranged for the following Sunday.

Tatav waited impatiently for the salad, so that he could sprinkle it with rubber maggots. After this he planned to behave himself until after the pudding. When coffee was served, he would renew the attack with some clever sugar cubes that changed into phosphorescent spiders when they melted.

'Very tasty, your leg of mutton, perhaps a touch over-cooked? Leg of mutton's got to be pink. I'm not saying purple, I'm saying pink. In any case, the beans are fresh from the garden. As for the bread, it's home-made and first-rate.'

When conversation flagged, the clatter of forks was interrupted every so often by a cascade of grating, dia-bolical, laughter. Tatav had a laugh-box on his lap and set it off with a cherubic smile. When the cheese arrived, he was unable to resist trying out his bow and arrow. Ludo got an arrow near his eye that drew blood. He was sent to wash himself at the pump.

He groped his way through the shop, passing between the counter and the shelves where a single overdone loaf remained from the day before. He identified the familiar bell as he opened the door, and then he was outside. His head was swimming in the giddiness of a drowsy afternoon awash in soft sounds. Then his heart leaped and the pain disappeared. Ludo held out his hands towards an over-whelming vision he recognized instinctively—sunlight on the sea . . . not a tree was in sight, the heaving, naked sea lay beyond the harbour roofs, immense, contained between himself and the horizon. It was like glancing into the fragment of shattered mirror.

Chapter Three

Michel Bossard had started out as an apprentice mechanic at the docks at Alangon. Michel, the mechanic: they had nicknamed him Micho. The summer residents left their boats in his care during the winter. The sailors did not really have confidence in him, but they liked him well enough. Micho checked the moorings, pumped out the bilges, scraped away at the rust, and kept an eye on the gear. In the end they accepted him as a specialist, and when his mattress began to get lumpy with banknotes, he was able to open both a current and a savings account.

Nobody really knew where he came from.

Soon he set up shop on the outer harbour by buying a building that had once been a lifeboat shelter. He camped out by the slip-rails, surrounded by his tools, and cooked his solitary dinner of mussels in beer on a hot plate. Apart from taking care of the boats, he provided a full range of domestic handyman services, and in the summer rented out bicycles at high rates. From Easter on, a banner announcing the availability of absolutely everything a holidaymaker might want floated over a shop where you could find anything from air mattresses to corned beef, and there was no longer any doubt in anyone's mind that Micho, with his less-than-clean-shaven face, had gone over to the other side. He was one of the filthy rich.

On Sundays he presided benevolently over the harmonium at all three Masses. He also provided musical accompaniment for weddings and funerals. He was as fond

38

of the rituals as if he had been born a sacristan. When the time came to get a new harmonium, the parish priest let him have the old one. Micho fixed the moth-eaten bellows, greased the knobs, and began to treat himself to Latin services in the evenings among the beach umbrellas and fishing rods.

In due course he sold his bazaar and built The Hedges outside the village. It was a bourgeois villa just off the road, surrounded by pines and by warehouses intended for farm and household equipment—maintenance and show-rooms. He installed leaky water pumps in people's houses and then came to patch them up with sealing compound. The repair would last for a while, Micho would stick on some more compound, and since his supply of charm was even greater than his supply of compound, his clients thought of him as a magician.

He was thirty years old before he let himself get ensnared by Mauricette, the postman's niece. And tongues wagged when Tatav was born six months later. Then came the accident. One squally evening, after an outing in a boat, Mauricette lost her balance going ashore ahead of her husband and fell between the planking of the slip and the hull. Micho was hurrying towards her when a sudden gust pinned the boat to the pier, crushing Mauricette to death. The mechanic lost two fingers in the accident.

The locals deeply mourned that mutilated hand, a trag-edy condemning the harmonium to silence—and every Mass to boredom. But Micho, a true professional, made it a point of honour to get things working again, spare parts or not. Eventually when he went back to playing the harmonium, no one could tell the difference. God is not fussy about a finger.

Micho had to hire a maid to help him bring up Tatav. Liliane was sixteen years old. She was a chubby little thing, a hard worker, and full-breasted. 'So, Liliane, how's it going?' When it got too bad, he could always go and visit the whores in Bordeaux.

Insomnia reared its ugly head. The mechanic longed for a body he could stow himself away in, where he could be berthed like a boat. He needed a nice, padded pier, with bowlines and cushy moorings . . . Mauricette had been too scrawny, a real beanpole! She had been so flat-chested she had not even been able to give Tatav milk! God Almighty, who would ever have believed it possible — a woman without tits!

So with eyes as big as saucers and all his senses on the alert, he began looking towards Peilhac. The baker's daughter was certainly round in the right places. René's girl had more curves than a rollercoaster.

The more he thought about it, in the sleepless nights, the more he felt that people's hearts were too hard, too grim and mean, and that the girl had been on bread and water for long enough and with tough crusts to boot. A flirt? They never changed their tune on that score, people of Peilhac! But I don't give a damn, he reflected, I think the flirt's pretty . . . And the rape doesn't bother me. I'd take the flirt and the rape, and the boy into the bargain.

Those bastards really botched my life, thought Micho who was secretly eating his heart out with bitterness and love. He refused to think about the innocent girl in the hands of rapists and so coming to him second-hand.

It was at the Sunday afternoon sessions of *pétanque* that he was able to see her, to see her and no more. The game ended regularly with the baker from Peilhac pitted against Micho, who let him win more often than he need have. Nicole was always there, on her mother's arm, silent and bareheaded, her eyes as empty as if she were blind. When the game was over, Monsieur Blanchard and his family slipped away.

The mechanic's saturnine charm began to have an effect on the baker. He came more often. Eventually he started turning up almost every evening at the *pétanque* alley, where Micho would be waiting for him. One day when it was raining down in buckets, they tossed back pastis instead of playing bowls, and the mechanic described his house as he showed it to the baker.

'I called it The Hedges, because of the bushes, of course, they're all over the place. On the left, there's the store. Completely new machines, and nothing but up-to-date stuff. I sell to as far away as Bordeaux. In the back, I've got my workshop.'

They were in a huge hangar, the rain clattering on the roof, and they had to shout their heads off.

'So—this is *my* bakery! That's a manure spreader. That's an electric milking machine. That's a water pump . . . Well, what about your daughter?'

'What about her?' said the baker suspiciously.

'That's a grinding mill . . . It is your daughter who comes on Sundays with your wife, isn't it?'

'Yes, that's my daughter.'

'Why does she never open her mouth?'

The baker toyed thoughtfully with the levers of a concrete spreader, as though he had just noticed something unusual about them.

'How do I know' he grumbled. 'Girls, come and go, who knows. Well now, I'd best be getting back.'

'Is it true, what they say, René . . .'

'The bread can't wait, I've really got to go.'

He straightened his cap and turned back towards the workshop exit without a nod.

'Is it really true, René, that she's got a boy hidden away in the attic?'

Monsieur Blanchard stopped. Micho had already caught up with him, and went on speaking as he poured out a glass: 'Come on, have a drink! We're just talking, that's all . . . So, it's really true?'

'That's right,' said the baker, sitting down heavily on a roll of fencing, his arms drooping between his knees.

'And is it true, as they say, that the brat's a bit simple?'

'Well yes, it is like they say, its true enough.'

'René, I'll tell you: as for Nicole, I would be glad to

marry her, and I'd take the boy along too, simple though he is.'

The pounding of the rain was hard on the ears. The baker's pink forehead folded into a pile of wrinkles, which slowly faded away. After a deep sigh, Monsieur Blanchard looked up, and at the sight of the mechanic's pleading eyes, he understood that he had indeed heard correctly.

'Well now, we'll have to see about that, Micho,' he said with a big smile. 'We'll really have to see about that.'

The ceremony took place in mid-November, and they were all up to their ears in melting snow. Nicole wore Madame Blanchard's wedding dress, altered to fit her. At the express request of the bride, Nanette was the only guest. Ludo was allowed nothing more than to watch the hectic preparations, slamming doors, people galloping through the place and shouting. Then he was left behind, alone in the empty house.

The next day, Micho drove him over to The Hedges. The van followed a sandy road through the woods, where the sea gleamed silvery between the trunks of the trees. A grinning miniature rabbit dangled from the rear-view mirror.

'What's the matter, Ludo—you feeling okay?' said Micho, surprised to see Ludo twitch and shake like a leaf every time he changed gear.

No one came to meet them when they arrived. Indoors Ludo found the remains of a party. A long table with a white cloth and crumpled napkins, a crystal bowl lined with the crimson sludge of melted ice-cream, and empty bottles tangled up in paper streamers.

The evening before, Nicole had looked at the room Micho meant to give her son: the bed was shaped like a boat, the view was of the sea . . .

'All this for him?'

'All of it! The boy's going to enjoy it here. And now you've got him all to yourself. In a real family. No more fighting with your parents because of the poor little thing. You'll be able to spend as much time with him as you like.'

Nicole was speechless.

Ludo did not like his room at first. He missed his attic. He did not understand that he was free to go out, to go wherever he wanted. Dejected, he paced up and down his unknown territory, hampered by its confinement, his steps accustomed to a greater range. He still felt like a stowaway on a voyage, but his eyes were already drinking in the milky sea, that immense maternal breast. The sky-blue freighters on the horizon seemed to have been carved out of thin air.

You've never had such nice clothes before Nanette said to me . . . Nicole gave me everything . . . you should call her Mama . . . it's not like where I was before . . . now Nicole's nice and Micho he's nice and it's me who takes Nicole's breakfast up in the morning on a tray with coffee and bread and butter and the medicines . . . I like bread and butter . . . you can't just let him rot in this attic . . . have you seen what lively eyes he's got no he's not crazy . . . it's nice the harmonium with Micho . . . Nicole does not like it . . .

In the evening he waited automatically for his daily mullet, hidden behind the curtains. 'Hey Ludo, come and eat, it's going to get cold . . .' He was always surprised when his mother came to call him. The corridor was empty, foot-steps died away. He forced himself to go downstairs, where he sat at the table between Tatav and Micho, who monopolized the conversation until the pudding.

'So, you're coming along all right, old fellow? You don't say much do you, but you'll get the hang of it. Why doesn't your boy talk more Nicole?'

'He's never been talkative . . .'

'Ah, but things have changed now! This little boy who

43

didn't have a father and whose mother didn't dare love him like she should have . . . Now he's got two parents and a brother, too. You can call me Papa, Ludokins.'

'You're not his papa,' grumbled Tatav.

'Course I'm his father. You lend him your father and he lends you his mother. So you don't lose a thing! I admit it feels a bit funny at first. With Mauricette it was just the three of us. Now there was another one who didn't talk much. The quiet type, Mauricette, and her feet were always cold. You got cold feet, Ludo? Her circulation was sort of sluggish. That's why Tatav's fat, of course. Something to do with the circulation. Mauricette was sickly, you could see right through her—her skin was so transparent. It's nice being here all together isn't it.'

He patted Ludo's head. The boy hunched down in his chair, exhausted and anguished, terrified by all these unfamiliar objects, by the food, by these strangers talking to him, and by Nicole, smiling and transformed.

'Why doesn't he go to school?'

'He's going to go, just wait and see! We're going to register you, aren't we, Ludo? Look, you've even got a napkin ring with your name on it.'

'Like the sand barge,' mumbled Tatav into his plate.

'I'll show you how to fold your napkin when you've finished eating. And . . .'

'How long are they going to stay?' cut in Tatav, bitterly.

'We've already been into that. They're living with us now. Papa has got married again. Take some more, boy — he doesn't eat enough, this lad. He must eat.'

Sitting on his hands, Ludo looked first at his plate of sausages, then—discreetly—at Nicole. He did not dare touch them, despite his hunger. He waited until she went to the kitchen before he stuffed himself, bent low over his plate, hiding behind his arm.

After supper, Tatav pushed the table out of the way and turned the dining-room into a model-railway network, with

44

the help of appropriate sound effects and an all-purpose signalman in training named Ludo.

Almost every evening, Nicole and Micho went into town to shop, bringing him back a new pair of trousers, a shirt, shoes, comics. The child never thanked them. He tended to hide the presents in his cupboard, unopened. 'Find anything on your bed?' Nicole would ask at the supper table. Silence. 'If you found something, say so.'
    'It's a package.'
    'And what's in the package? Find anything?'
    'Yeah, I found it.'
    'Well, go on, what was it?'
    'It's a package.'
    Micho left for work early every morning, was gone all day and came home tired. 'So, how's it going, lad? Is your mother around?' Ludo answered with a smile. The man with eight fingers would stuff sweets into his mouth then go off looking for his wife or sit down to play the harmonium while waiting for her. The sweets had praline in them, which Ludo did not like.

The reorganisation of his family life exasperated Tatav. Having lost his mother, he thought that paternal affection was a privilege not to be shared.
    Tatav was a real fatty-puff, sausage-plump from head to toe, hair of a washed-out mouse colour, piggy-blue eyes, sharp and piercing through the rolls of fat. His thighs and knees rubbed lard against lard, and gave him a penguin's waddle. The slightest effort left him out of breath and sweating. A sourish smell warned of his approach.
    Tatav loved animals, but with a love that moved on to barbarity. He cut the fins off his goldfish with scissors. He caught lizards and brained them or pierced their hearts with a hat-pin. He starved quails after having fattened them for months. He kept rabbits, always seven of them (named after the Seven Dwarfs), which he seemed to love more

45

than everything else, taking each of them in turn for walks on the road, with a long pink ribbon for a leash. If one of them happened to die of cold, Tatav was prostrated with grief. That did not prevent him, however, from going off alone to a special shed with Bashful or Grumpy and skinning it with a paring knife. In Micho's eyes, unwilling to see this cruelty, the death of Tatav's mother absolved his son from everything.

Tatav had a sweet tooth. He had once written a triumphantly well-received school composition about a cake-shop counter, from which the teacher had read this passage aloud:

'The cakes gleam with a thousand lights. The éclairs, turnovers, strawberry tarts, the cream swans, the shining mocha cakes, the powdery millefeuilles, have all put on their Sunday best and their sweetest perfumes. They look like Christians at Mass. It is like a Sugar Mass, with nuns, those fat bellied chocolate éclairs, stuffed with whipped cream.'

Between cakes, he chewed 'globos,' a brand of gum he kept stockpiled in an aquarium, whose original occupants he had tortured to death.

Little by little, Tatav struck up an odd friendship with Ludo, as the Pygmalion of a gullible scapegoat to whom he would make amends, when necessary, through the stupendous gift of some well-chewed gum. On Thursday mornings, when there was no school, he took his Mickey Mouse comics and shut himself up in the downstairs bathroom, the one used by the two boys. He would climb out of the window an hour later and come whistling casually by Ludo, who, thinking the coast was clear, found himself locked out. Alternatively Tatav put pepper on the lavatory paper Ludo would be using. Some days he hid outside, and just as Ludo thought he was finally alone, Tatav would fling open the window and shout: 'NOT YOUR FATHER.'

After a few months, the house held no more secrets for

Ludo. He knew all its noises, recesses, and surroundings, including the workshops and stores he had visited with Micho. On the side facing the road, terraced lawn ran along a drystone wall planted with hydrangeas and willows dried out by the sea air. In the back, the garden encroaching on the courtyard was a tangle of pines overrun by brushwood, ferns, and brambles, separated from the woods on the property by an abandoned railway station with moss-grown platforms. To kill time, Ludo would go there and pretend to be a chugging train, setting out for exotic destinations. Sometimes he pretended that all his carriages had been derailed down an embankment.

Pompously dressed in a showy outfit, Tatav might decide to play Indians and attack the train. At first Ludo got beaten up whenever he emerged from a collapsed tunnel, but then he worked out how to even the score. The train conductor scouted out all the ambush points, and when the Indians charged, the train sped up imperceptibly, just enough so that the fat war-whooping Cheyenne would not give up the chase. When Ludo went full steam ahead, the whoops would grow fainter, until the Redskin collapsed breathlessly on to the grass, coughing his lungs out.

Tatav burst in on Ludo, who was ready to go to sleep. The visitor had slipped head-first between the sheets without taking off his slippers. 'It's frigging cold tonight. Papa used to store potatoes in here!'

'This was my bed before. What's that you're reading?'

Ludo was looking at the pictures in *The Crab with the Golden Claws*, which he held upside down. He did not much care for having Tatav's legs near his face.

'It's the wrong way up . . . I've got all the *Tintin* books. And all the *Spirous*. My father bought 'em all for me. And all the *Mickey Mouses*.'

The sea murmured, in the silence of the night.

'And for Christmas, my father's going to buy me a TV, idiot. Ever seen a TV?'

'What's that?' asked Ludo with a yawn.

'It's a box. You can see everything on it. You can see soccer, serials, cartoons. You see everything on TV. The priest's got TV. And my father's going to get me the same one as the priest's.'

Tatav let a few seconds slip by.

' . . . I'll put it in my room, and you won't be allowed to touch it. Anyway I forbid you to touch any of my things. It's my father who bought everything for me. And what about your father, who's he?'

'It's Micho,' said Ludo, as if stating the obvious.

'No it's not Micho, liar.'

'My mother said it was Micho.'

'Well it's not true, idiot! You're the son of a kraut, that's who you are! You ever seen him, your father?'

'Sucks to you!' shouted Ludo, losing ground fast.

Tatav had started coming every evening to torment him about his background, his real parents and where they used to live.

'We lived in an attic.'

'That's not so hot, an attic. So where's your father now?'

'He's in the attic.'

Tatav like to make Ludo squirm with questions he could not answer or escape.

'Your father, what's his job?'

'It's in the attic.'

'And what's he do in the attic?'

'He does the laundry. And he shells peas.'

'Your father's a drip! My father's got tractors and harvesters and reapers. And he's the one that fixes them. He's the richest man in all of metropolitan France.'

A history course on the colonies had taught him the euphonious-sounding *metropolitan France*.

'Why do you scream at night?'

'I don't scream.'

'Your mother says you're crazy. Anyway I don't like your mother.'

This rapid fire of obscure but malevolent shots sometimes sent Ludo to sleep. Tatav poured water down his
neck to wake him.

'You ever been with a girl?'

'Where?'

'You're really an ignorant idiot! Me, I've been with one.
We even touched our dickies. Well, I mean I touched her
nunnie. And it cost me a lot . . .'

'Nunnies,' repeated Ludo, seduced by this unusual
word.

'Five bubble-gums for the nunnie, and two for the titties.
I wanted her to touch mine, too, but she didn't want to.
She said "You're disgusting and I'm going to tell my
mother on you." And I had to slip her another two pieces
of gum not to get ratted on.'

Conversations like these usually ended in a pillow fight.

After Tatav had gone, Ludo stretched out on the parquet
floor. Staring into the darkness, he could see his father on
the horizon. He saw him from the back, a big man, in
white duck trousers, he saw him walking alone on the road
with loose-limbed steps, walking on and on without ever
drawing away, followed determinedly by his shadow. It
was a beautiful day, the scent of resin was in the air, he
saw the sunlight on the back of the man's neck, he saw the
man briskly swinging his arms, and surely it would have
been enough simply to call out in order to see his face, but
Ludo did not know his name. Suddenly he was only a tiny
dot in the distance, swallowed up by sleep.

Early one morning, Tatav entered his room while it was
still dark.

'Time to get up!' he cried. 'The bus will be here soon.'

Then, seeing Ludo go back to sleep after barely opening
his gummy eyes he said: 'Hey there, hurry up. You've
already forgotten that today's your first day of school.'

Laughing loudly, he tipped the mattress and its burden
on to the floor.

49

'Nanette's going to take you. In fact, here she is. You're going to be with the little boys, *I'm* with the big boys. This morning we have gym but that's for morons. I get excused.'

Ludo got dressed and went downstairs. Nanette was waiting for him in the kitchen. Tatav was having his breakfast.

'So, Ludokins,' she said, giving him a kiss. 'You've just time to drink your coffee. Mustn't be late.'

'Where's your car?'

'Haven't got one. I took the bus, it's not far, you know.'

'Look, I'm a train.'

Holding his arms out like the wings of an aeroplane, Ludo began soaring round the kitchen with loud humming noises.

'What a clown you've become, just look at you! But today, you've got to be on your best behaviour.'

She buttered his bread and sat facing him, smiling or opening her eyes wide in mock astonishment when he chewed noisily. She never tired of looking at him, or of patting his cheeks. They had filled out a bit but were still rather pale. Tatav watched her from his seat, angered by an intimacy that he thought of as poaching on his territory.

'You look healthy, you know, and your appetite's good, too,' Nanette continued playfully.

'And you too,' said Ludo. Nanette's face fell.

'Me?' she said sadly. 'Not me . . . I'm not in good shape and never have been. Come on, time to leave, it's eight o'clock.'

The sun was up. They had been walking along the road for a few minutes: every now and then Ludo pretended to be a glider.

'It's one kilometre to the school,' explained Nanette. 'One kilometre, that's a thousand metres. Tomorrow you'll go with Tatav.'

'And you?'

50

'I've got other things to do. I have to go away for a little while . . . Hey, not so fast, I can't keep up with you! And that's why I'm going away.'

'Why's that?'

'To rest. It won't be too long, I hope. But I'll write to you.' Nanette was going away for her third operation.

'You're coming back?'

She stopped, short of breath, and took Ludo in her arms.

'Come here, sweetie, come to me. We'll see each other again, you know, we'll even see each other every day. And I'll help you learn to read and write. I'll teach you lots of things. You can spend your holidays with me if you want to.'

'Don't want to,' he murmured as he wriggled free.

'Why do you say that, it's not very nice.'

They didn't speak again until they arrived at the school, a silent, greyish building out in the open countryside, surrounded by a bare courtyard.

'Come along, the bell's going to ring. We'll say goodbye now.'

'Here,' said Ludo. Rummaging in the pocket of his new school smock, he presented her with a pine cone.

'I'd like to introduce you to Ludovic Bossard, a new pupil,' announced the teacher to the class. 'Go and sit at the back, my boy.'

Their eyes fastened on Ludo, who did not dare move a muscle.

'Therefore, we call a term that is linked to the subject the . . .'

Suddenly noticing Ludo's immobility, the teacher raised an eyebrow. 'I said: "Go and sit at the back, my boy!" '

The child seemed paralysed.

'Are you deaf?' he asked, holding up his hand to quell the beginnings of derisive laughter from the boys.

'Are you?' answered Ludo, so softly that the man thought he had misheard.

'Another shining light,' he sighed, getting up from his desk. He pushed Ludo briskly to an empty bench near the coat pegs, and returned to his seat.

'The complement is a word or group of words completing a predication. I said, a word or group of words completing a predication. Can you repeat that, Bossard?'

His tongue hanging out, Ludo was rolling a snake out of the modelling clay he had found on the squeaking table. Laughter broke out again. Hands behind his back, the teacher proceeded solemnly down the aisle to Ludo, who looked up politely, though he was bothered by the smell of hot chalk dust the teacher brought with him.

'So, Bossard, you can't repeat it?'

'Can you?'

The metal ruler slammed down on Ludo's knuckles.

He barely flinched but began licking his bruised fingers. The class held its breath.

'Follow me.'

Ludo followed him

'Get up on the dais.'

He did not move.

'Will you do as I say!'

The teacher twisted his ear and forced him down on all fours.

Mama says he's cracked . . . Mama says he fell all by himself . . . I'm the one who does the bread and butter . . .

He made no protest when the dunce's cap was put on his head. There was an eruption of hilarity when he said of his own accord that he was sorry.

'The complement is a word or group of words completing a predication. If I say: "Ludovic Bossard is as ignorant as a donkey," what is the complement?'

When school was over, Ludo got a beating from the big boys.

*

One morning Ludo was fixing his mother's breakfast. Everything on the tray had to be just so: the buttering of the bread, the cooking of the bacon, the temperature of the coffee, the half glass of water for the ampoule of Sargenor, a vitamin tonic. He was proud of this task which he performed every Thursday. When Micho took over on Sunday, Ludo's jealousy showed in his sullen silence.

Holding the tray, he waited patiently for Tatav to stop blocking the door. 'You're going to bring me my Ovaltine in bed, too. Promise and I'll let you pass . . .' Tatav finally moved out of the way, racing ahead to the foot of the stairs. 'Here's where I trip you up and you land on your stupid face, idiot! And for starters, I don't like your mother.'

Ludo put the tray carefully on the floor at the top of the stairs. He listened. The corridor was empty. Kneeling down, he spat silently into the bowl of coffee, mixed in the foam with the little spoon and wiped the spoon with the lining of his pocket. Then he went on to Nicole's room at the end of the passage.

The voice drifted up from the bed, peevish and thick with sleep. 'What's it like out?'

'It's nice outside.' Ludo had left the tray on a small round table and drawn back the curtains: he looked at the red hair spread out on the pillow.

'You always say it's nice. I'm sure it's windy. I can hear it from here. Have you noticed, this house is more exposed than the bakery. It's on higher ground.' Nicole coughed. 'First of all, help me get up.'

Ludo went over to the bed, took Micho's pillow as his mother held it out to him and settled it behind her. In passing he breathed in the smell of warm skin scented with soap.

'Now the tray. Sit down on the footstool. How's it going at school? Well, answer me, at least! You're anything but a chatterer. But I like the way you butter the bread. My

53

mother knew how to do it too. What's this, then? A sprig of heather? Did you put that under the plate?'

Ludo nodded, blushing. Nicole smiled.

'It's for me? At least you're sweet. But heather isn't a flower. The flower I like best is the rose. You ever seen roses?'

Papa got married again . . . you've even got a napkin ring . . . you can't just let him rot in the attic . . . have you got cold feet . . . Mauricette's circulation was sort of sluggish . . .

'You're really not a talker at all. How're you getting along with Tatav? I find him strange, don't you? The coffee doesn't taste the same as at home. Ludo, why do you scream at night?'

'I don't scream.'

'Yes you do. It's weird. In the middle of the night. Mama used to say you were crazy.'

Through half-closed eyes, Ludo was slyly watching the woman stretched out on the bed. His mother. She was so beautiful. He remembered Tatav and the mean things he said: 'She's not your mother, she's your sister. Not even your sister. You're not my brother. My father's not your father. You're all lying toads.'

She had on a nightgown buttoned up to the neck. Her arms were bare, with naturally golden skin. A drop of coffee glinted at the corner of her mouth.

'There's too much wind here, it's exhausting. That's why I'm always getting colds. My mother used to cup me. D'you think you could learn how to do that? It's just a bit of cotton-wool burned in a little glass pot, and you press it on. You put them on the back, ten of them, you drape a towel over them, and to get them off you let the air in with your finger.' Nicole was wracked by a fit of coughing.

With his hands between his knees, Ludo furtively stroked

54

the bed-sheet hanging over the side. To lie down for a moment in this big, almost empty bed . . . To snuggle up in the warm sheets, if only for a moment, on the other side, where the coverlet still showed the outline of an absent sleeper . . . He pulled the material gently towards him, watching the folds stretch over his mother's body, around the tray. Two sneezes in quick succession almost tipped the bowl of coffee on-to the sheets. Ludo made no effort to help.

'You're really not too bright,' snapped Nicole. 'Get going, take away this tray! I've finished. Then go and get the cupping glasses from the kitchen, they're somewhere there tied up in a cardboard box.' As he reached the door, she called after him: 'Whatever you do, don't throw away the crumbs. I save them for the birds.'

I just don't like school and besides Tatav's with the big boys . . . the teacher breathes like the baker it makes a noise in his mouth and his mouth smells bad . . . I don't like the stories he tells . . . he hits with his ruler and the girls up front have got a cross on their smocks . . . I've got nothing . . . the principal came the other day and the teacher gave her his place and she said here are your places for the month . . . head of the class Roumillac that's very good Roumillac your parents can be proud of you I'm very pleased you've earned the Cross of Honour and Roumillac sat down again and all the pupils stood up one after the other and the principal said to each one well done I'm pleased for your parents and they got a cross and I thought I'm going to get a cross too but towards the end the principal didn't say well done any more she started saying I'm very displeased your homework is badly written you ought to be ashamed . . . next to me there was a little blond boy who was crying I asked him why are you crying I'm afraid I'm going to be last . . . and then she named the little blond boy and she told him this is very bad but he stopped crying anyway ... everyone was looking at me ... I was happy because the little boy wasn't last and then the ones in the first row they had pretty crosses they were touching them then the principal said the last is Bossard get up Bossard I feel sorry for your parents Bossard and I don't know what else she said but everyone was listening and looking at me and she went on and on about how it was a disgrace and the teacher kept nodding his head and his beard ... so I closed my eyes and I didn't hear any more it was like being back in the attic.

He drank the rest of Nicole's bowl of coffee in the kitchen, being careful to place his lips where his mother's had been. He found the box of cupping glasses on top of the kitchen cabinet, ten little pots that had once held yoghurt. He dusted them off, arranged them on the clean tray, then went back up to Nicole's room.

'Took you long enough. You're really a slowcoach. Now go and get my hairbrush and the cotton-wool balls from the bathroom.'

After that, he had to go downstairs again for matches. 'I can't help it, as soon as I wake up I have to brush my hair. You understand how to do it? The cotton-wool goes in the pot. You light it, then you press down hard. Well, not too hard. Try it out once on yourself, I'll feel safer like that.'

He set a scrap of cotton-wool on fire in the bottom of a pot, then clapped it firmly on-to his thigh. The flushed skin immediately swelled into an orange dome under the blackened cotton.

'Slide your finger under the rim of the cup ... that's right ...' There was a sucking noise. 'That's fine, turn around, and close your eyes. I'll tell you when to open them.'

He heard the rustle of cloth and the creaking of the bed.

'All right,' said Nicole after a brief silence.

56

She was lying on her stomach, the sheet drawn up to her waist, her arms lying beside her body, her face buried in the pillow. Her nightgown lay crumpled into a ball next to her. Ludo looked at the bare back, the tousled red-gold hair lying between her shoulder blades as if it, too, were naked. Captivated by this vision, he trembled as he lighted the first cotton-wool ball so clumsily that he burned himself.

'It's not working?' asked a muffled voice. 'If it doesn't work stop immediately.'

Applying the cup, he saw the flesh become distorted as if cooked by an invisible fire.

He soon finished attaching the ten cups, moving aside her curls to get to the skin just below the nape of the neck. He felt heady with a sense of victory and pride in a job well done. Nicole was momentarily in his power.

'That's good, I feel better already,' she sighed. 'Cover everything with a towel and wait ten minutes before loosening them. It's hot, but it helps.'

A slight snoring sound showed that she had gone back to sleep. Ludo went to get the towel and returned on tiptoe to gaze at his workmanship — all those pots clinging like snails, all those imprisoned cotton-wool balls, all those discs of scarlet flesh, and the golden skin, so sensitive to cold, rippling as she breathed. Leaning over the bed, his throat dry, he slowly reached out his open hand to touch, just once, his sleeping mother. He could already feel the heat from the naked body rising towards his fingers when she woke.

'What on earth are you doing? I'm frozen stiff. That's enough, anyway, get these things off me.'

Relieved of its burden, her back looked like butcher's meat.

'Now turn round and close your eyes.'

Turning his back to her, he kept his eyes wide open.

With his heart pounding he stared at the floral pattern on the wallpaper.

'All right, take the cups back downstairs. You're really lucky, you never catch cold!'

She had slipped into her nightdress again. Ludo noticed that the top button was unfastened.

'I catch cold at the slightest draught. I had bronchitis over and over again when I was a baby. The doctor couldn't do anything for me. Later they put mustard plasters on my chest, but that burns, I didn't like that. I didn't like inhalations either. I couldn't breathe under the towel. I must have been nine years old ... or maybe ten ... How old are you now?'

'I'm five years old.'

'No, you're not five, stupid! You're eight years old now. Eight years! It's been eight years ...' Her voice broke, and she fell silent. 'So hot, that summer ... we couldn't walk on the road anymore, the asphalt was too sticky. Eight years ... We went swimming ten times a day but it didn't cool us off. I went to the beach with Marie-Jo. She's an auctioneer now ... There hadn't been any wind for months, not one breath of breeze, we waited for thunderstorms, we ate ice-cream at the Fairway Café ... Look at me for a second.'

When Ludo raised his head, trying to look into his mother's eyes, she collapsed suddenly on to the pillows, her features distorted, her nostrils flaring and clenched teeth showing between her white lips.

'Get out of my sight,' she whispered.

Chapter Four

Winter plunged The Hedges into torpor. The spontaneity of their first days together had given way to the monotony of a family swept along by habit. Assigned to household duties at first, Nicole burned several joints to a crisp, inadvertently cooked a plaster soufflé, forgot a laundry tub on the gas burner (it melted into a pool of metal), wreaked havoc with the dishes and finally dumped all the chores on to Ludo. The problem of what to do about meals was solved by the delivery of an enormous refrigerator that Nicole had ordered without even consulting Micho. The latter was astonished to see his stepson always hard at work.

'He's got to be kept busy,' said his mother. 'While he's working, at least he's not screaming.'

Ludo's nightmares were a subject of daily discussion.

'If he's crazy, he's got to go to a doctor,' Micho said. Nicole did not hesitate to wake up Tatav and Micho so they could watch the phenomenon. The three of them stood in their pyjamas in Ludo's room, watching him utter loud, plaintive cries, huddled up in a ball on the floor with all his clothes on.

'Used to cry even louder at the bakery. Even used to grind his teeth . . .' Then she would shake her son: 'That's enough. You're making an awful row, do shut up!' Ludo flinched as he woke up.

'Doesn't bother me,' said Tatav. 'Anyway, it's not as loud as Papa's snoring.'

For Christmas Micho wanted to have a celebration, a real party in honour of his beautiful wife and new son. Nicole seemed enchanted by the idea at first but then changed her mind. In any case, she did not want to invite her parents. So why spend all that money? Micho asked what possible reason the Blanchards could have for not wanting to spend Christmas Eve with the family.

'At their age the last thing they need is trouble!'

When he pressed her further, she lost her temper, claiming that her parents never came up to The Hedges, that her father no longer played *pétanque*, and that the sight of Ludo made them sick.

'Are you trying to say that he can't come to the party?'

'One thing's for sure, my parents won't spend Christmas with him. Think about it from their point of view!'

'They can stay at home then, if that's the way they feel about it.'

This was the first major difference of opinion between the newlyweds. Nicole sulked. Micho sent to Bordeaux for a fir tree so tall that it touched the ceiling. He set it up in a corner of the dining-room and spent two days decorating it with artificial frost and fairy lights made from roots swathed in silver paper. Ludo stood staring open-mouthed at this ornate tree, which Micho said was connected in some way to a certain Father Christmas who came down the chimney once a year to cover the tree with presents.

The morning before the great day, Ludo brought breakfast up to his mother and tried to sit down.

'I'm tired, buzz off . . .' After he had gone, she snatched up the little flower he had put in a glass of water, twisted it and stuck it back in the water upside down. 'Twisted as he was, inside me. Hold up your arms, daughter, hold them up higher!'

That evening, as he did every year, Micho played the harmonium for Midnight Mass. He had invited the priest to the party instead of his in-laws. 'Why,' asked Tatav, 'did you say in the sermon that Christmas shouldn't be a scandalous feast?' Wrapped in haughty silence, Nicole picked at her food. When the pudding course arrived, they distributed the presents from the tree. The priest got an envelope, Nicole a gold chain bracelet, Tatav and Ludo a table-top soccer game. Micho got nothing. There was also a box of chocolates for Ludo from Tatav. Most of the chocolates were missing. In the bottom of the box was a grinning white plastic skeleton.

In the break periods at school, Tatav usually ignored Ludo, who was well able to amuse himself. Ludo played all alone, pretending to be a twin-engined aircraft by twirling strings round in front of him as though they were propellers. He also liked to watch the girls skipping and humming songs. He scrounged old bits of chalk from the blackboard trays to scribble twisted lines on the cement. Sometimes he played games of knuckle-bones with little peasant boys who bet in chocolate and paid him off with kicks from their wooden shoes if he managed to win. At lunch time, he always sat between two girls whom he left overcome with admiration for his ability to polish off the congealed lentils left on the edges of their plates.

In the evening, Tatav waited for him on the road, where no one could see them. They went home by cross-country routes that took them as far as the harbour, where they dawdled by the boats tied up to the quayside. Tatav would pull a bit of fishing line out of his satchel and hook greasy mullet, whose eyes he put out with his pen-holder before dropping them back in the water.

Not content with being cruel, he also had scatological tendencies. Once a week, armed with a saucepan attached to a huge pole, he took Ludo behind the workshops to stir up the septic tank. He claimed that this kept it from exploding. He had a collection of dried excrement under glass, each specimen the product of a different kind of animal. He hunted dung-beetles—beautiful glossy black insects that lived in cowpats. In March, Tatav and Ludo, armed with soupspoons, rummaged meticulously through bovine bowel movements with the euphoria of gold-diggers. In the evening Tatav pinned his prey alive to his dungodrome: a big sheet of white cardboard glued to the wall, where each specimen was mounted with a Latin patronymic. He had a passion for taxidermy which applied to all insects, crushers, stingers, lickers, or suckers. He organized cockroach round-ups in the warm oven, tempting them with crumbs of cheese. After sorting through them carefully, he mummified his catch in hair-spray.

Ludo went by himself to catechism classes every Thursday afternoon in the church halfway between the town and The Hedges. He stumbled through the acts of faith and contrition, getting them mixed up with each other. He never did learn *Our Father*, but he could whip through a *Hail Mary* with one breath. His favourite prayer was the two times table, which he recited to himself each evening before going to sleep.

In church he watched old ladies light wobbling candles on a big black tray studded with sharp spikes: sometimes he put candles on the empty prongs, elated by this burning bush that did not arouse in him even the tiniest flicker of piety.

On the way home, he would take a detour through the village and go window-shopping in front of the Paris Bazaar—Micho's former store—where luminous watches and scuba-diving knives hung on invisible threads. Behind the shop a shallow slip once used by rowing-boats sloped down into the water, intermittently reflecting the red flash of the jetty light.

It was dark by the time he got home. Micho, busy at the harmonium, sometimes mentioned the lateness of his arrival in a friendly way. Nicole interrupted her solitary apéritif to remind her son that they were not running a hotel, that he should at least be polite and show her some respect, that the table had to be laid before tomorrow morning, that the laundress had complained about his underwear again, and that if he kept it up he was going to have to wear nappies like a baby.

'Where was you?' asked Tatav.

'In my hiding-place.'

'If you tell me where it is I'll show you my submarine.'

'You always say that. You've never shown it to me. Don't believe you've got a submarine anymore.'

Tatav was pretending to Ludo that he and his friends were building a fabulous ship, able to sail into the depths of the seas and up into the constellations. 'It's the first flying submarine. It's got buttons with the names of the stars on them. All you do to get there is push the button.'

'What colour is it?'

'It's a chameleon submarine. It's the colour of wherever it is.' When he went off to play with his friends, leaving Ludo behind, Tatav would mention the various finishing touches still to be made to the submarine. 'I can't take you along, or I'd be giving away the secret.'

'Where is it?'

'Deep in the forest. There's a huge grotto, with a passage underneath filled with water that goes all the way to the sea. Have to be a bit careful, in the grotto, because of the monsters.'

'What kind of monsters?' pleaded Ludo.

'There's shark-elephants, with fins and an elephant trunk on their back and teeth all round their eyes. They can eat you up with their eyelids. There's also cat-crabs. The front paws are pincers.'

One day, Tatav showed him an old bicycle gear-lever, claiming that it was a marvellous machine. 'Mustn't touch it. That's what's used for the engine in the submarine. It's got a thousand like this one.' He had made Ludo listen to the sweet sound of the ratchets, which he had oiled beforehand. 'Not bad, eh? If you make my bed every morning until April, I'll let you have it.'

No sooner said than done. Ludo carried the gear-lever

round everywhere with him for several days running, not letting go of it even at night, dreaming of the *Nautilus* and interstellar travel. In the mornings, cleaning up Tatav's room, he drooled over the aquarium and its stock of chewing-gum. One afternoon, during break, a marbles player whom he had hoped to amaze brought him down to earth with a bang: 'A piece of a submarine? I've got the same thing on my bike, go and look.' At supper that night, taking advantage of a moment when Tatav was looking the other way, Ludo stuck the gear-lever into the traitor's mashed potatoes, hoping to make him feel guilty. Tatav must have suspected something, because he neatly ate the mashed potatoes around the hidden gear, leaving it untouched.

Madame Blanchard often came by bus to spend the afternoon at The Hedges. 'How are you? Nanette's in a tight spot, this time. Might not even make it through the winter. The surgeon telephoned your father. He wanted us to go up to Paris. Who'd take care of the shop if we did? And I've never been there before. When he says we ought to come, it means the end is near. You're not looking so good yourself, you know.' She was always insinuating that Nicole was ruining her health by having a husband who was so much older then she was. 'It was one of your father's ideas, this marriage. You know how he is when he gets an idea into his head. And of course there was the idiot . . . It's not too hard on you is it?'

Nicole protested weakly that Ludo was not an idiot and that everything was all right.

'If he wasn't an idiot, you wouldn't have a face a mile long. It's your father who won't come here as long as *he*'s around! He's stubborn, you know. Anyway, I'm not the one to say he's wrong.'

'And what about me,' exploded Nicole, 'you think I want to see him, my father? It's all his fault, so far as I'm concerned he can drop dead!'

'Of course,' Madame Blanchard went on, 'you're well

fixed up here. The mechanic has money to burn. He's kind at least? He's not a bully like your father?'

'Absolutely not,' answered Nicole, 'he's not rough at all. He goes through the whole church service every evening. He sits down at the harmonium and there's no stopping him. And when he's had a drop or two to drink, it makes him cry.'

On every visit, her mother asked to go through the house. Ludo's room always gave rise to sighs of indignation.

'You're too good, my girl, you'll pay for it. As if one mistake wasn't enough: you're making it worse. And what with prices these days!' They went back to sit in the sitting-room where Madame Blanchard took out her knitting. Ever since Nicole was a baby, every year, she took up her knitting-needles to immunize herself against the winter with a handmade garment. 'I found the pattern in a fashion magazine. It'll be perfect for you, with your delicate lungs.' They gossiped until five o'clock, drinking one *café-au-lait* after another, one pulling on her wool, the other polishing her nails or leafing through Tatav's *Mickey Mouse* comics. 'Enough of this, I don't want to miss the bus. And there's the bread to think about. It's so empty now, at home. Your father's going to kill a chicken. Why don't you and your husband come and eat it with us on Sunday?'

'What about the boy,' ventured Nicole, 'could he come too?'

The baker's wife curled her lips in disgust. 'Certainly not, what an idea!' She put away her knitting in a flurry and her daughter saw her to the door. That night, the sight of Ludo gave Nicole palpitations.

She had been married for less than six months and she was already getting bored. She had the impression that she had somehow been saddled with someone else's fate. Nothing in her life was settled, neither past nor present. She believed that one fine day she would awake with other memories, on the verge of a new and better life. Clinging

65

to the dreams of a spoiled child, she ignored her birthday and every year applied make-up to the first wrinkles of passing time, which she attributed to the chores of daily life. At twenty-three, her beauty was already facing her with a thousand minute betrayals whereby a life suddenly stops blossoming and begins to show the effects of wear and tear. Tiny blue lines wove themselves round her eyelids. Her eyes were always slightly red as though she had been crying. Her hair was no longer quite so lustrous. Tobacco smoke stained her white teeth brown. She weighed herself every morning, but had decided the scale was wrong by about five kilos. This gave her back her youthful weight and her passion for strange whims. She ate very little—sweet things, mostly, but enjoyed red wine and towards evening drank Sauternes or Monbazillac to block out the harmonium. The Gregorian outbursts made her hate her husband. Nicole never went out anymore, except to church on Sunday. She saw no one but her mother. She lived at The Hedges as though it was a prison. She was even jealous of Ludo, who came back from school with ink-stained hands and rosy cheeks.

Micho's nights were not triumphant: Nicole's responses were tied up in knots. It had been a long time before she had allowed him to touch her. In bed she slept with socks on and said no, not yet, and so the nights went by. Micho was getting impatient. The first time he made love to her she left the bedroom and sobbed until morning on the living-room sofa. Afterwards, she was docile to his love-making, but without desire, without pleasure and lost in a frozen passivity unstirred by emotion. 'Finished?' she would ask him coldly.

Released from desire, the mechanic talked himself to sleep. 'I think he's happy here, your Ludo.'

'I'm tired,' Nicole sighed.

'You always end up loving a child if he's a good sort . . . I knew everything would work out . . . A boy needs his mother.'

He smiled in the darkness. It was good to come home in the evening. To stretch under the shower, which got rid of the filth and soothed his chilblains. It was so good to have a pretty wife with a warm body, and a little brother for Tatav. The two boys were getting along well—an occasional row maybe, but usually good-natured. Nicole did not like the harmonium? Each to his own, and anyway, she'd get used to it. It was the little boy who loved it. He was always hiding under the stairs to listen on the sly. During the day, no doubt he touched the knobs and pedals. The stops were often out of alignment. One of these days, he'd teach the boy how to play. Then he would be able to accompany Mass just like Micho. Too bad Tatav showed no interest: serious music was not one of his hobbies.

Ludo woke up one night bathed in sweat. He had seen his father. The loose-limbed walker had turned round, but his face had been hidden by the pouring rain. Ludo went into the hall, groping his way blindly in the darkness. A doorknob turned under his hand. He slipped into Nicole and Micho's room, which overlooked the courtyard. Rain lashed at the roof, and the drops played a tune on the shutters. He was asleep on his feet, vaguely disturbed at not hearing breathing noises from the shadowy bed. An armchair seemed to swim towards him. He recognized his mother's scent and buried his face in the clothes draped over the back of the chair, cuddling the material against his cheek. Then he wandered round the room on all fours, rubbing himself along the edge of the mattress like a dog until, frightened by a sudden snore, he went back to his own bed.

Tatav and me are blood brothers . . . that's how the Indians do it he said . . . you cut your wrist you put it on mine and that way we're brothers and that way Micho's sort of your father a little and that way we got the same blood . . . have to have the same blood in a family and I

cut my wrist I put it on his and I said the multiplication
table . . . then we followed the Gabarou sisters . . . Tatav
said which one d'you want we'll take them for a ride in the
submarine . . . me I don't believe in the submarine anymore . . . the Gabarou sisters were turning round Tatav
was saying which one d'you want we were soaked . . . they
ran off in the rain Tatav said it's a good time for hunting
snails . . . Nicole didn't want to eat them . . . your trousers
are torn . . . now they've gone off to the hairdresser's with
Micho and she cut his hair before you couldn't see his neck.

At supper the next day, Nicole complained to Micho that
her gold bracelet had disappeared. 'I thought maybe you'd
put it away somewhere . . .'

He hadn't seen it, or put anything away.

'Well, it can't just disappear into thin air!'

'Maybe it fell off your wrist,' he suggested.

'I always close the safety catch. Besides I clearly remember taking it off last night.'

'And where'd you put it?'

'If I knew that, I wouldn't have to ask! I've looked
everywhere.'

'Children, anybody seen Nicole's bracelet?'

'No!' answered Tatav and Ludo.

She was still looking a week later. Ludo helped her move
chests of drawers, crawled under the double bed, emerged
empty-handed and poked around under the rugs.

Two weeks went by. That Thursday, Nicole was astonished to see her bracelet on the breakfast tray, neatly presented in a pretty saucer between the coffee and the bread.

'How did that get there?'

'I found it,' said Ludo. 'I found it all by myself.'

She held the bracelet at arm's length between two fingers,
suspiciously. 'But where did you find it? We looked
everywhere.'

'It must have fallen from your wrist. I'm the one that
found it.'

'At least tell me where you found it.'

Ludo tried to look mysterious. 'By the front door, where the shoes go. I picked it up inside a shoe.' Opening his shirt, he produced a filthy old shoe and held it out to his mother.

'Get rid of that disgusting thing, it's full of germs! Don't hold it over the coffee, you idiot! But what gave you the idea of looking in the shoes?'

'While I was searching. I wanted to search everywhere. I started downstairs, and I found it all by myself.'

Nicole looked at the bracelet and smiled. 'First thing I'll do is wash it in vinegar. I still don't quite understand your story. Anyway, thank you. Perhaps you're a good boy after all . . .' She waited, embarrassed, holding her arms out awkwardly. 'What would you like as a reward?'

Ludo blushed. 'Would you come up and say goodnight to me in my room this evening?'

She burst out laughing. 'That's easy, but you'll be sorry if I find your room in a mess! You know how I hate that. Now run along and play.'

He was on his way out of the room when she called him back. 'Ludo, I forgot. Hand me my purse. There's a letter for you . . . from Nanette. She's in Paris.' Nicole had had the letter for a week, and had read it several times. 'I'll read it to you.'

In guarded terms her cousin explained to the child that she had to rest a while longer and that she would be back a bit later than she had expected. She also mentioned *The Little Prince*, and wondered anxiously how Ludo was doing at school. Did he know how to read and write? Luckily he had his mama to help him decipher her letter. Blushing, Nicole skipped the part where Nanette told Ludo that she loved him very much and could not wait to give him a kiss.

'There . . . Did you wash this morning?'

'Yes,' he answered, showing her his scrubbed finger-nails.

'I'm not so sure. A nice letter like this, mustn't let it get dirty. I'd rather keep it for you.'

At supper that night, Ludo announced several times in a loud voice that he had cleaned up his room, expecting some sign from Nicole that she would keep her promise. Then he went upstairs for the night.

Sitting on his bed at two in the morning, he still hoped that she would come, that the clean windows, the clothes neatly hung in the wardrobe and the polished floor were calling her, as a late guest is drawn to his empty place at the table. He waited for another hour and then wrecked all his preparations. He emptied the toy box on to the crumpled bed, dumped his clothes in a pile on the floor, went to sleep in the bottom of the wardrobe, on top of the shoes, with tears in his eyes.

Ludo wanted to punish his mother by ignoring her. He did not spit in her Thursday morning coffee any more and he did not glue his lips to the rim of the mug where she had drunk. He held his breath when their paths crossed. It was a point of honour to him that henceforth all intimacy should vanish from the things that he did for her every day.

Nicole pretended not to notice. It was as if the feud started by her son suited her perfectly. Since his coldness could have no effect on him but sadness, he clung stubbornly to his hostility simply to ward off his sorrow for as long as he could.

'You're right,' Tatav told Ludo. 'Your mother's silly. I didn't want my father to marry her.'

'Really,' answered Ludo.

'Have to drive her up a wall,' Tatav said one day. 'She's got to say she's sorry. It's the law.' He laughed crazily: 'We'll stick earwigs in her things. Come on! You keep an eye on the stairs, I'll see to the bugs.' Ludo kept watch. 'She'll never dare put on her panties again,' said Tatav exultantly, coming back a few moments later. 'I

70

put in a whole army of insects. Okay? I'm off to the submarine.'

After he had gone, Ludo slipped into the bedroom and removed the earwigs scattered among Nicole's underwear.

'She's pretty sneaky,' remarked Tatav on their way to school the next day. 'Didn't say a word. Even gave me a kiss. We'll have to put stink bombs under the sheets. When she gets into bed, it'll squish the bombs. What a night they'll have, the two of them!'

Ludo almost got caught clearing Tatav's booby traps from under the bedding.

'I don't understand it,' fumed Tatav.

'Me neither,' said Ludo.

'I've got a new idea. I'll get behind her on all fours. You race at her from the front so she steps back and falls over me.'

The plan was carried out, but just when Nicole was about to stumble over Tatav, Ludo shouted a warning, and the trap was sprung. Tatav barely got away with pretending to have been stooping to tie up a shoe-lace, but he started giving Ludo dirty looks.

'It's just that I got scared . . .'

The days got longer. The warm weather returned, and brought with it the scent of pines on the breeze. The air tasted of honey and the Atlantic was drowned by the rasping noise of cicadas. Waves of turbulent blue rolled crisply on to the shore. In the evening, flights of cranes struggled across the sky, streaking the azure with violet. Tatav and Ludo went swimming. Although he claimed he could swim like a fish, Tatav was barely able to splash around treading water, which fooled Ludo until he discovered that he could dog-paddle too. Ludo had no trouble immersing himself completely in the cold water. Tatav, on the other hand, was more sparing with his dips. By the time he had waded up to his thighs, his fat, milk-white

71

skin would be covered with goose-pimples. One teasing remark from Ludo and he would give up, saying that he had had enough.

In the long balmy twilights, the two boys played table-top soccer until dark. Tatav slaughtered Ludo, thanks to elastic rules which allowed him to replay any points his opponent seemed to have scored. Their matches were accompanied by the reedy throbbing of the harmonium. Towards midnight, Micho often suggested that they have a cup of herb tea. Tatav boiled the water, while Ludo put the tea bags in the cups. 'Be quiet on the stairs so you don't wake your mother,' Micho would remind them. Standing at the kitchen door, Ludo hurled the used tea bags out into the night. They hung by the score from the branches of the lilac bush in the courtyard.

At school, the pace of work had slowed down. Summer was coming: the teacher chatted with the students, asking them questions about their future and letting them go home early. At the first sign of unruliness, he clamped down severely with long dictations.

Barely able to scribble a few words, Ludo would draw pictures instead.

Nanette still isn't back yet ... what's your drawing supposed to be ... why's the hand so black ... Tatav's scared of the dark I'm always the one who gets the cider from the basement ... I like it when it's night ... I've almost finished my nigloo ...

After a lesson on the Eskimos, he had dug out a *nigloo* in the sand at the far end of the garden. It was a hole closed off by pine branches interlaced with seaweed. There was just room inside for a man, if he crouched.

One morning, his attention was drawn to the words *Mother's Day*. 'And so,' the teacher went on, 'each of you will now weave a raffia basket for your mothers. I'm going to distribute the material now.' By the end of the next afternoon forty baskets were finished and gift-wrapped, with cards written in nice round handwriting: 'Happy Mother's Day.' The children set out proudly for home, carrying their presents. Two bullies, Maxime and Jésus, were waiting for Ludo at the gate.

'Your mother's a kraut and don't get no present.' Ludo was beaten up and his basket trampled upon. He arrived home in a sorry state, his face badly bruised. Nicole was in the sitting-room, cutting pictures out of women's magazines.

'You've been fighting again and your shirt's torn to shreds.'

'Boys will be boys,' Micho said peacably. He was working on the circuits of a second-hand television set acquired from the parish.

'He's a troublemaker, my mother was right. She always said he was violent.'

For some time now, a derisive tone had been creeping into her voice, tingeing everything she said with irony.

Ludo went upstairs to wash his face and change his clothes. Then he slipped into Nicole's room, spotted the handbag on a shelf, and reached inside to grab a handful of money. He met Tatav on the way out.

'What the hell were you doing in there?'

'Nothing to do with you,' he mumbled, rushing down the stairs.

He left the house by the back door and ran to the village with awkward strides, arriving drenched with sweat at the Paris Bazaar. On a bed of starfish, amid the diving masks, flippers, guns and gaudy bathing suits, lay a superb knife. It was unsheathed lying next to its black case. The handle was moulded so as to fit a human grip. Nicole was always complaining that the knives at home were worthless. Ludo opened the door. A bell tinkled.

'It's about the knife,' he said to a middle-aged lady with an artificial-looking tan.

She looked the child over from head to toe—the flushed

73

face, the crumpled shirt, the wrinkled trousers flapping round matchstick legs. 'Which knife?' she asked.

'It's outside,' he said, turning on his heel.

The lady followed him, smiling, and led him back inside when she had identified the knife in question. 'Don't you think it's a little big for you? Why don't you pick one of these instead.' A complete array of penknives with open blades was spread out under a glass counter.

'It's the other one I want,' insisted Ludo.

'For you?'

'No. It's a present.'

'If it's a present, I suppose its all right,' said the shopkeeper, and took the dagger out of the display window, holding it out to Ludo on the palm of her hand. 'Do you like it?'

'Oh, yes,' he breathed.

'Is it for your father?'

'No.'

'For your big brother?'

'No, it's for my mother.'

The lady looked into the child's deep green eyes. 'For your mother?' she exclaimed.

'Yeah.'

'She likes underwater fishing, your mother?'

Ludo murmured something inaudible.

'What did you say?'

'That's the one my mother wants, she told me so.'

The shopkeeper hesitated, wondering whether to put the knife back. He was on the young side, her client, but seemed to have set his heart on that particular knife. 'Do you realize that it's a very expensive knife? It costs fifty new francs.'

With the greatest solemnity, Ludo turned round to count his stolen money. The numbers got all muddled up. 'Don't know how much this is,' he sighed, facing the woman again and holding out his handful of crumpled bills.

'You've only got forty-seven francs,' she told him after counting them.

74

'Is it okay,' he said beseechingly.

'No . . . not quite. You need three more francs. Are you sure your mama doesn't want a smaller knife, one for cutting things up?'

'No, that's the one she wants.'

He was a touching child, he must have broken into his money-box for Mother's Day. 'Well, all right, it's yours. I'll even wrap it up nicely. And if your mama wants to exchange it, tell her she can.'

When he got home, Nicole had not yet noticed the theft. He hid the dagger in his nigloo at first, then under his pillow. All night he longed to open the parcel.

The next morning, as soon as Micho had left for work, Ludo laid the parcel on his mother's lap and ran away without a word. He went outside into the garden, beside himself with nerves, and galloped off to the abandoned station, where he worked off some steam playing at trains and ocean liners.

A few minutes later, he retraced his steps and lay down under a pine to keep a close watch on the house. Not a sound to be heard.

She ought to be looking for him. Calling out to him. It was the most beautiful knife in all the world. His heart pounding, he got to his feet and started walking towards the courtyard. Standing beneath Nicole's window, he whistled as loudly as he could, but in vain. When he went back into the kitchen, he found Tatav seated at the table drinking his Ovaltine.

'Seen my mother?' asked Ludo, very casually.

'Your mother only bothers to talk to me when my father's around.'

He went upstairs again. The passage was quiet: listen as he might at Nicole's door, he heard nothing. He almost shouted, or went in without knocking, but instead he sat down on the floor next to the door-jamb, imagining for the hundredth time Nicole's hands opening her beautiful present, finding the marvel hidden in the parcel, lovelier by far than all the raffia baskets. Then he heard the parquet creak behind the door and stealthily returned to his room. A morose voice called his name. He answered only the third call and dashed to his mother. She was trying on high heels in front of the wardrobe mirror.

'Where were you? I've been calling you for an hour.' The unsheathed knife gleamed on the bed, nestling in the opened parcel. 'Where'd you get this?'

'At the Paris Bazaar.'

'And why'd you give it to me?'

Ludo blushed. 'You always say the knives here don't cut. That one'll cut all right.'

She turned the dagger over in her hands. 'But this isn't for eating . . . What's it for, anyway?' She seemed disconcerted.

'It'll cut, for sure.' he said.

'And why'd you give it me today?'

'It's Sunday,' he announced.

She dropped the knife on the eiderdown. She posed before the mirror, looking at her feet in their new shoes. Catching sight of Ludo behind her, she was struck by a sudden suspicion.

'Wait a minute, what about money, where'd you find it? A knife like this must be expensive!'

He muttered something incomprehensible between his teeth.

'You can't afford a thing like this. Where'd you get the money?'

Ludo did not answer.

'I bet you stole it!'

'It'll cut anything,' said the child imploringly.

'So you did steal the money . . .' Her voice was suddenly quite slow and deliberate, almost lascivious. 'Who'd you steal it from? Micho? Tatav? Who?'

Ludo's green eyes gave nothing away.

'I've got all the time in the world, you know. If you won't tell me, it's 'cause you're really a thief. A dirty little thief.'

Ludo wrung his hands, staring at the dagger: he was happy that it had got this far, at least. No doubt it would go back into the shop window eventually, but for the moment it shone brightly on the eiderdown. Could she see how shiny it was?

'So, where'd you get the money? From my purse?' she shouted.

'The lady said she'd give it back,' he explained, his eyes glued to the dagger.

'What lady?'

'The shop lady. She said you could return the knife and she'd give you back the money.'

'But you got the money from my purse, didn't you. You went and took money from your mother's purse!'

Ludo shivered.

'A liar and a thief, that's what you are!' she shrieked, shaking out her empty handbag. 'Just you wait, you're going to be punished. I don't know exactly how, yet, but you're really going to catch it. It's disgraceful! Micho's going to drag you by the ear to that shop and tell the lady everything. Imagine stealing money from your own mother!'

Distraught, he ran and hid in his nigloo. What would Micho think? And Tatav? And what would the lady in the shop think? He did not go home for lunch or dinner, and slept shivering under the sodden branches.

When he reappeared in the house the next morning, the atmosphere was strange, no one scolded him for anything. The news of Nanette's death, announced the evening before by Madame Blanchard, had overshadowed the unpleasantness over the knife. Tatav had been asked not to mention Nanette's death to Ludo.

The body was brought back by train for burial in Peilhac, her native village. The funeral cortège was an almost perfect replica of the bridal procession that had followed Nicole and Micho the previous winter. Madame Blanchard scolded her daughter for coming bareheaded, without even a little black veil, and for standing dry-eyed in front of the open grave. Nicole was nauseated. She looked at the silver holy-water sprinkler, the clods of dry earth raining down on the coffin, the tightly-laced shoes of the priest who had baptized her, the torrid bright blue sky, and there, making the sign of the cross at the edge of the hole, was that stranger, almost an old man, whom it frightened her to think of as her husband. Ange, the gravedigger, leaned on his shovel while he waited. 'So, that's it? Nobody else? Can I close it up now?'

They returned to the bakery for a light meal. The men played *pétanque* in the courtyard after their brandy; Nicole helped her mother wash up. She slipped upstairs to see her old room, and stood out on the landing, staring at the highly polished steps leading up to the attic. She shed her first tears at the sight of Ludo when she got home.

'You ought to be told about Nanette. She's gone upstairs. She's pegged out. You won't ever see her again.'

Chapter Five

When he was thirteen, Tatav went off to Tivoli, a Jesuit boarding school in Bordeaux. Ludo walked back and forth to school by himself. He had to do each year's lessons again. Since he did not understand the alarm clock Micho had lent him, it went off at two-fifteen on the dot every morning, so he arrived either after the bell or well before dawn, but never on time.

The bus dropped Tatav off at noon on Saturdays. Ludo waited for him at the front door, pretending to be there by chance. The schoolboy's chief concern, even before sitting down to lunch, was to go and make sure that no one had meddled with his fish bowl. After this formality had been taken care of, the two boys would settle back into their squabbling intimacy.

At first glance, Ludo's room at The Hedges seemed tidy with his bed properly made. But tidiness was not Ludo's strong point. He crammed a tangle of toys and clothes into the wardrobe, shoving it shut with both feet. This mess gave out a stench that Nicole attributed to a dead mouse. Ludo did not smell it.

After Tatav's departure, Ludo switched from wetting his bed to peeing under it. When Micho pointed to the damp parquet, Ludo said: 'That's not me, its the mouse that's not dead.'

'And this,' Micho asked, 'What's all this?' He was looking at a strange row of crudely coloured portraits drawn on the wall. All were identical, with red hair, a long neck, the features partially hidden behind a large hand. Shining black eyes looked out from between the fingers.

'It's a drawing,' answered Ludo, as if he had had nothing to do with it.

'What's it supposed to be, your drawing—can't see a thing because of the hand!'

'It's just a drawing!'

'Okay, but stop mucking up the walls, you're not supposed to draw on them. There's special paper for drawing.'

Suppertime was now enlivened by television. Ludo adored all the programmes indiscriminately, lapping up whatever images came along. At the first screen kiss, Nicole turned off the TV with a sigh of exasperation: 'Clear the table and go upstairs to bed.' Ludo got up regretfully: after he had gone, she turned the programme back on again.

One night Nicole woke up shivering: 'Is there someone there?' The darkness pressed in upon her, impenetrably. She felt something. A presence. A light touch. She shook Micho, who was not snoring, for once.

'You had a nightmare, it'll go away.'

'It's not a nightmare. I wasn't sleeping . . . I'm sure there's someone in the room . . .'

He turned on the light. 'See for yourself: no one's there.'

'I could've sworn there was,' she murmured. 'It doesn't matter, I suppose, but there's a smell. A smell I don't like.'

After the business with the dagger, Micho had let himself be persuaded that his stepson was a little crazy. This did not affect his relationship with him at all, however. 'You seem astonished,' he said to his wife. 'I knew it when I married you. Everyone knew. I expected worse. I even worried because of Tatav. But you know, your boy's not completely round the bend. It's more as if he's just a little different from the rest of us. We ought to send him to a good doctor.'

One Thursday, Nicole and her son went to see Doctor Varembourg. 'You'll answer his questions politely. And don't put your hands in your pockets,' she told him.

The doctor was a plump man who gave the impression of constantly pursuing two ideas simultaneously, linking them with intermittent 'Well-well-wells.'

'What's your name, young man?'

'His name's Ludovic Bossard, Doctor. It's not easy for me, I can assure you. The boy is . . . I don't know how to put it. There's something wrong with him, he's not right in the head.'

'What makes you think that? Well, well, well.'

Looking out of the window with its half-drawn net curtains, Ludo tried to see the sea through the pines. Doctor Varembourg listened politely to Nicole and, well, well, well, set about seeing for himself how things stood. He made Ludo cough, checked his hearing, his eyesight, measured him, weighed him, then finally announced that the case was not one for a general practitioner but should be referred to a specialist. Nicole took down the address of a colleague, a psychiatrist in Bordeaux.

'One thing's for sure, at least, you're perfectly healthy!'

'They're all jealous,' answered Ludo.

It was Micho who drove them into town the following week. They were going to take advantage of the appointment and have ice-cream in a café.

'What's a psychiatrist do?'

'Heads,' said Nicole. Then, turning towards her son, who was sitting behind her in the back seat she said: 'You see what we have to go through because of you!'

After a short interview with the three of them, the doctor had the child shown into a kind of drawing-room, magnificently furnished with carpets and bibelots standing on a low table. A smell of resin and fresh paint floated in the air. Ludo sat down on a couch, the man at his desk. When he smiled, his upper lip looked false, somehow. He smoothed his bald forehead frequently with a languid palm.

He quizzed Ludo affably about a thousand indiscretions: did he touch himself at night, had he already seen his stepfather's penis, did he lust after his mother, was he a battered child. Finally, leaning his shiny bald pate towards Ludo, he informed him that Freudian symbolism concerning the phallus well and truly included bald heads, 'whence the ambiguity of the relation to female, and even male patients . . .' The consultation cost three hundred francs: Nicole had to write down the address of another colleague, a specialist in 'paranoid dysfunctions.'

'Didn't follow any of that,' said Micho after they had sat down in the café.

'Problem is he's not right in the head.'

'Well it hasn't hurt his appetite, that's for sure!'

His mouth ringed with whipped cream, Ludo had just finished his coffee ice-cream soda before anyone else.

'Want another, sonny?'

Ludo nodded. A rosy wad of chewing gum was stuck to the seat, impressed with a fingerprint that Ludo replaced with his own. Then he picked off the gum and popped it furtively into his mouth.

'He shouldn't eat too much, he'll get worms.'

'That's not going to give him worms. What does the doctor mean when he says he's not right in the head?'

'He gave us the address of another specialist. He's the one who'll say what's the matter.'

'You know, it costs a lot, being crazy. And what use'll it be when we do know?'

'No use at all. Anyway, we know already. Ice cream makes me so thirsty, I'd like a glass of Sauternes or Dubonnet.'

Nicole and Micho had an apéritif. It was Ludo's first visit to the city. He watched the passers-by, all those faces, all those eyes, all those footsteps, all those people coming in, going out, the waiters shouting, coins jingling, coats being slipped on, explosions of laughter, the air aswirl with different smells. Two old ladies appeared, one holding a cardboard box of cakes by its string. Ludo watched them settle down comfortably on a banquette, loosen the collars of their fur coats, and polish off some enormous cream puffs. Their jaws worked in a strangely lateral and circular movement, rather like cows chewing, accompanied by flickers of their tongues, tiny chin quiverings, a brief pantomime with the eyebrows, and nods that set the feathers on their hats dancing.

'It's so upsetting, having a boy like that,' muttered Nicole.

'No need to moan about it. He's a nice boy. There's plenty that are nasty.'

When it was time to go, Ludo stuck the gum back under the seat, pressing his thumbprint in it once more like a seal.

The winter mists threw a cloak of gloom over colours and souls. In the afternoon, night fell quickly in a landscape already glowing with harbour lights.

It was Christmas again. The Blanchards were quite willing to spend Christmas Eve at The Hedges, provided that Ludo was not there. Once more, Micho stood his ground. 'The boy's staying here. He hasn't done anything wrong. And you couldn't say that about everybody!'

Nicole slapped her husband, told her parents not to come after all, and shut herself up in her room on Christmas Eve. She even refused to go to Midnight Mass. Micho, Tatav and Ludo spent a miserable evening sitting by the gaily decorated but now quite meaningless, fir tree. Micho made up a bed on the downstairs sofa.

Nicole did not reappear until two days later. She looked positively cadaverous. After wishing them a Merry Christmas she emptied a chamber pot full of cigarette butts over the kitchen floor.

Madame Blanchard came to The Hedges several times a week. 'So, how're you doing? Your father's feeling a bit under the weather. It gets to his back—it's the damp that does it, the doctor says. But round our place damp's as common as crabgrass. You eating, at least? There's not much flesh on you, you know. If you want to give your husband a baby, you'd best get some meat on your bones. Listen, the other day I saw your . . . you know who I mean, the idiot. It's amazing how much he looks like . . . well you know who. He mustn't stay in the house if you get pregnant.'

Nicole was irritated. 'I don't want a child, it's only Micho who does.'

'Well, I mean, I'm just saying you shouldn't be looking at an idiot when you're pregnant. Anyway, they have places you can put them. He'd be all right there. And then you could see your father again.'

'The doctor says there's nothing wrong with him.'

'What do you expect him to say? If you will go to a dentist for an earache! I'm telling you, this is going to end in tears.'

One Thursday morning, Ludo seemed to stumble as he was setting down Nicole's breakfast tray, spilling scalding coffee on his mother: 'You're not only an idiot, but a dangerous one . . .'

The next time, he got up early, put on his Sunday clothes, and went downstairs to get the breakfast ready. The tray was always perfectly laid. The arrangement of the plate and knife symmetrical, the bread perfectly buttered, even the sugar cubes in a saucer made a pattern. The whole thing showed his obsessive attention to detail.

Ludo went carefully up the stairs. Just before knocking on the door, he set the tray down, pulled a safety-pin from his pocket, and pricked the ball of his thumb over the bowl and watched the drops of red blood mix into the steaming coffee. Then he closed the pin and knocked on the door.

Nicole was in a chatty mood.

'Don't forget to polish the furniture downstairs. This afternoon you can go out and play. My mother's coming.

If you behave yourself you can watch TV tonight. What're you going to do now?'

'Tatav lent me his train.'

'What about your homework?'

'I did it all.'

'Okay. Was it you who washed in my bathroom yesterday?'

'No—wasn't me.'

'It certainly smelled like you, I had to air the place out.'

Ludo swivelled in the rocking-chair and looked her in the eye. 'It was my father who washed himself.'

Nicole looked puzzled. 'You mean Micho?'

'Who's my father?' he murmured, turning away.

Nicole turned pale. 'What're you talking about, you idiot?'

'Nothing,' he said in his normal voice.

Ludo had been making veiled references to his father more frequently lately, playing on the confusion with Micho in everyone's mind. One day, he announced coldly that his father had come to get him after catechism class. Another day he claimed to have gone for a ride in a car with him. In the face of this provocation, Nicole scolded Ludo icily, but went no further than that.

'Don't be a fibber, Ludo.' She settled back into her pillows. 'You're getting sly and that's not right. What're they teaching you at catechism?'

'It's the Romans with Jesus. How Pontius Pilate washed his hands. They put Jesus up on a cross, she said. It was in the field of the skull. The Pharisees were jealous!'

'You certainly know a lot of religion, but I hope they also teach you obedience and respect.'

'I don't know that they do.'

'Do you know your prayers?'

'There's one I just can't learn. It's too boring.'

'Which one's that?'

'The *Our Father*.'

'Really? It's just a question of working at it. You're the lazy type. And stop rocking, you're making me feel dizzy.'

He sat still in the rocking-chair, looking at his bleeding thumb with an enigmatic smile. Then he became absorbed in looking at the window-panes. Nicole's reflection was superimposed on the monotonous view of the pine trees.

'If I learn the *Our Father*, can I learn to play the harmonium?'

'After you know everything else. Reading, writing without spelling mistakes, and arithmetic, most important of all. The harmonium is not a career.'

Micho had wanted to teach his stepson music, and thought of using him as his assistant at the church. The first lesson took place late one Sunday afternoon. After half an hour, Nicole appeared with a glass of Sauternes in her hand. She said she was not some priest's housekeeper, and that if Micho was a priest that still was no excuse for turning her only son into a lousy priest as well. Still muttering threats, she had slammed the keyboard cover down on Ludo's fingers: 'Whatever possessed me to marry an old man!' The fight went out of Micho when he heard those cruel words and he capitulated on the spot.

'What do you want to be when you grow up?' Nicole asked Ludo later that week.

'Aeroplane pilot.'

'Why?'

He did not answer.

'You could be a sailor. It's nice, being at sea. They wear pretty trousers and blue collars and they see the world.'

'Where's that?'

'In the Navy I mean, they travel a lot. They wear white berets with a red pompon. Of course, with your jug ears . . .' she sneered.

Ludo scowled. His ears made him miserable. Now that he could see himself in real mirrors, he spent hours studying this face. He was handsome and grotesque at different times, his face moulded by his feelings. In the playground at school, he was careful to present his profile to the girls, constantly pretending to be interested in something off to one side. An attempt at plastic surgery on his ears with glue had resulted in a mongoloid appearance for a few hours one morning, followed by two raw wounds behind his earlobes that had taken almost a month to heal.

'What's the weather like?'

'I haven't looked.'

'Well look now, stupid! No, not out of the window, go outside and tell me if it's cold.'

He went downstairs, recited a *Hail Mary* standing on the last step, counted to ten, and went back to sit in the rocking-chair.

'It's very strange weather. Not as cold as yesterday. It's not raining just now and there's a little wind.'

'You always say the same thing. Why can't you tell your poor mother whether she's liable to get a sore throat or not! You probably do it on purpose.'

She raised her voice. 'You're really just a little pest, Ludo! You don't talk, you never do what you're told, the way you wash is beyond belief. Don't turn round, whatever you do.'

In the window-pane he could see Nicole push back the covers and stretch.

Now you're my blood sister . . . even though you're not nice we're married . . . Tatav's my brother . . . and I'll put some blood in my own father's coffee when he comes back . . . Micho's not my father so I don't put anything in his . . .

Tatav had a birthday party in mid-February, and blew out all fourteen candles with one breath. Ludo wondered if *he* would ever get to stretch his lungs over a festive, twinkling cake. He did not know the real date of his birth, he simply assumed that his age moved on with the New Year. Nicole had rejected Micho's suggestion that they should give a little party once a year in his honour. 'You know what it means to me, the bastard's birthday, especially one like this? Do I have to explain everything to you?' Micho made up for the lack of birthday celebrations to his stepson as best he could. He gave him a little pocket money, and admired his well developed biceps. It was Micho who gave him the coloured pencils and felt-tipped pens Ludo used for his extravagant wall decorations.

At school Ludo did badly in drawing classes, scrawling preposterous babies and impossible houses with doors on the third floor. Once, trying to draw a picture of Christ, he had been carried away by his favourite obsession and drawn a woman's face glimpsed through the outspread fingers of a black hand. Another bad mark.

In his room at night he kept refining the invisible portrait, stroking it, talking to it, cursing it, endlessly correcting the expression of the eyes seen between the fingers, the number of which varied from seven to nine. The general appearance of what could be seen of the face was now firmly fixed: red hair, eyes of a panicky blue, the whole thing slightly larger than life-size.

I know Nanette's not pegged out . . . she'd have told me if she'd been going up above . . . when she gets back I'll tell her we've got the same blood my mother and I . . . what would my mother say if she knew we were married like the Indians.

As Easter drew near, Madame Blanchard had to cut down on her visits to The Hedges. The Parisians were turning up again. Not a single brioche left by nine in the morning . . . 'Then with the holidays, *he*'s going to be there during the day. I don't want to run into him. When're you going to send him to a home?'

One afternoon Nicole was sorting a bundle of laundry spread out on the kitchen floor, busy separating the whites from the coloureds. Raising her head, she screamed with fright when she saw Ludo standing outside the window, staring fixedly at her.

'What are you doing there?' she shouted.

'We're on holiday,' he said, smiling strangely. 'Like the church bells—they've gone to Rome to fetch the Easter eggs.'

'How long have you been standing there? I've had enough of being stared at! Why don't you make a noise when you walk! You're just a dirty little sneak! You're like a spy here. I'm fed up, d'you hear. If you're mad you belong in a madhouse.'

That evening, in bed, she refused to let Micho touch her. 'My mother's right. He's dangerous. He's got to be sent to a home. I don't want him eating with us any more. I'm scared when he's around.'

Ludo heard every word, with his ear glued to the door.

For the rest of the holidays, Ludo was farmed out with an old peasant couple in the neighbourhood. They were astonished by his avoidance of work, his huge appetite, his silences, and the apathetic cries they heard from his room in the night. He spent ten days digging carrots, weeding, lifting potatoes and earthing up cabbages. He rigged up a scarecrow out of an old pitchfork that scared even him and made him sleep badly. He came home tanned, fit, and longing to talk about his experiences, but nobody wanted to know. Tatav had gone back to Bordeaux the evening before he arrived, leaving the page cut from a girlie magazine pinned to Ludo's pillow as an April Fool joke. The picture of the nude mermaid upset and bewildered Ludo.

As time passed, Nicole avoided her son more and more assiduously. The more she schemed the more he tried to see her. During the week she arranged for him to have supper by himself. On Sunday, when he ate with them and stared at her as he held out his plate, she made her irritation plain. He no longer got anything but the least appetizing morsels of food. Micho pretended not to notice. A truce was declared on Thursday mornings.

I knocked on the door . . . she was already awake with her hair all brushed . . . in bed with her shawl round her shoulders . . . she smiled and drank the coffee and said your coffee's still as good as ever Ludo . . . she didn't ask me if it was nice outside . . . her clothes weren't on the chair and when I sat down she said don't bother waiting I'll bring the tray down . . . I left and afterwards I saw her leave the house with Micho . . . she came back on the midday bus . . . she had her handbag with her and that evening I found out that she's learning to drive and she wants a car when she gets her licence.

Tatav's attitude to Ludo was also changing. Irony took over from friendship. He treated Ludo as a king did his Court Jester. Ludo was there for his amusement and for him to vent his spleen on now and then. He liked to inspect Ludo's room regularly, paying particular attention to the walls with their constellations of eyes. If he happened to open a cupboard, he found a nauseating mess. If he looked in a desk drawer, he found shells and semi-fossilized banana skins covering schoolbooks and papers: 'Your desk's a sort of pantry!' he said. One Saturday evening, to Ludo's intense embarrassment, he triumphantly rooted out a kind of pink rag that proved to be a bra when he unfolded it.

'You wear this?' he cackled.

Ludo stuttered and stammered that he had found it on the road.

'That's fantastic. I don't find bras lying about on the road.'

'Maybe it was in the hall, must've fallen out of the laundry waiting to be ironed.'

'You're just a liar! Lying's a mortal sin. You'll go straight to hell.' Holding the bra up to his plump chest Tatav said: 'I must admit, your mother's got a good bosom. Go on, admit you swiped it off her!'

'No! That's not true.'

'Yes it is. If you don't want to go to hell, you've got to give it back and say you're sorry. If you don't, I will.'

Ludo's teeth started to chatter. 'I'll take it back. I'll put it back where it was.'

Tatav turned the garment over in his hands as if trying to find an answer to a thorny moral problem. 'That might work, but only if you go to confession.'

That was the end of the incident so far as Ludo was concerned. He never knew that Nicole had been terrified when she found the bra, with its sucked-on cups, and inevitably filthy and stinking after a long stay in a desk drawer with rotting fruit and sausages. It was as though her memory was being dragged up from an abyss . . . Fingers crawled all over her . . . Will's green eyes twitched . . . his friends heavy breathing and laughter stifled her . . . she kept hearing the sound of her dress ripping . . . she saw the yellow lightbulb swing . . . saw a blood-red light coagulating, and it was she who was being endlessly torn apart. Eventually, she slammed the drawer shut, vomited and fainted.

She said nothing to her husband, but refused to be left alone in the house with her son, or to let him get her breakfast from then on.

June was so beautiful that Ludo preferred the seashore to school or catechism classes. He finally managed to get expelled from both for truancy. He had three days of happiness before the information reached The Hedges.

'Why didn't you tell us?' asked Micho.

'Didn't know I was supposed to.'

The problems caused by this silly idiot of a stepson were beginning to try Micho's patience. Ludo prowled the corridor at night, listening to them agonize over the imbecile who was making life impossible. Now that he had been expelled there would be no respite from him and God knows what trouble he would get into! It could not go on like this, an idiot was capable of just about anything. Micho had to promise Nicole a speedy solution.

I'd like globos like Tatav keeps in the aquarium . . . Nanette said I'll bring you all that for Christmas but since she pegged out I didn't get anything anyway it's not true she's pegged out . . . she didn't say your ears stick out she didn't say you're crazy as a loon . . . she said you have the most beautiful green eyes in the world . . . at school they kiss their mothers at the gate and even their fathers . . . I wouldn't want to kiss my mother . . . when he gets back my father'll find out everything . . . my mother tells Micho everything I'll tell my father everything and we'll be blood brothers.

The summer blazed on. One horribly hot August evening, Tatav and Ludo were having dinner alone at The Hedges. Thunderclouds churned up the sky without dissolving into rain. It was black overhead with a coppery sheen and the sea was flat and lifeless, forgotten by the wind.

Micho had been persuaded to spend the day with his in-laws. 'We won't talk about the boy,' Nicole had promised. 'We ought not to be quarrelling over an idiot.'

Seated at a table on the terrace, his head wrapped in a towel, Tatav watched the sweat form on his forearms. 'Got a date tonight,' he sighed, pouring himself a glass of lemonade.

'Where's that?' asked Ludo.

'You can come along if you want to. It's at Milou's place . . . Maybe something will happen,' he announced mysteriously. 'His parents are at a wedding in Arcachon.'

Ten minutes later, they heard a raucous whistle.

'That's Milou, let's beat it before it rains!'

Milou's real nickname was Lowflying Milou, a reminder of a crack-up on a stolen Vespa. 'But that's the nutcase!' he cried when he recognized Ludo.

'He's not dangerous,' sneered Tatav. 'When he bites he's only playing. Anyway I have his leash and muzzle.'

'You've got the pen, at least?'

'Of course I've got it,' replied Tatav, showing him a ballpoint with four different coloured inks, twirling it to make the chrome glisten. Milou held out his hand. 'Later, mate!'

'All right, let's go. But no noise. Last time it was a narrow escape.'

They walked along the highway for five minutes, cutting across towards the sea between steep embankments shrouded in the gathering dusk, and arrived in a farmyard beside a long, white, two-storey house. A silhouette passed back and forth in a lighted window downstairs.

'She finishes the washing up and then it gets good,' whispered Milou. Bending over, he signalled to his accomplices to follow him.

Night fell swiftly, a throbbing, sticky darkness beneath a black sky charged with electricity.

They had stationed themselves at the left wing of the farm, using a hayrick for cover while they kept watch on the house. Milou became impatient when a light went out, but another went on almost immediately in the next window. 'That's it,' he said, 'there's Gisèle.' A girl of about twenty appeared, in a pink cotton jersey and khaki skirt. She was untying the scarf that bound up her red hair. She flung the window wide open and leaned her elbows on the sill, studying the night and sighing noisily. Then the three voyeurs, breathless with anticipation, watched her slowly remove her jersey, step back with a flourish, and stand barebreasted right under the ceiling light. At that moment an even brighter light seemed to split the sky open, and the storm, held in abeyance for so long, crashed down on the burning night. Gisèle receded into a muddled and watery shimmer. Tatav, now soaking wet, protested that he had been cheated.

'But you saw her tits!' cried Milou.

93

'You said we'd get to see her bush as well!'

'I've already seen her bush,' said Milou, 'It's not as sensational as her tits.'

'Well I came for the bush,' Tatav insisted.

'You'll see the bush next time, don't be a spoilsport. Come on, give me the pen!'

'I'm not slipping you a pen like this for a pair of tits!'

Lightning interrupted this shouting match.

'Listen,' shrieked Milou, 'Berthou's coming over tomorrow, she's really ugly but what does it matter. I'm sure we could get to see her bush!'

'Okay, what time?'

'After supper. Let's meet at the wine press, in case my parents come back early.'

The pen changed hands, to be passed on later to Gisèle, who made a habit of marketing her charms — to please her brother whose reward was lessons in kissing on the mouth.

That night, Ludo woke from a fitful sleep. He had been seeing visions: Nicole in the attic, Gisèle taking off her jersey, Nicole in bed at breakfast time. A wave of desire flowed through his body, he turned towards the wall, curled up, and fell back to sleep with a sob.

The next evening, Nicole and Micho had a violent argument. Ludo had not closed the sitting-room windows during the storm, and the furniture was ruined.

'And my nice ballpoint pen, the one I got as a present from the newspaper, he's stolen it.'

'You accuse your son automatically without any proof!'

'Why shouldn't I accuse him, Tatav even saw him coming out of my room! He won't stop stealing, spying, going through my things . . . He's a maniac. Micho,' she lowered her voice, 'you haven't forgotten your promise, have you? You're not going to try and get out of it, now.'

Micho rolled up his eyes. 'Of course I remember. It takes time, that's all.'

Chapter Six

Ludo was living at The Hedges now as though it were a hotel. He was no longer supervised by anyone and he was saddened by the loss of his Thursday morning duties. Sometimes he saw his mother, who greeted him dryly, like a next-door neighbour. He no longer went to Mass on Sunday, but in the afternoon he often sat in the church and had a nap. Tatav had fallen madly in love with a peasant girl, and had taken to wearing cologne and spending the day off on his own. By midday, Ludo was alone. He ferreted through the house, played bellowing cacophonies on the harmonium, then helped himself to apples and went off to roam along the shore.

Scorning the barbed wire and DANGER signs, he strolled along the wharf: an enormous municipal mains drain that carried the sewage far out to sea. Ludo often fell asleep in the shade of the huge bituminized pipe, which he had resolved to explore to the very end.

He rarely went down to the beach, scared off by the swimmers lounging on the sand where he wandered like a king in the winter. He preferred the deserted and dangerous spots, off-limits to the public. He loved to collapse, fully clothed, into the quicksand sinkholes warmed by the sun, his head on a level with the sand-hills ruffled by the gusting winds, waiting for the tide that loosened the deep sand. He used to scramble free at the very last moment with a rush of fear. He walked along the shore, scratched huge drawings in the fresh sand which were soon disfigured by the flying spray. Then he started again, higher up the beach, disconcerted by the rising tide that still sent waves to rub out his frescos. He wandered around, oblivious to the sun or the passing of the hours, chewing on sunbaked seaweed. He picked up an exploded piece of a practice grenade, imagining that Nicole was going to appear suddenly, just like that, beyond the next sand-hill. Shouting nonsense to the sea or running until he was out of breath, he sometimes went as far as the firing ranges and found himself in the middle of fixed targets, with bullets whistling by his ears and soldiers pointing their guns at him from the distant ranges.

It's for his own good she said . . . have to take care of him before it's too late . . . he's unhappy because he does everything backwards he's cracked . . . when he does the washing up he breaks the plates poor thing . . . I only broke one plate and it was already chipped . . . who knows where he spends his days he's going to get us into trouble again he can see for himself he's not like the rest of us . . . Mama said he fell out all by himself . . . but don't want to have a baby with an idiot still in the house . . . he has to go and live somewhere else . . . I don't want to go somewhere else myself and anyway it's not me that's crazy.

He returned home when the sun began dipping towards the west driven by the feeling that he was all alone with his footsteps.

At about twelve one morning, in a cove near the wharf, Ludo came across a drowned swimmer abandoned on the sand by the tide. He had never seen a corpse before. The man was young and tanned, wearing a wedding ring and a green bathing suit. The second hand was still ticking on his watch. Ludo sat down near the dead man, whose left eye was wide open, and stroked the skin of his arm, warmed by the midday sun. The man had come from the

96

sea and the sea would carry him away again. The sea was his nigloo, his hiding place, and he had lost his way. Seeing flies settle on the swollen lips, Ludo floated the body out into deep water and watched his dead man drift back out to sea. He did not mention this to anyone.

'Come and help me. I only need a little push to get the old motor bike in. It won't go straight so I'm pushing it.'

Night was falling: Ludo had just found Tatav, dead drunk, staggering by the front door.

'Fuckin' bitch! She told me she didn't screw fat boys. And that I was fat and I wasn't good-looking. She even said I had blackheads on my big fat nose. But she's just a scarecrow, Berthou. A scarecrow and a fatso, ought to work.'

'I'm not good-looking either. And I . . . apparently I'm simple-minded.'

'Besides that—you're a Jew!'

'Really?' said Ludo, who did not know what that meant.

'Yeah, a stinking Jew and a dirty kraut! I can't remember if being a kraut is the same as being a Jew, or if you're a Jew you're not a kraut, but whatever you are you're a real jerk, idiot!'

'A real jerk of a Jew,' murmured Ludo, delighted to add new words to his vocabulary.

'What's it feel like?'

Ludo stared at him in surprise.

'Being a Jew? Is it true they trim your prick?'

'Not true at all.'

'Well I'm telling you you're missing a bit of brain. Anyway, I don't give a damn, doesn't help me and my weight problem.'

'There's plenty of people that're fatter than you. And you're not as fat as you used to be.'

'Don't bother trying to cheer me up,' sneered Tatav, flopping down on the lawn. 'I'm an expert on my own figure. It's a disease. I'm full of water. My fat rolls, my spare tyre, it's all water. You can call me the oasis from now on. Monsieur Oasis! If it keeps up, I'm going to sprout a palm tree! The opposite of Baby Jesus. I drink wine and change it into water. Where's your mother?'

'Dunno.'

'At her parents' again? I don't believe it. Her papa driving her back every evening makes me laugh. Come on, let's go and check on her.

'Who.'

'Not your mother, stupid. We're going to check out the cesspool. Mademoiselle Cesspool. We're all set, there's no one around. Micho's at the church with the choir.'

'Don't feel like it.'

'Yes you do. And we're going to have a little something to drink, both of us. You don't drink enough for your age.'

'I'm thirteen,' answered Ludo proudly. 'I'm almost six feet tall.'

'That just makes you a big idiot,' said Tatav, who was quite a few inches shorter.

Ludo had to support Tatav as they went through the house. Tatav wanted to go past the drink cabinet, where he groped blindly among the bottles, knocking some over, before carrying off a decanter of banana liqueur. They went out by the kitchen door, passing the silent workshops that Tatav treated to a flurry of kicks: 'These confounded workshops should've been put somewhere else.'

A translucent darkness lay over the countryside and made the stars seem close enough to touch. They came to a strip of wasteland thick with clumps of nettles.

'Here we are!' exclaimed Tatav, holding his nose.

There was a wooden rectangle in the grass, a sort of trap-door, with a floral-patterned soup tureen lid in the centre. Tatav lifted the cover, releasing a powerful stench. He stood on the hatch and took a swig of liqueur. 'Now it's your turn.'

The first mouthful was a revelation for Ludo. Tilting his

head back, he saw worlds spinning round and felt he was going to sink and drown in a bowl of ink where his memory still lay.

Tatav had opened the trap-door and was parading round the cesspool. 'Where'd he go? I can't see him. Come and help me.' Leaning forward, his hands on his knees, he peered into the gaping hole. Big flies were buzzing around, drugged by the fumes.

'What don't you see?'

'The ghost! Sometimes you can see him when the weather's clear.'

'What's a ghost?'

'I think that's him. Look!'

Tatav had already grabbed Ludo, pushed him to the edge of the pit and was trying to throw him in. Struggling frantically to get away, Ludo slipped, bumped into Tatav, who was off balance and with a shriek toppled into the pit.

'Tatav, Tatav, you all right Tatav?'

'Get me out, idiot, quick, get me out of here!'

Ludo lay down on his stomach and held out an arm. He could not quite reach the hand of his would-be persecutor and could barely see him in the gloom.

'I'll go and get the pole, hold on.'

'Don't leave me, idiot, I want to get out, don't go away.'

Ludo rushed to the workshops with Tatav's cries echoing in his ears. No pole. He remembered that Micho had locked it up, complaining that he had had enough of his son behaving like a cesspool cleaner.

It's his fault . . . it's him again . . . he's the one who killed him . . . Mama said he fell out all by himself.

He ran to the brightly lit house. There was no one there. He did not notice that he was knocking into the furniture in his frenzied haste, or that a vase fell and broke as he

99

passed. He went outside again. Tatav's cries had stopped. Scared stiff Ludo ran back as fast as he could.

'Tatav, Tatav, are you all right?'

He was beside the hole but all he could hear was the buzzing of flies. He had to find Micho. He set out on the road, haggard, his nose stuffy from alcohol and anxiety, and headed to the right because the only memory that pierced his fear, was the memory of the church on the right as you leave the house. Farther on was Peilhac, and farther still the dunes and the sea, and then ... but how can you single out a memory from among so many stars?

The guild room came into sight with lights jumbled up with snatches of music. The choir-boys with their short hair, the girls in the choral society, the priest, and Micho —at the harmonium, proud as a pilot at the controls of a plane—saw a terrified boy burst in, stare up at the vault where the paper cherubs were left over from last Christmas, and bellow: 'TATAV ... TATAV'S FALLEN INTO THE CESSPOOL!'

The firemen from Bordeaux took twenty minutes to arrive, but by then Micho had fished out his son using a ladder and a brand new tow truck he had had on display. Naked and shivering on the grass, Tatav was coming out of the faint caused by the noxious gases and the commotion.

As soon as he came round, he claimed that Ludo had pushed him into the cesspool on purpose and that he wanted to get his revenge sooner or later.

Nicole directed such melting looks at the police sergeant who came to take their statements, that he positively bubbled: 'Such a nice lady, Monsieur Bossard. Why take the risk? You're asking for trouble. Put the poor boy in a home.'

The policeman grilled Ludo who told him they had been drinking banana liqueur with a ghost and that the ghost had pushed Tatav.

The next day, Tatav retracted his accusation feebly,

complaining that Nicole was getting everything mixed up
and knew nothing.

'Did you or didn't you say he pushed you?'

'It's hard to see when it's dark.'

'You don't want him punished, that's why you're
changing your story!'

'Drop it,' said Micho, 'it's not that serious after all.'

'You won't be satisfied until something terrible happens
and then that'll be it. For him, for you, for everyone. That's
what happens when you try to keep lunatics at home.'

The mechanic began to have his own doubts. Perhaps
the boy really was dangerous? If he was really crazy maybe
he ought to be locked up for good?

Ludo was put on a diet of dry bread, but Tatav slipped
him food in secret, alternating table scraps with old rabbit
food pellets that Ludo thought were biscuit crumbs.

In the days that followed, Nicole was conspicuous by her
absence. 'It's quite simple!' she said to Micho. 'You just
have to make up your mind about the lunatic, that's all.
You're the boss.'

'What do I have to decide?'

'You know what. You promised me.'

The family circle was complete again at Sunday dinner.
Despite Micho's efforts, the situation was deteriorating.

Ludo helped with the harvest. He spent ten nights
sleeping in a hayloft, bundled straw, carried sacks of grain
on his back and caught a hare with a flying leap. He failed
to understand the advances of a seasonal worker, a female
law student who came to the house every evening to
challenge him to arm-wrestling. He was thirteen years old,
a strapping young man tanned by the sea air, moulded by
work in the fields and chores at home. He had a swimmer's
broad shoulders, but his chest was slightly sunken, as
though he were ashamed to breathe. His long legs with
their well-developed muscles could move with feline speed.
His strength was concentrated around his neck and

shoulders with an exuberance that contrasted strangely with the features of a face gnawed by anxiety. He had an uneasy mouth, sad, sea green eyes. His chin was smooth, to Tatav's great delight. Tatav periodically cut away at his own downy growth with a razor.

Nicole got her driving licence at the first try. Because the butcher drove a Mercedes, she chose a white Renault *Floride* convertible with leather seats, a radio, and a cigarette-lighter. She spent her afternoons in Peilhac, fleeing Micho's harmonium, fleeing Tatav and fleeing Ludo who she left loaded with chores.

'Oh, it's you,' Madame Blanchard would say. Mother and daughter stayed in the room behind the shop drinking *café-au-lait* until the evening. They were not thirsty, it was their bitterness they were quenching. They felt they were sharing a kind of intimacy.

'I admit that you've had a hard time. First that business with the . . . and now an idiot child. That doesn't come from our side of the family. No idiots on our side. You really didn't have much luck . . . It would please your father if you stayed for supper.'

While Madame Blanchard prepared the soup, Nicole went upstairs to her old room, and with a pounding heart, told herself *not to go up to the attic*. Once, but only once, she ventured up there with lugubrious relish. It was a cursed place, left to drift into oblivion. The smell had not changed. A mixture of dead dog and must. The wind whistled through a loose window-pane. A greenish film coated the scene of disorder left untouched since the departure of the last occupant. Clothing lay in a shapeless heap in front of the open wardrobe. The canvas aerie still cluttered up the rafters, rotting and spectral in appearance. The deep fryer, the washbasin on its pivots, the pram, the cupboard, the smell of fear, the years . . . all the memories of a blasted childhood were there, alive and malignant, rattling the dice from that first throw when everything was lost to her.

The memory was still raw to Nicole as she waited for the vision to fade, for the screams to cease, for her torn skin to stop hurting, for the shame to recede. But the shame persisted, waking her up at night like a cruelly guilty conscience. For thirteen years the memory had softened only to strike harder when it caught her off guard.

She left for The Hedges without a word of explanation, nearly crashing into the bakery as she manoeuvred out of the courtyard, driving home as fast as she could. Her son was not there. She had a glass of Sauternes, then another, then finished off the remaining half-bottle and went out into the garden. She found Ludo hiding in his nigloo.

'Come on. We're going for a drive.'

It was the first time he had been taken out in the *Floride*. She grazed the stone pillars going out through the gate and they sped off towards Peilhac by the coast road. They caught sight of the little harbour boxed in behind a spit of sand and barely slowed down as they drove through the village. Then they turned back towards the dunes, driving flat out over bumpy wasteland that fell away at the far end in a stony escarpment. Nicole jammed on the brakes when she came to the edge. She was out of breath.

'Go on, get out.'

Ludo drew near the edge, followed by his mother, her arms crossed over her chest for warmth. They could hear the surf beating on the cliff beneath their feet.

'You've been here before?'

'No,' he replied.

'Before, there was only a road for cars. For pedestrians too, really, but there weren't many.'

Ludo was silent. He squinted straight ahead at the evening sun touching the horizon.

'It wasn't a very safe place. There were drifters, not locals but outsiders. We'd come here to see the lighthouses. The beacons aren't lit yet, we're a bit early. That's Cordouan over there, right next to it is Saint-Pierre. When there was good visibility we could see the buoy over the wreck.'

'What's that over there?' he asked suddenly, pointing to an enclosure off to the right, with several rows of fencing with the wire tightly drawn over closely-spaced stakes disappearing into the foggy distance. Nicole did not answer. 'What's that?' Ludo asked again.

She sighed bitterly. 'It's a military base, you can see that for yourself, can't you?'

'There's even a French flag,' he cried, still pointing, 'and white houses.'

'So what?' she cut in hoarsely. 'Come on, I'm cold.'

They got back into the car. She lost her temper over the gear lever, which she had never learned to manipulate smoothly, and pounded on the steering-wheel in her exasperation.

'I'm thirsty. Let's go and have something to drink. There's a café not far from here, on the channel. Do you know it?'

'Where's that?'

'It's near the harbour, five minutes from here.'

They went back to the cliff road leading to Peilhac.

'It's nice in a *Floride*, don't you think?'

'I drove the tractor on the farm.'

'Once, I know. You turned so sharply the back wheel lifted up the trailer and spilled the grain into a ditch.'

'That's not true!'

The café faced the harbour from a dusty strip of land used for drinking and dancing in the summer. She did not park the car but left it where she had pulled up in front of the entrance. She put on her dark glasses and told Ludo to get out of the car.

'It's so hot today!' Her voice sounded strained. 'You go in first.'

When they reached the door, she had her hands thrust deeply into the pockets of her cardigan. She hid behind her son, directing him in a whisper, overwhelmed by memories.

She felt alienated from every passing moment. They went through a large room where tables were set up under bay-windows. Two couples navigated round the dance floor, the partners closely entwined, while Gloria Lasso moaned over the loudspeaker. Some seedy-looking young people were smoking and drinking, watching listlessly as the two strangers sat down. Nicole seemed exultant when she gave their order: 'One Sauternes and one beer.' The waitress was about sixty years old, as swarthy as an old Indian. Bells rang on the pinball machines; the bowling game assaulted their ears. Through the window they could see boats come into port and berth at the quay. Holding one hand over her mouth, Nicole gazed at Ludo. Her dark glasses bothered him, she seemed to have no eyes. The waitress brought their drinks.

'The beer's for you,' said Nicole briskly. 'I know you like it.'

Ludo had never tasted any before. He forced himself to finish the bitter liquid, which made him cough. She had drained her glass of white wine in one gulp.

'Things have changed around here. Before, they didn't have all these machines, or all this racket. You could talk without shouting. D'you like this place?'

'It's fine,' answered Ludo, trying to listen to the songs.

'The waitress is the owner's mother. She hasn't changed. Everyone used to be afraid of her. She was the bouncer, and no one gave her any trouble. She liked me a lot. She called me "sunshine". I didn't come here very often, though, except in the summer, after the beach. We drank lemonade with grenadine. They call those "diabolos" now. My parents knew her, too. When there was a dance or a wedding, they let me on to the dance floor with Marie-Jo . . .'

'Who's Marie-Jo?' asked Ludo suddenly.

Nicole fell silent, as though she had seen a ghost. 'I'd forgotten you,' she said dully, 'I thought I'd forgotten you . . . it's a bit hot in here . . .'

She ordered another round for the two of them and began to smoke. 'When I was three years old we were already playmates. She told me I had ugly hands because she was jealous of my hair.'

'They're all jealous,' murmured Ludo, enchanted by his mother's faraway voice.

'She was always jealous. We had more money than they did. Her father was a labourer at the naval yard. My pretty dresses and shoes used to drive her crazy. She was two years older than me, but she was shorter, and that bothered her too. She always tried to copy me. She did her hair like mine, she talked like me, she did everything I did. If I wore pink hair-slides, so did she. If I took a purse to Mass, so did she. She used to tell the boys we were sisters, but they'd just laugh at her. We really didn't look alike at all.'

Nicole stubbed out her cigarettes after a few long drags, exhaled smoke in endless streams, talked, fell silent and looked nervously from side to side. Drowsy from the alcohol, Ludo kept smiling at his mother and was beginning to feel sleepy.

'Then I went off to school, and we didn't see each other any more except in the holidays, with my new girlfriend Simone. We'd go to the beach together, and meet at the Fairway. This is where we ran into him, Marie-Jo and I. The table next to the bowling game it was. His accent made us laugh.'

'Who was that?' asked Ludo without thinking.

'Who'd you think? The American of course,' she blurted, her voice breaking. Her dark glasses gleamed in spite of the smoke rising from the full ashtray. She got out her lipstick and calmly retouched her make-up. The spell between them had somehow been broken. Feeling her invisible eyes on him, Ludo tried to smile again. Nicole seemed paralysed. It was then that the corners of the freshly painted mouth began to tremble, and two tears trickled out from beneath her glasses, coursing softly down her cheeks. Appalled, he was reaching towards his mother when she stood up so violently that her chair flew over backwards.

'Don't touch me, you lousy bastard!' she shrieked wildly, and went staggering out of the door.

Chapter Seven

When the summer was over, Tatav went back to boarding school. Ludo spent the autumn doing the manual labour assigned to him daily by Micho. He uprooted tree stumps, filled in a ditch, dug a trench to lay an electric cable, scraped paint off the shutters, repainted them and then painted them again because the first colour had not met with approval. The priest called for Ludo's strong arms to repair his roof, which was falling to pieces and leaked like a sieve. More than satisfied with the results, he hired Ludo to do other odd jobs, pleased to have found someone as strong as he was cheap. In payment, Ludo was invited inside to share his employer's evening omelette. 'He really doesn't seem malicious,' the priest reported to Micho. 'Or even stupid. I'd almost say he was afraid.'

Nicole was often angry with Ludo but without any real passion, as if the divorce from her son were final and the abcess drained. It simply did not seem worth getting upset about him any more.

In October he had toothache, but did not dare say anything: it was Micho who noticed his swollen face and drove him to the dentist in Bordeaux. Ludo had a dozen cavities, some of them eight years old. The treatment took two months. Ludo also suffered secretly from indigestion.

Berthou wanted to take a little walk in the country but her girlfriend didn't want to she said no not with that one he's crazy . . . its not true that I'm crazy. I know how to read and count . . . I remember everything with my memory and the girls laughed when I recited the *Hail Mary* all the way through . . . you can see he's crazy he's always snooping around the school . . . anyway his mother's sick to death of him.

One night, hearing Nicole and Micho talking, Ludo got out of bed to listen.

'I want you,' said Micho. 'I can't sleep when I want you.'

'Well I don't want you. As long as he's here, I won't ever want you.'

'So you don't want to do it.'

'Absolutely not! Are you the one who has nightmares? All night long, sometimes . . . I feel I'm not asleep, but wide awake. I can see green eyes that get bigger and bigger, like balloons and inside each balloon there's the idiot, with his green eyes whirling round and round, all night long.'

Micho sighed. After a long silence, he said: 'I've got an idea.'

'You're full of ideas.'

'It's my cousin, I haven't seen her in donkey's years. She works in an asylum. Well, it's not really an asylum. It's for rich people's children who're off their rockers.'

'Why didn't she come to the wedding, if she's your cousin?'

'You're the one who didn't want anyone there.'

Nicole's voice was coy as she said: 'Why didn't you say anything about her before?'

'I'd forgotten about her and I thought it would work out with the boy. I'll drop her a line and we'll see what happens.'

'It's settled, Micho.'

'We'll bring him back on Sundays and for holidays. He won't be unhappy.'

'And it'll stay in the family. Less expense.'

After a few moments of silence she whispered: 'So it's a madhouse!'

'They're not crazy, just a little slow. And it's private. My cousin's a nurse. She was having an affair with the director before he died. The boy'll be fine there.'

'It's a really good idea, Micho, a very good idea. You can come over to this side of the bed if you feel like it.'

Tatav came home in mid-December for the Christmas holidays. On the twenty-fourth, after lunching alone with Ludo, he told him slyly: 'I've got a proposition for you.'

'What's a proposition?'

'A little stroll over to the cesspool. To celebrate Christmas. Okay?'

Ludo refused, claiming that he had to lay the table and shell the peas.

'You're scared. I'm warning you, if the mountain won't come to Mohammed . . .' He winked jauntily at Ludo, drank a large glass of beer and disappeared for the rest of the afternoon.

The Blanchards had been persuaded to come over for Christmas Eve, it being understood, of course, that the bastard was to be kept out of sight. But Tatav had insisted on laying his place at the table. 'I'm sick of all this, I want him here!' After Midnight Mass, he had gone to wake Ludo from a comatose sleep induced by the massive dose of barbiturates given him by his mother to keep him away from the festivities. 'You didn't want to go to the cesspool with me,' Tatav sneered, throwing back the sheets, 'but you've got to get up now! It's Christmas, I've got a surprise for you.'

The turkey was burned, the **pudding** poorly cooked and Nicole's mood was foul. 'Well, daughter, you'd be more at home in the kitchen if you'd listened to me when you had the chance, instead of traipsing all over the place.'

'Shut up, Mama.'

'Come on now, it's Christmas!' said Micho, trying to smooth things over.

'And Christmas is Christmas,' sighed Monsieur Blanchard, who was being very careful not to let the bastard's eyes meet his, since he had solemnly sworn never to see him ever again.

The fir tree Micho had decorated twinkled with bluey-green lights near the harmonium. It got on Nicole's nerves by stirring up her memories: the lighthouses that flashed near the Atlantic. They had been flashing in her head as far back as she could remember. She hated lighthouses, fir trees and memories.

At the end of the meal Micho served the yule log cake brought by Monsieur Blanchard; they celebrated with champagne and exchanged presents. Tatav got a remote-controlled motor boat, a package full of a new brand of chewing gum, a Jerusalem Bible and an envelope he tore open immediately to see how much was inside.

The grown-ups were feeling more relaxed now thanks to the wine, and unwrapped their presents noisily: a fishing rod for Monsieur Blanchard, a lizard wallet for Nicole, a Winchester rifle for Micho. Then Tatav suddenly asked that his brother have a turn.

For the sake of appearances, Micho had vaguely re-wrapped the puppet-theatre he had given to his stepson earlier that evening: 'from all the family'—lowering his voice so that Nicole could not hear. Ludo took up the theatre for the second time.

'Here's my present,' boasted Tatav. 'You could eat it.' Gleefully he handed over a pretty box with a lamé ribbon, the kind used for expensive chocolates. Then he set off his laugh-box and shouted at Ludo: 'Vengeance is mine!'

Ludo had hardly opened the lid when he recognized the horrendous, nauseating smell of the cesspool. The seeping stench overpowered the smell of wine and cheese and the sweeter smells of the women's scent, stupefying everyone at the table.

'What the hell did you do?' Micho swore dully.

At the bottom of the box, grinning on a bed of filth, lay the eternal little white skeleton that Ludo knew only too well.

'That's my revenge,' cackled Tatav. 'Chocolate shit without the chocolate, pure cesspool . . .'

Nicole shivered and bit her lips, staring at her son still dazed by Gardenal, by injustice, his pyjama sleeve dragging in his plate—the boy who, just a little while before, had placed an armful of ferns tied up with wheat-grass in front of her bedroom door.

'Pure cesspool,' repeated Tatav with gales of laughter.

A mighty three-fingered slap landed across his face. Micho stood up suddenly, shaking with rage, glaring at everyone. 'Get out of here, all of you!' he shouted in a hollow voice. Then he himself stalked out.

After dark a phantom felt its way through the gloom. Ludo moved barefoot along the corridor, certain that he had heard Nicole and Micho arguing. Farther along was Tatav, and that well-oiled snoring he had been displaying since last Christmas, a nasal mimicry reminiscent of the motor boat he clutched in bed like a teddy bear.

'It's not my fault that the letter came back.'

'But why'd you say you'd sent it?'

'Well I was quite sure about it, I mean really sure . . .'

'Don't lie, Micho. I found it in your jacket pocket. You hadn't even changed the address.'

'All right, all right, I'll mail it tomorrow.'

There was a rustle of bedclothes and then Nicole spoke again in a lower voice: 'What's her name again?'

'Come on, I'm tired. It's Poupette. Poupette's not her real name. She's got an unusual name: Hélène Rakoff.'

'That sounds Russian, is she a commie?'

Micho yawned. 'It's her grandfather, or her grandfather's grandfather, I don't know. He stayed in France after some war or other. He was a bear-leader. He had a trained bear and lived in Bordeaux.'

'You'll see, he'll be fine there. We'll go and see him on Sundays, and he can come back here for holidays. It's no life for him here.'

When the breathing degenerated into snoring, Ludo crept back to his room, drew on the wall for a while, then buried himself between the sheets.

I'm not crazy . . . my name isn't the idiot it's Ludo . . . I know how to read labels and even write a little . . . I've got a good memory too . . . a coffee with character from beans of superior quality grown in the best coffee-producing countries in the world a distinguished and subtle blend six sardines in oil with anchovy fillets three capsules within a twenty-four period to be taken with a sip of water before meals promotes the reconstitution of muscle fibre and blessed be Jesus the fruit of thy womb mix the flour and remaining sugar in a bowl add the whole eggs and the zest of one orange mix with milk to obtain a thick batter . . . when I'm too hungry I go and help myself to apples from the neighbour's tree . . . I'll have a profession too and a house . . . I know how to climb trees and make sling-shots . . . I'm the one who can make stones skip the best on the pond and who spits farthest . . . the other day I got up on a cow's back she bolted when Tatav tickled her behind with a stick, I know how to cut wood, not Tatav, and how to grease a sawblade and sharpen the scythe for the alfalfa and since my mother said that I was dangerous they won't let me anymore . . . I don't want to leave the house . . . I don't want to go where they're talking about at night . . . Tatav said it's not his fault he's an idiot.

One morning, Hélène Rakoff's answer arrived.

Saint Paul Centre, February 11, 1961.
Dear Michel,
    Today is Our Lady of Lourdes. I received your letter and it gave me great joy. I had almost forgotten that I

had a cousin living so close to me. It's true that we live very secluded lives at Saint Paul, in our own little world of innocence and friendship. Here at the Centre, we do not have, as you put it, the 'mentally retarded.' What an awful expression! If God created innocents, it was not so that we should call them mentally retarded. Therefore, we have only children here, no matter how old they are. The Centre belongs to them, just as I belong to the children. The Holy Spirit watches over us. Could you send me the medical file on the child you mentioned and put me in contact with his family? Is he baptized? Enclosed please find a pamphlet concerning the admission requirements here. Are you still in charge of the parish harmonium? I would very much like to obtain any old missals or hymn books you might have. Sincerest best wishes to you all and to the child. May God keep you in His most holy protection.

Your cousin,
Hélène Rakoff

'Take a look at this,' said Micho to Nicole: "May God keep you in His most holy protection". She's changed one hell of a lot, has Poupette. When I knew her she was a real gadabout.'

The next night, Ludo overheard this conversation:

'I'm not really the mother, since it was an accident.'

'So maybe I'm the mother, or Tatav? We must tell Poupette.'

'We give her the identity card with your name on it, and that's enough.'

'She also wants the birth certificate and medical records.'

'Well why don't you tell her the whole story, while you're at it? There were three of them on top of your wife!'

'Shut up!'

'All night long, you hear? Three of them all night long!'

114

'I said shut up!'

'And why not tell her everything they did to me, too, and everything they made me do?'

There was the dull sound of a slap followed by a cry. Ludo slipped silently away.

His mother called him early the next morning. She was standing near the window in her nightgown, chipping the old polish off her nails and studying her fingers as if they were tarot cards. Her mouth was set in a hard line.

'I'm hungry. Get me something to eat. Make the coffee good and strong. Is it nice out?'

'It's cold,' he answered at random.

'I suppose so.'

Ludo looked at his mother, her hair about her shoulders, that beautiful dishevelled red-gold already threaded with silver. She had bags under her eyes; a pimple stuck out on her lower lip.

'What're you looking at?'

'Nothing.'

'Liar—it's a pimple. A fever blister. They come and go. Have you looked at yourself lately, with your jug ears? Go on, hurry up!'

My father drives the bus he has a gun and he also pilots planes . . . even battleships he can drive them and when he asks me to help him I'm the one who drives but I don't drive quite as well as him . . . my father won't have anything to do with the *Floride* . . . I've seen planes on TV and it's him driving them . . . and my mother knew very well it was him . . . Tatav says a plane is bigger than a tractor and even bigger than a reaper . . . my father . . . I don't know where he is . . . oh yes I do . . . he hasn't got time to call but he'll really come here one day and I'll do everything just like him.

*

Taking up the breakfast, he found her sprawled on her bed. The neck of a bottle was sticking out from behind the pillow.

'Sit down. I've got something to say to you. It's for your own good, you know. We don't often talk, but it's not my fault. You've a right to know the truth. So I'd better start at the beginning. When I was four years old I sang on a radio talent show at Yquem. That has nothing to do with it but it's still important. I even won a scooter . . . One day Nanette took me to the pictures in Bordeaux. You remember Nanette? She's gone now. I slept all through the film and had an ice-cream in the interval. I never wanted to go fishing with my father. It bored me, each to his own . . . Marie-Jo and I used to play princess . . . I was ten when the cherry tree froze and split, it was dangerous. Papa put cement in the crack and I never wanted to eat the cherries after that. I said they tasted of cement. Like your coffee. You hear? Your coffee tastes of cement! I don't like your coffee anymore. You made bad coffee on purpose. You're bad on purpose, and you don't put enough butter on the bread on purpose! And anyway you don't even listen when I talk to you. You're heartless, Ludo, that's what you are, heartless. You'll be happy when you've driven me to my grave!'

The Hedges, February 23, 1961

Dear Poupette,

I think it's better you should know everything as they say in the newspapers. Nicole, my wife, was molested by some creeps when she was a girl and you can guess the result, along came a baby. His name is Ludovic, but we call him Ludo. What's weird is that it's the name of the sand barge Mauricette and I went out on when she had her accident. So, as to a father, he doesn't have one. We've taken him to several different doctors, and each time it's the same rigmarole, impossible to make head or tail of it. Let's just say he's the quiet type. It's hard to tell what goes on in his mind, but he's nice. It's no life, for Nicole. And it rakes up memories for her. So, I'm enclosing a cheque in advance and if you could tell me when to send Ludo along it would be appreciated. Love and kisses from Nicole and me.

Your cousin,
Micho

Hélène Rakoff replied by return.

Saint Paul, February 17, 1961

Dear Nicole and Micho,

Sainte Honorine, a day of rejoicing. This morning there is blue sky over Saint Paul. Our Lord is offering this beautiful day to the children. We would like to share it with you. I've already spoken to the children about the arrival of a new child. I made them pray that he would soon be among us. I'm already eager to meet Ludo. We'll do without the commitment papers, that's all. Doctors are not always clear-sighted about innocence, a point on which I trust my judgment more than I do theirs.

We have at Saint Paul, moreover, a marvellous psychiatrist who comes each month and who will tell us quite sincerely what Ludo's problem is. We will see whether God had intended him for society at large, or whether his true place in the future is with us. And innocence by the way, is a gift that so-called normal people would do well to envy. As to Ludo's arrival, it's up to you to set a date. The best time would be at the end of March, because at present many children are on holiday at home with their families. I want them all to be here to welcome their new little brother. May God keep you in His most holy protection.

Your cousin and friend,
Hélène Rakoff

P.S. Thank you for your deposit.

*

Tatav was upset by the departure of his scapegoat, but the full truth was kept from him. The correspondence with Hélène Rakoff was kept locked up. No mention was made of the psychiatric oubliette to which Nicole was determined to send her son. At dinner on Sunday, the subject of boarding school came up. A boarding school like any other. Ludo would be happier there. He would learn things, improve his manners and make friends. On Sundays, maybe, perhaps not right at the beginning, he would be coming home to The Hedges. Or the family would visit him. How about that, Ludo? The boy kept his head down in uneasy silence.

Tatav promised we'd go down to the harbour at night and that we'd go aboard the fishing boats moored at the quay . . . they were sand barges so black . . . what a noise they made, creaking . . . the wind was blowing . . . Tatav showed me a big sand barge he undid the ropes at both ends and he told me this one's the Ludovic it's the longest in the harbour . . . watch this Ludo it's doing like you it's leaving and Tatav sat down on the quay to push the barge off with both feet . . . then I did it too with both feet and the wind took hold and the boat drifted away . . . we could hear it bump into another and it disappeared into the night . . . This morning the police asked if it was Tatav who was setting the boats adrift at night and Tatav said maybe it's Ludo so Nicole answered don't worry about it he's going to a home so I can have some peace.

Micho could no longer sleep at night. Overcome by insomnia, a guilty conscience, and sexual blackmail, he lay awake torturing himself over his stepson. Maybe he was crazy but then again maybe he was not. If he was not he should not be sent to Poupette, an old hag who went overboard for the good Lord so He would not give her a hard time later on. He was dying to make love to Nicole, and exasperated that she slept so soundly that he could not even hear her breathing.

One day, he said casually that as Ludo had not been in any trouble lately, there was no hurry to send him away.

'You're an old man who doesn't understand a single thing! I'm going to find someone younger. I'm not going to spend my life with an old goat who doesn't even know how lucky he is. Anyway, I'm pregnant and I'm going to Switzerland for an abortion!'

Micho saw red, being one of those fathers who become fanatics at the prospect of an heir. 'What's this nonsense about going to Switzerland? You'll have the baby just like everyone else!'

She shouted back that Ludo's presence spoiled all her maternal instincts and that she would walk to Switzerland if she had to.

The next day Micho wrote to confirm Ludo's arrival at Saint Paul.

The next phase was exhausting for Nicole. He was leaving. Her unconscious, once held in check by pride, began to crack open. She had never dreamed so much. The faces of drowned bodies floated up from the depths of a slack sea. She saw green eyes slowly opening and closing like the valves of an underwater seashell. Sleep carried these death-masks away.

She began to count the days, crossing them off on the wall calendar hanging in the front hall, convinced that Ludo's departure would make it up to her for her blighted youth. Life would return to normal. The feud with her parents would be resolved. She would no longer be a nervous wreck. She would have the courage to have friends again, to invite people to the house. She might even look up Marie-Jo . . . Micho's snoring was too loud to put up with, she must have a room of her own. He could move to the empty bedroom. They would have it disinfected, repainted so those hideous frescos did not disfigure the walls. They could do the same thing for the attic at Peilhac. On Sundays, Ludo could sleep in Tatav's room or on the sofa downstairs.

Twenty more days to go. Luckily she had the *Floride* in which to let off steam. She went to see her parents or spent the day in Bordeaux where she daydreamed on the terrace of the Regent Café, drinking apéritifs and scowling as she watched the crowds. A stranger's glance would drift towards her now and then like a bubble and come and burst at her feet. Sometimes she felt hungry and ordered sauerkraut or a toasted ham and cheese sandwich, but in the end she usually left the food untouched. Sometimes she took a hotel room, turned on all the lights, closed the shutters, and locked herself in with her demons. She smoked cigarette after cigarette, she dodged away from her memories and then pursued the frightening images, seeing herself again at thirteen — a bloody corpse under a yellow light. Then she drove away the horrors by undressing in front of the mirror, tasting the bitter pleasure of loathing her prematurely faded beauty. As if flesh, deserted by desire, could only perish.

Sometimes, in her hallucinations, she and her son formed a single being and she was forced to kill herself to forget him.

'Are you seeing someone else?' Micho asked when she returned after dark.

'Why would I pick up someone else when sex leaves me cold?' It was true that any adventurous man who dared to speak to her met with a chilly reception. Nicole's eyes were so icy and vacant that no one ever spoke to her twice. At the Regent, frequented mostly by stylish clients, she was known as the housewife with the *Floride*. The routine of the drinks, the untouched meals, the solitary room inevitably led to gossip. Seeing her so gloomy, so stiff and affected, and stingy in spite of the large banknotes she liked to wave around, the waiters imagined she was a widow on the prowl, frightened by what people might say.

Ludo did not know when he was leaving, or even where he was going. Nobody told him anything. He waited. He got out of bed every night to spy, but Nicole and Micho talked more and more softly. What was this boarding school he was being sent to? Who was this cousin of Micho's? He was not crazy, he knew that. What was so different about him that they always kept him away from everyone else? One Sunday, he went to see Micho in the workshop.

'When am I going away?' he asked point-blank.

The mechanic was hard at work underneath a tractor.

'When are you going away?' he replied evasively. 'What the hell are you doing here, anyway? If your mother catches you, you'll be in trouble!' Micho looked up at him. Dropping from the engine, a long trickle of black oil made its way across his cheek. He got to his feet, winced as he rubbed bis back, wiped off the oil with a rag. 'Now you've got me drinking oil, with your questions. You get on my nerves, Ludo!' He gathered his spanners together on the hard dirt floor. 'I'm not angry with you,' he went on in a kinder voice. 'There's nothing I can do about it.' Avoiding the boy's eyes and busying himself at the workbench, he asked: 'How did you know you'd be leaving soon?'

'It's at night. I hear you talk.'

'Really?' said Micho. He hid his embarrassment by puffing at a lock of hair hanging over his forehead. 'I'll tell you, Ludo,' he began huskily, 'I like you. If it were up to me, I wouldn't send you away.'

'Of course,' answered Ludo, who did not understand at all.

The mechanic turned to face him. 'What I would've wanted was for her and you to come and live with us, and then Tatav and you sort of cancelled each other out. We'd start afresh all round, you see? What does it matter if you're a disaster at school, we'd work it out; you could be my apprentice. But it just didn't happen that way. That's not good enough for her! She says you're crazy. Maybe you are, slightly. But it's not serious, you know, we're not sending you away for a long time. And it's a nice place. You'll be well taken care of, you wait and see. And your mother won't be picking on you all the time.'

'Of course,' murmured Ludo with a lump in his throat. 'When am I leaving?'

Micho managed a smile. 'It's not settled yet, Ludo, and personally I'd rather you didn't go at all.'

When his wife was not around, he tried to regain his former control over a household she ruled with a rod of iron, ignoring his futile rebellions. Between then and Easter, he would have arranged things. He was a born fixer. He could patch up pumps with wire, mend anything and he still had enough time to get the boy's future back on an even keel.

'What is it, the place where I'm going?'

'It's not settled yet, but it's a centre, so to speak.' He nodded his head and continued softly. 'A centre where children live.'

'But I'm not a child any more.'

'No, you're already a big boy. It's the others.'

'They'll all be jealous.' murmured Ludo. 'Will I be coming back?'

'What a silly question!' Micho laughed. 'If you don't, I'll fetch you myself.'

'And you'll come to see me?'

'Of course I'll come and see you. I'm not going to wait around 'till doomsday for a visit, and neither is Tatav.'

I'll hide in my nigloo so I won't have to leave or I'll hide on the big pipe at the wharf and I'll eat gulls eggs to stay alive but then the gulls might eat me . . . what's a centre where children live and what's doomsday.

That evening Nicole got home around midnight. Ludo had

just gone to bed. Like a condemned prisoner ignorant of the date on which his fate was to be decided, or an old man tired of waiting for death, he was beginning to enjoy life again and refused to think of the future. He heard the *Floride* approaching from afar, heard the squeal of brakes, the slam of a door, heard the metal pin from the gate drag across the gravel, then the engine once more and metal scraping against the granite columns. Nicole had been drinking again, her car was a wreck. He burrowed down between the sheets when she started shouting his name on the ground floor and kept on shouting as she climbed the stairs.

'Ludo!' she was there, wheezing on the threshold, silhouetted by the light in the hall. 'Ludo! I wish you would just go away.'

He heard Micho protesting feebly, Nicole having a fit and telling him to go to hell, followed by footsteps fading away and an order delivered at a distance in a shaking voice: 'Tomorrow, Ludo, tomorrow you're to bring coffee to your mother. Don't forget.'

It's windy on the wharf I don't know if I can get to the end . . . when you turn round you can't see the coast anymore and the seagulls attack . . . they don't like it when you step on their nests but what about me I have to keep going . . . underneath the sea's grey and makes a nasty noise banging against the pilings . . . I put a potato sack over my head with holes to see through I put rags under my shirt and around my hands and it's all right . . . I'd like to get to the end of the pipe no one's ever gone all the way to the end apparently there's giant fish that come to eat the rubbish where it spills out even whales and sharks . . . it's not true about the cat-crabs or the submarine either . . . my mother wouldn't believe me if I told her I'd seen whales at the end of the wharf where all the freighters are lined up along the horizon . . . my mother and, me we're married.

*

Ludo put the tray down on a small round table. An icy sweetness hovered round the woman watching him through half-closed eyes, her face glazed with insomnia.

'Sit down. Not that way, silly, facing me. Don't be so shy.'

Ludo swung the rocking-chair towards the bed.

'So, come on, there's no need to be afraid.'

He looked up, astonished by the softness of her voice. Nicole looked straight at him as if his green eyes no longer grated on her memory. 'You'll be leaving for the Saint Paul Centre the day after tomorrow. It's a boarding school for . . . problem children. Micho will drive you there. That's what's going to happen. I suppose you're big enough to understand. Things were getting impossible round here. You'll be better off there. And besides, the person who'll be taking care of you is a relation, on Micho's side of the family.'

He did not move a muscle, keeping his eyes riveted on her. Nicole was busy rearranging her pillows.

'It's for your own good, you know. We didn't enjoy having to make this decision. This kind of home is very expensive. They're specialists. You'll be well taken care of. You poor boy, I'm not even sure if you realize how crazy you are.'

She threw her head back, and her voice became harsher. 'What did you expect? It's not much of a life with a child like you. You're a liar, a thief, always snooping around, you get sent home wherever you go, you don't tell us what you're thinking . . . You've never once called me "Mama". You do know that, at least, that I'm your mother? And even then you don't give a damn!'

She was almost shouting. Her hand shook as she lit a cigarette. Her eyes darted all over the place like a bird that does not know where to perch. 'Hand me the tray before it gets cold.'

He obeyed.

'Of course the coffee's stone cold now, that's splendid! And you sit there with nothing to say, as usual . . . You're to take only the bare essentials with you, they'll give you clothes when you get there. It's about an hour's drive from here. Then there's a bus, but you'll see all that when the time comes. Someone from the Centre will come to get you. Try to be polite, at least. In any case, you'll have all your belongings again at the weekend. I'm not quite sure yet how it's all going to work out, but believe me, I'm not enjoying this.'

She examined the slices of bread and butter disapprovingly.

'You never put on enough butter,' she said, dunking the bread in the coffee, which slopped over the rim of the mug. 'At home I used to have fresh croissants every morning, and homemade mulberry jelly.'

He had heard that bit about the good old days a hundred times. He had watched her turn her bread into a sponge and lift the dripping mess to her mouth a hundred times, and he had suffered the shame of this breakfast a hundred times, a breakfast she ate disgustingly on purpose, to degrade him, sometimes getting so carried away it was as if he did not even exist.

'Are you listening to me.' She was getting worked up again. 'I'm talking to you, Ludo, do you hear?'

'Yes,' he said.

'"Yes *Mama*," Ludo.'

The bread and butter lying forgotten in the mug collapsed soggily on to the tray-cloth. Ludo did not answer.

'Well, what's so strange about it? It's polite to say: "Yes *Mama*". What're you waiting for? Say *"Mama"* Ludo.'

Ludo gritted his teeth and stared at the ceiling.

'You have never,' continued Nicole in a toneless voice, 'ever, called me *"Mama"*, have you, Ludo? Why not? Come on, you idiot, say it! Once won't kill you! Say *"Mama"* to your mother, just this once, say it!'

She went pale with rage at the sight of her son huddled in the chair, shivering silently.

'You win! You're quite right. If you won't speak, it's

because I'm not your mother. And that's the truth, Ludo, I'm not your mother . . . So you won't say anything? Well, you asked for it! Your mother's an accident, d'you hear me, it's as if it was you, got that? Every time I see you, I see all three of them, I hear them, under the yellow lamp. Every time I look at you it's those three sons of bitches I see, it's as if it was you who beat and raped me. I'm not your mother, you hear me? Your mother's those three sons of bitches!'

Her voice was hoarse, poisoned by hatred.

'Now get out you bastard. Get the hell out of my life!' she screamed, sitting up so violently that her coffee spilled all over the sheets.

He left the room in a daze. Blundering down the stairs, he missed a step and slid all the way to the bottom on his back without feeling any pain. He decided he was thirsty. Turning on the two taps in the kitchen, he watched the water fall in iridescent spirals into the sink, then turned them off again, confused and unable to remember what it was he had wanted in the first place. Bastard, bastard, his heart hammered out the cruel word, he pounded his temples with his fists, repeating bastard, bastard, and a blinding red light swam before his eyes. He found himself out on the terrace. The silence crackled in the sun. He beat his head against the corner of the stone wall, on the sharp edge, get out bastard! The blood he drew made Ludo feel better and so he went on slamming his head with terrible force, like someone mesmerized crushing a snake to death.

There's three of them they've got axes and they start with the arms . . . they're cutting logs under the yellow lamp little ones like yule logs . . . they chop right up to the shoulders and then they hack up the legs they hack up the bodies but the yule logs turn back into arms and legs and the three of them underneath the yellow lamp start all over again with their axes and the head they leave alone and it watches them hacking away . . . there's three of them they've got axes.

When Ludo regained consciousness an hour later, Nicole's car was gone. It never even occurred to him that she might have helped him. Looking in the bathroom mirror, he was pleased to see that he had done a good job on himself. His face was black with blood. There was a nasty gash running down his forehead and his shirt seemed glued to his skin. Without washing himself off, he leaned back against the wall and slid down to sit on the floor.

It's not true . . . I haven't got three fathers . . . but if it's true they've got to tell them where I am they've got to come and get me . . . Tatav says they're krauts and Jews but I didn't get born inside her all by myself . . . anyhow it's not true that's not where I was born . . . it must be freezing in there . . . I never could've hidden inside her nigloo.

When he came home that evening, Micho was upset to find the house empty once again. Despite her pregnancy, Nicole was never around anymore. She wanted a car? She got a car. But she used the *Floride* mostly to get away from her house and family. One fine day she was going to end up in a ditch and it would be the end of the baby. A pregnant woman is supposed to rest, not tear around on the roads after dark. Was she really pregnant? He played the first few bars of the *Veni Creator* on the harmonium, then gave up: even his favourite pastime was beginning to pall.

On the offchance, he set the table for two. She might get back in time for supper. He considered adding a third plate, thinking of Ludo due to leave the day after tomorrow but decided it was better not to expose him to any more quarrelling. Besides, the boy probably preferred being left alone. He would take a bit of cheese up to his room as he always did and spend hours scribbling like a madman on the walls. Everything would be settled in a few more days. Soon Nicole would have another child, that was what she needed, a child who was right in the head, one who was really hers, instead of a poor idiot. He was not a bad boy, but he did have bats in the belfry and he just could not help it. Even Tatav had been having trouble getting on with him lately.

Losing all those verbal sparring matches with his wife had slowly embittered Micho. He now prudently steered clear of his stepson's doings, the cause of so many affronts he had to put up with at home, and he unconsciously held a grudge against him because of his own cowardice. After all, the boy *was* odd. A bit too odd. He had intended to take him on as an apprentice, but what would people have said? He had already lost some clients since his marriage to the Blanchard girl. Some parishioners had complained, others had even switched to another church.

At nine o'clock he turned on the television, heated up a tin of stew and ate without enjoyment, casually watching images flit across the screen with the sound turned off so that he could listen for the car. He was always afraid there might have been an accident when she was late getting back. He ate slowly, to give Nicole a last chance to keep him company. She arrived just as he had finished peeling an apple.

'Ah, there you are,' he exclaimed, getting up to go and kiss her.

'My parents have invited us to dinner on Sunday,' she shouted from the front hall, 'so don't waste time when you drive Ludo to the Centre. I'm exhausted.'

He could not help asking her: 'Where were you?'

'That's my business, leave me alone. And I'm not hungry. You can clear everything away. Good night. I'm going to bed.'

She had thrown her coat on the sofa, turning on her heel after blowing a vague kiss in his direction. He stood quite still, holding his piece of apple, swallowing in his dismay. He heard her go up the stairs and down the hall, then open the door. Her sudden scream made him drop his apple and dash upstairs. All the lights were on. Nicole was still shrieking in the bedroom door, her fists clamped to her temples. Pushing her aside, he stood rooted to the spot at the sight of Ludo lying on their bed, his head a mass of congealed blood.

Part Two

Chapter Eight

The Saint Paul Centre was in the middle of a forest. Silence, pine trees, and thick bramble bushes shrouded the approach. A sandy lane linked it to the main road, a kilometre to the south. The wrought-iron gate, of vaguely Moorish design, opened on to a gravelly avenue leading straight to the manor, a former hunting lodge with spacious wings on either side. It was a two-storey building with a garret, a new slate roof, and a façade covered in small cracks. Forty rooms in all, including a refectory equipped with a huge fireplace that had not been used since time immemorial, or so they said. Two doors opened on to a terrace paved with gravel that creaked underfoot.

Looking down towards the river, there was a neglected park with a dilapidated tennis court. At the far end sat the car that had once belonged to Colonel de Moissac, the founder of the Centre: a Versailles sedan, now up on blocks near an overturned bathtub. An old cat named Dopey lived under the car.

Here, like sleeping beauties in the woods, lived 'the children'. The youngest was twenty-one; the oldest in his fifties.

They were children in spirit only. Simple souls. Simple-minded. They were as innocent as Adam and Eve in the early days of the Garden of Eden. They were the lily-white hope of atonement. They were thoroughbreds of the beatitude preached by Christ. One day they would redeem the world, as the colonel used to say, while he was in charge.

No one ever referred to a 'girl' or a 'boy' at the Centre, only to a 'child'. A strictly enforced segregation prevented any real co-education, however.

They all came from well-to-do families, those able to afford the lifelong expense of full room and board in protected surroundings. Their parents lavished melancholy adoration on them and took it upon themselves to defray the cost of paying for abandoned 'children' out of a communal fund.

The violent inmates were sent back home or transferred to the psychiatric hospital in Valmignac.

When the Colonel died, Mademoiselle Rakoff, the nurse, had taken over the running of the Centre. Two employees, Adolphine and Doudou, shared the household duties and supervised the girls' and boys' dormitories, which were on either side of the dining-room.

Depending on the severity of their mental condition, the boarders were assigned different tasks to help the staff.

On Sundays, the old father-confessor of the asylum arrived on his bicycle, cleansed their souls, said Mass, and had lunch with the visiting families. In the afternoon, depending on the season, Mademoiselle Rakoff invited him to play dominoes or croquet.

Ludo had been living at the Centre for a month. He had left The Hedges on the appointed day, against the advice of the doctor called in to sew up his wound. Nicole had refused to take part in any farewell ceremony, she said it would be out of place. She argued with Micho when he begged her to say goodbye: 'He's not going to prison!' she shouted, 'I'll say goodbye the next time round.'

Tatav had handed him a heavy sock tied with a knot: 'Stash this away carefully, it's my savings . . . so long!' The savings, all in five-franc pieces, had come from a piggy bank belonging to Nicole: nuts and bolts had replaced the stolen money.

Micho had driven him to the beginning of the forest road leading to the Centre, an hour's journey which took place in complete silence. A stout woman was waiting for them when they arrived. 'It's a real labyrinth,' she said. 'You have to know your way. So that's the boy!'

Micho suddenly began to check his watch, shifting his feet uneasily. 'It's just that I've got more driving to do . . . and you know what your mother is like if I'm late!' He kissed Ludo, promised to visit him on the following Sunday or the one after that. And, of course, he promised that they would fetch him home for the holidays. Then he drove away.

'Come on,' the woman said, turning back towards the woods. 'It's quite a walk to the manor house, but you've got a fine pair of long legs. They call me "Fine". The children like me. I do the cooking and the housework, and whatever's needed, really. It's a lot of work but that's all right. Mademoiselle Rakoff likes things to run smoothly. What's your first name?'

'Ludo.'

'Why not? You'll get used to it, you know. It's a bit strange at first, but in the end you're the lucky ones. Nothing to worry about, no bills to pay, no arguments with anyone, nothing . . . Little birds that're kept nice and warm . . . What's your problem?'

'It's the others . . . They say I'm crazy.'

Ludo was beginning to feel feverish. The path fell away under his feet.

She didn't say goodbye to me but I saw her . . . she was watching through the window and I didn't give her the present I made . . . so I won . . .

'What happened to your head?'

He told her he had been in a fight.

'That's not very nice. You'd better calm down if you want to stay out of trouble here.'

'She's the one who started it.'

'A fight with a girl? That's even worse!'

'She's not a girl, she's my mother.'

Fine shook her head disapprovingly. 'Mustn't fight with your mother, only leads to unhappiness . . . I see the way you're looking at me. I look like an old woman, huh! That's what slaving your life away'll do to you. I was just twenty when I arrived here, twenty years old. Now I've seen forty come and go, and white-haired as I am I remember it as if it was yesterday. That was before Rakoff's time. I didn't think I would stay on, either. Just long enough to look around for something more suitable, I told the Colonel. He's dead, poor man, and I still haven't found anything more suitable.'

Fine was red-faced and chubby. A few hair combs showed under her washed-out pink scarf. Big veins twisted on the hands clasping a black purse of imitation leather. She was wrinkled and heavy and had let herself go, but her body still had a certain charm, despite its faint smell of sweat and dishwater.

' "Away with you, slut!" they told me at home. Life on the street or at the sink, and not a coin for a bite to eat. You don't always get what you want in life! Anyway, men are okay. Then I took up dishwashing and I've been at it for ages. At first it was the Colonel and his wife who supervised the children. You'll see their twins, "the ninepins" we call them!' She laughed resignedly. 'Drive me potty, those two, never seen an appetite like theirs. Always underfoot, pinching bread when it's not whole dishes I've set out to cool! Don't worry if you're hungry, you'll get a snack when you arrive. We're almost there, anyway.'

Gingerly, Ludo felt the wound on his forehead.

Micho said I'd be coming back to The Hedges soon . . . maybe my father'll come back too but it's not true that I've got three fathers and it's not the three sons of bitches . . . she was lying . . . to make me leave . . . she

136

said it's for your own good I don't want my own
good . . . I don't want her to find my father again when
I'm not there . . . don't want her to tell him he was crazy
so we put him in a home.

There were twenty of the 'children' standing on the front
steps. They cheered as Ludo drew near, making a show
of twittering delight while they studied him from head to
toe. They glittered colourfully like the motley birds
stuck in Tatav's scrap-book album, with eye-catching caps
and bow-ties that seemed almost alive. A narrow space
separated the boys from the girls; the latter, bareheaded,
were fragrant with eau de Cologne and kept their eyes
lowered. There were more cheers and clapping when Fine
introduced Ludo. One of them, almost a dwarf, bizarrely
dressed in a red jacket, stepped forward and held out his
hand as if it were a racquet. He said he was happy to
welcome him to Saint Paul on behalf of all the children.
He was the Marquis Odilon d'Aigremont, of impeccable
aristocratic lineage from Nantes, and at fifty years old their
senior member.

At the sound of a whistle, the joyous animation ceased
immediately. Hélène Rakoff appeared behind them, smiling
like her charges, but more severe-looking and tightly
buttoned-up in a grey suit.

'This is our new friend Ludovic,' she announced. 'Come
closer, my boy.'

Ludo climbed the steps, shaking hands here and there,
bewildered by the uproar.

'You're so tall! We were all impatient to meet you. And
vice versa, I hope . . . Here we celebrate the arrival of every
new child. You'll soon see that the Saint Paul Centre, your
new family, is a harmonious refuge.'

The children had gathered round them, still chattering
away; Ludo could hear them laughing and whispering.

'Now don't catch cold,' Mademoiselle Rakoff told them,
clapping her hands. 'You'll see Ludovic again this evening.

Now I must tell him all about his new life with us. In the meantime you can go for a walk with Fine.'

'For a walk with Fine,' echoed the Marquis d'Aigremont emphatically.

'Ludovic, you'll come with me.'

Somewhat bewildered, he found himself on the second floor of the manor house, in a little room arranged with the finicky tidiness of a study and the messiness of a lumber room. His legs were giving way beneath him. He looked longingly at the well-polished parquet, not daring to lie down on it.

Standing regally at her meticulously tidy desk, Mademoiselle Rakoff looked him over closely with a soldierly eye.

'You're not feeling well?'

'My name's Ludovic Bossard,' he said faintly. 'I'm almost six foot tall, but I'm not mad, it's my mother who . . .'

'Now let's not get everything mixed up, please. Tell me about that cut on your forehead first.'

'It's my mother,' stammered Ludo. 'No, it's Nanette! She's dead now . . . No that's not even true.'

'I see. From now on you will call me Mademoiselle Rakoff, do you understand?'

He nodded.

'Yes Mademoiselle Rakoff,' she said irritably.

'Yes Mademoiselle Roff.'

'Ra-koff, if you please. Mademoiselle Rakoff.'

She must have been about fifty-years-old. Her hair was greying but thick, cut short and swept back. She had blunt features and a horsey face, piercing grey eyes, and a boxy silhouette in her tailored suit which was symbolically held together by a little chain at the bust. An unctuous smile preceded everything she said.

'You already know Fine. Presently I'll introduce you to Doudou, our oldest employee, a black man.'

'And you?' murmured Ludo.

'And me, of course,' she added indulgently.

He suddenly noticed the huge cut stone gleaming like a third eye on the middle finger of her left hand. It looked as if it was streaked with congealed blood.

'Salmordine,' the nurse informed him, placing her hands on the desk. 'This ring belonged to Colonel de Moissac, our founder. He gave it to me several days before his death. It's supposed to have magic powers. A very rare stone, in any case. But let's get back to you. According to Micho you're a strong boy: well, we'll find out. Fine will wake you in the mornings. You'll help her make the children's hot chocolate. After breakfast you'll help in our various workshops like everyone else.'

The words fell from her lips in slow motion, melodious and suddenly tinged with a nasal twang. She fiddled with the whistle hanging from her neck on a leather thong. Ludo was exhausted and no longer listening; to his right, seen through the mica windows of a cast iron stove, a fire seemed to be chewing on the coal with a noise like grinding bones.

Anyway Micho said he'd come on Sunday with Nicole and Tatav and he said that afterwards I'd be the one to go back there . . . but it's not the same with me I'm not a child I drove the tractor at the farm and I know how to drive my mother's car, even . . . she doesn't know how to change gear she's going to strip the gear-box.

'A few words about our rules. You must make your bed every morning. If you know how, so much the better; if not, Fine will show you.'

'I know how to!' he cut in tartly.

She looked at him in surprise, and continued: 'You have a large park to wander about in, but you are forbidden to go outside its boundaries. That would be dangerous in any case. It is also forbidden to run, to hide, to go near the girls' dormitories, to laze in bed, and to lie down during the day. Other than that, you are free to do as you please. You'll soon feel at home here and you'll see that we're a happy family. Do you have any questions to ask me?'

'No,' answered Ludo. 'What do you eat?'

'That depends on what day it is, on Sunday there is cake.'

'At home I had croissants and jam every morning,' he murmured.

'Really?'

'My mother brought me my breakfast in bed.'

Mademoiselle Rakoff smiled maliciously and softly chimed in as if Ludo were not telling her anything she did not know already. 'And on high days and holidays she cooked you stuffed lentils . . .'

'With orange-peel stuffing.'

'You're the one who's stuffed—with silly ideas! Is that what you wanted to tell me?'

'What're the children?'

The nurse's face brightened. 'At last, a good question.'

She patted her hair. 'Children are those whom the good Lord has placed on this earth . . . to set an example. What example you may ask? That of purity, sincerity, simplicity and, of course, innocence. You have been chosen to set an example.'

Ludo had a temperature and began seeing double, triple, and eventually an infinity of Mademoiselle Rakoffs. 'They're all jealous, all of them,' he asserted. 'The Pharisees were jealous. I'm fifteen years old. Tatav even said they were mad. I'm not mad.'

'Who is this Tatav? He's the one who sounds jealous to me! Well don't you worry about it, none of that is very important anymore. Why don't you come and see the lovely room we've given you instead.'

He went downstairs, following Mademoiselle Rakoff across a large room where bowls and wooden spoons were set out on a row of tables; at the far end, on the hearth of a colossal fireplace, a Christmas scene was on display.

'That's our conscience,' she announced without stopping. 'I'll explain it to you this evening when all the children are here.'

One detail caught Ludo's eye. Beneath the folds of painted material, spangled with gold stars, the eager visitors to the manger were not those Wise Men, but a flock of roughly carved sheep.

They went down a corridor, their footsteps making a rubbery sound.

'Here is where the boys live. The girls are on the other side.' She opened a door decorated with an imitation stained-glass window made of paper. 'The games room. Over there, the door with the red cross, that's the infirmary. Doudou is just across the passage. Your room overlooks the park.'

She went into a room with pale walls. Simple curtains, standard furniture: a wardrobe, a table, a stool and a bed. There was a gaily-wrapped packet on the pillow.

'Go on, don't be afraid, open it! It's from all the children.'

Inside, protected by rags, Ludo found a toy made of wool and cardboard, a sheep as big as a rat. His name was carved on a small wooden plaque with serrated edges.

'What is it?' he asked suspiciously.

The nurse beamed with angelic sweetness. 'Children are the guardians of purity,' she whispered. 'The lamb symbolizes purity, you'll understand it all this evening. Don't forget to bring your lamb when you come down to dinner. One last thing: your window doesn't open. The door must always stay open, even at night. On the other hand, the door in the hall stays closed after curfew until the next morning. I'll leave you now. You have a wardrobe and several boxes under your bed, I don't want to see anything left lying about. And hurry up, there's a musical session in the chapel. That's the building you can see outside.'

'What time?'

Mademoiselle Rakoff burst out laughing. 'What time?

Where do you think you are, my boy? There's no time at Saint Paul, you'll never see a watch here, what would you do with it? I give the signal for all our activities with my whistle. Any other questions?'

'Where's the sea?'

'You're not by the sea here. The sea is miles away. You can see for yourself, we're in the middle of a forest.'

'It's not true,' said Ludo.

Mademoiselle Rakoff's eyes narrowed. 'I'd advise you to be polite,' she snapped. 'Don't forget that you're lucky to be at Saint Paul. Your parents could just as well have sent you to the psychiatric hospital. If you cause any trouble, you'll get what's coming to you.'

She left without closing the door.

Fever racked Ludo's body. Exhausted, he glanced round the room. A crucifix was painted on the wall over the bed. The eiderdown was blue, the walls a creamy white; the floor gave off a friendly smell. He imagined himself back at The Hedges smoothing butter on to slices of bread with the blade of a wet knife. He breathed in the smell of coffee, of fresh sheets, of his mother's room. She would probably have taken advantage of the fine weather to drive down to the coast, she would be home late, she loved to come back late. He would not hear her come in tonight.

He thought he saw a grinning face with a green cap on its head at the window.

He opened his suitcase and emptied it into the wardrobe as if into a dustbin. Micho had packed it the evening before, adding food and felt-tipped pens to his personal belongings.

Ludo stood there, weak and disoriented. Then he slowly pulled a necklace of mussels and periwinkles from his pocket and kissed it with closed eyes. He had spent months choosing the shells, matching them, scraping them, washing them, drilling holes in them, stringing them on elastic thread, and varnishing them. He had tried on his sea ornament himself to see how it looked, convinced that with this present he would at last dazzle his mother and earn her forgiveness.

He hid the necklace under the mattress, along with the picture of her he had stolen from an album, and the sock full of money. Then, feeling dizzy, he curled up on the floor, wrapped his arms round his head, and fell asleep.

Of course he's not an idiot just look at those bright eyes . . . Mama said he fell out all by himself . . . you can't hear the sea as you could in the attic but that's because it's low tide . . . sometimes there was banging on the wall and I had to lean on it so it wouldn't collapse . . . I talked to her there in the wall and I scratched with the nail to let her in but I didn't know who it was . . . I'll ask Fine where I can see the sea from.

The storm had finally engulfed the pier, blowing the gulls' eggs to kingdom come and knocking Ludo down as he reached the end. The waves buffeted him so fiercely that he opened his eyes. The seagull's face was next to his, about to strike. He opened his eyes, recognized the Marquis d'Aigremont and stifled a cry.

'It's forbidden to lie down,' the voice said softly. 'I won't say anything, but the others might . . . Anyway you missed a really lovely performance, beautiful music. Now we're going to have supper, everyone's waiting for you in the refectory.'

It was dark outside and the overhead light was turned on.

'Don't forget your sheep!'

The children seated at the tables greeted their entrance with a round of applause. Their caps which hung on pegs, looked like birds perching. The manger was garlanded with twinkling lights. A pot-bellied black man was pushing a large trolley loaded with steaming dishes.

'I'm Doudou,' he said with a huge smile. 'Who are you?'

He had a youthful expression but grey hair. His bellybutton stuck out from under his jersey like a nipple.

'I'm Ludo.' He shook the black man's hand somewhat apprehensively: he had never seen one close up before.

The children were craning their necks to get a better look at Ludo. With a pompous flourish, the Marquis waved him to the empty seat next to his own. 'My name is Odilon. On your left is Gratien. He doesn't talk much, but we like him a lot.'

Ludo turned towards a melancholy figure with thick, beetling black eyebrows.

'Gratien's cap was taken away from him,' whispered the Marquis.

Just then there was a light blast on the whistle. At the girls' table, over by the manger, Mademoiselle Rakoff had risen to her feet. Everyone was silent.

'Now you have all met Ludovic, our new friend. I'm going to ask him to be good enough to come over here with his lamb.'

Trembling with fever and anxiety, Ludo left his seat to join the nurse in front of the manger. As he went by, his eyes met those of an adolescent girl with black hair, who blushed. She had pretty features, but an ugly scar on her mouth.

Ludo saw a dimpled Jesus, the ox and the ass, and a whole procession of lambs like his own.

'Watch carefully, children,' said the nurse. 'Like all of you, Ludo has a soul.' She brandished the fetish in front of them like a censer. A murmur of approval rose from the tables. 'To celebrate his arrival, today I am putting Ludo quite close to Baby Jesus. He's with Myvonne and Rosalie, right behind Odilon. For twelve years now they've held the same place. Let's hope Ludo will do as well.'

Myvonne and Rosalie were two poor girls so thoroughly robotized that every speck of freedom had been taken from them. They showed the same blind indifference to absolutely everything.

'Now I'm going to give Ludo his cap. At Saint Paul, every child has a cap.' She repeated in a louder voice: 'Every child has a cap, and every child has a lamb.'

At these words, a ripple of agitation ran through the audience.

'That's right, children, every child but Gratien. Gratien took his lamb from the manger. He stole his soul from the good Lord; he'll never see Baby Jesus.'

There was no doubt that Gratien was afflicted by some hereditary aberration, but the fog in his mind was occasionally pierced by a sudden gleam of light. His particular sheep had always been the last. Try as he might, despite his fondling and coaxing, even though he stealthily placed it in front of Myvonne and Rosalie, every morning the sheep had returned to the back of the flock. One day the animal disappeared altogether, and the mystery was never solved. Gratien had hidden it in an abandoned bird's nest, with a mini-Jesus he had acquired one year when he found the charm hidden in his slice of Twelfth-night cake. He had tied the charm and the sheep together with string, and his soul, thus closely bound to God, no longer had anything to fear.

'Unless Gratien finally tells us the truth.'

All eyes were on the melancholy boy with the bushy eyebrows, who seemed completely absorbed by adoration of his wooden spoon.

'So you've nothing to say?'

He did not even raise his eyes. He had never admitted his mystical larceny, and in any case he had forgotten it the moment afterwards. He mindlessly continued visiting a sheep that had ceased to exist, having melted away in the wind and rain. Gratien patched up the battered nest with little wads of bread, fiercely protecting a secret he himself had lost.

'Well that's just too bad for you! No confession, no cap.'

Gratien made up for it at night, secretly wearing in bed

a red cap he had found in the chapel.

'It only remains for me to give Ludo his own cap, and then we may eat our supper.' Producing a hat topped with a yellow pompon as ceremoniously as if it were a diadem, she solemnly placed it on the newcomer's head.

Boys and girls began to sing in chorus at the signal, while Ludo returned to his seat, crimson with shame.

He sat through the entire meal in stupor. Like all the others, he swallowed a white tablet first. He had been fasting since dawn and was no longer hungry. The boring chatter of the Marquis d'Aigremont exhausted him, and he was mortified by the stares and laughter of the other diners, who stared attentively at his every move.

He's in a home now . . . that's what he needed . . . that's what he deserved . . . he was put there for his own good . . . now he won't break the plates anymore . . . he won't cry out at night anymore . . . he won't snoop anymore . . . leaving the doctor's office she said they're all cowards about the certificate but you're crazy Ludo you know you're crazy . . . it's not true I don't know.

After the meal Mademoiselle Rakoff released the children with her whistle, 'And now,' she said, 'off to the chapel with Fine. Quickly! I'll be with you very shortly for prayers.'

Every evening she rearranged the manger according to her mood, consigning everyone in turn to disgrace and defeat. The falling-back of some opened a path to the front for others. Every morning they came to find out what their position would be that day *vis-à-vis* the Almighty. Having power over the children reconciled Mademoiselle Rakoff to her fate. She had once been the mistress of Colonel de Moissac. She thought of him day and night, she was the keeper of the flame, she took perpetual revenge on his memory for the solitude in which he had left her by dying.

146

Had he ever loved her? Perhaps, in the beginning. How he had sweet-talked her when he used to come and pick her up in his car at the hospital in Angoulême . . . He wanted to marry her. Those were honeyed words. She was forty years old, he was sixty, he wanted to start a new life. Of course he was already married. An error he had made in his youth, one for which he had been forced to pay too high a price: two retarded sons. Now he wanted to have a child by her. They must not rush things, or cause a scandal, it was better to move quietly for the moment and keep their love a secret. She could take care of the sick inmates of the Saint Paul Centre until everything was sorted out and he had divorced his wife.

She had gone along with it. She had loved him. She had given him everything, abandoned everything else, built castles in the air and rashly given up her position in charge of the nursing staff at the hospital.

It was difficult now to remember that she had believed him!

When Colonel de Moissac's wife died of an embolism four years later, her despairing husband had put a pistol in his mouth and pulled the trigger, leaving her to discover the resulting carnage.

She had had awful nights to get through when, tormented by desire, her body wept over its own fleshly passions. She awoke drenched in sweat, imagining her lover holding her in his arms and pleading with her. Then she remembered the mutilated corpse again and her imagination took her to the brink of delirium. She took endless walks.

Ever since then she had slept with the light on.

The photographic studio he had in the cellar—a bachelor's den in fact, with a folding bed under the workbenches. She had always been afraid that his wife would walk in.

Old coward! He had put a bullet in his head rather than keep his promises to her. Pretty clever, though, he had not missed a trick: everything he wanted was at home. Their's had not even been a real affair, a healthy frolic without the risk of nasty gossip. She had been a frolic to someone who took his pleasure like an old man—to enable him to sleep better.

After his death she had not gone to her hairdresser in Mérignac for over two years. One day, however, she had been seized by a thirst for youthfulness. She telephoned the salon for an appointment with Ivan, the handsome young man with the clean-shaven skull who had taken care of her before. She had gone back there every week since then, on Saturday afternoons. What pleasure to have her hair washed by male hands, and, with closed eyes and a mind at ease, to think about the marriage she had never had, the dinner parties at the prefecture, the jealousy of an ex-wife, and all the wonderful responsibilities of a life spent moving in high society.

Chapter Nine

Ludo never did understand the clinical differences between autism, delirium, melancholia, and delusion; for that matter, no one ever explained them to him. At Saint Paul, illness or injury applied exclusively to minor ailments with cut-price solutions: a sprain, a cavity, a stiff neck. The children were proud to wear big bandages, a plaything allowing them to say, 'I'm ill,' the magic formula briefly abolishing the abyss where reason was dashed to smithereens.

They seemed untouched by time, without past or future, excused from memory and death, all of them—young and old—hovering at the same childish age. They were going grey without growing old, without any future beyond the present moment, only occasionally subject to momentary flashes of doubt.

Ludo knew some of them by name: Gratien, Myvonne and Rosalie, quiet Lise, Maxence, Antoine, the twins Bernard and Barnabé, who stole food and sang Mass like nightingales. But some of the children were so shy that they seemed to have taken on the colour of the walls, silent and impenetrable like ancient packages no one thought to open anymore. That was the case with several girls whom Ludo never did sort out. Which was Nadine, Angélique, Mireille? He avoided them all superstitiously. They were skilled in the art of rolling into a ball and disappearing into a shadow where no eye cared to look for them.

Ludo had a weakness for Antoine, a sort of gloomy hermit who always seemed to be alone, even in a crowd.

His eyes gleamed with unshed tears that might overflow on to his cheeks for no particular reason. He shaved the right side of his face, leaving the other side bearded; brushed his upper teeth but never the lower ones; and bathed only with extreme repugnance. One day Mademoiselle Rakoff and Doudou tried to shave both cheeks and wash him by force. He turned into a wild beast, bit the nurse savagely, and the project was dropped. He had a habit of committing make-believe suicide by hanging. He would get up on a stool, knot his tie loosely round a coat peg, and wait patiently, standing in the dark, for the gallows to take effect. This trafficking with the great unknown, even so safely, gave him a sort of funerary magnetism in the eyes of the others and was much envied by the dwarf.

There was also Lucien, who spent all day reading *Count Kostia*, by Victor Cherbuliez. 'You're faking,' Ludo said to him one day. 'You can't read.' Lucien began to reel off the text at top speed, and Ludo went away slightly chastened. But that was the extent of Lucien's prowess: he understood neither the words nor the story, and for ten years had been endlessly rereading the same novel as a priest returns to his breviary.

Odilon was the secret leader of the children, whom he treated with condescending formality. He made up for his diminutive height with the arrogance of a Roman tribune. His pallor was tuberculous. His face looked like a big turnip sprinkled with long, twisted hairs, and split by a cunning smile so tight-lipped it might have been a wrinkle. He was passionately fond of music and claimed to have studied with Cortot, although he could no longer remember what instrument he had played. He believed himself to be a close friend of Mademoiselle Rakoff. She found in him the most deceitful and zealous of stool pigeons. He informed on others for love of her compliments. He paraded in front of her preening himself like an old turkey. His obsession was with the girls: he believed that they hated him. He never ventured out alone into the park, convinced that they were waiting there to tear him to pieces. He blackmailed the boys who spoke to them.

The boys and girls were allowed to talk to each other on the terrace before meals, but they felt so oppressed by anxiety and the innumerable rules and regulations that they did not know how to enjoy their freedom.

Ludo had shown Lise his seashell necklace on the first day. 'I made it myself. It's for my mother. We're married like the Indians marry. I put some blood in her coffee.'

Without answering, she had stroked the shells one by one, as if they were talismans. She was eighteen years old, and said to be anorexic. Unable to bear life either with her family or on her own, she had come to Saint Paul of her own free will. A harelip marred her mouth, enhancing the perfect lines of the lower lip. She always kept her hands in the pockets of a loose jacket that disguised her femininity. At the bottom of her pockets she crushed breadcrumbs or clenched her fists.

'When I'm back home,' Ludo went on, 'I'll make a necklace for you. There's lots of shells by the pilings under the wharf. I went out almost to the very end.'

The whistle blew, calling them inside to the refectory; Ludo took his seat next to the dwarf, who was sulking.

'I don't want you talking to that one,' he told Ludo during the meal. 'She's bad; in fact they're all bad.'

All through the day Mademoiselle Rakoff's whistle divided up the hours and directed the daily routine. The mornings were devoted to outdoor activities. The afternoons began with the children falling into line for a constitutional in the park, after that they reported to the workshops behind the chapel for pottery, drawing, weaving or writing letters, depending on the day. The more gifted among them sent their families little illustrated notes that gave them a feeling of closeness and accomplishment. In the evenings there were films and music: an audio-visual montage uniting Mahler or a Mozart opera to scenes celebrating Genesis and therefore innocence—the pristine seas of the first days of Creation or the purity of the desert. Next came the obligatory pre-prandial shower, the boys taking their turns first. Ludo saw them stark naked: flabby flesh and waxen white bellies. After the meal, prayers and communal singing, held out of doors in the summer, re-emphasized the idea of angelic unanimity. Then the children were at last free to go to their rooms or to the lounge to idle away the time before lights-out.

A new edifying theme highlighted each day, and recurred inexorably every week to haunt their memories. On Monday, a day of peacefulness, they practised serenity through devotion. On Tuesday, a day of kindness, time was devoted to helping one's neighbour. Wednesday was a day of hope, and they gave thanks to Jesus, the father of innocence and the gentle conqueror of Satan. Thursday was a day of collective penitence. Children wandered in the park, red-faced, overwhelmed by guilt for the most minor of offences, like stealing biscuits or eating greedily. Friday was spent praying for *outsiders*. Saturday was the day for joy. Everyone made a point of feigning happiness even if this was at odds with their deepest feelings.

'What's joy?' asked Ludo.

'It's being here, all together and safe from outsiders. Do you have anything to regret?'

'How would I know, I don't remember things.'

'Nevertheless, I want you to look more cheerful on a day like this for everyone else's sake.'

Sundays were set aside for parents. They arrived early for Mass, parking their cars on the tennis court between the bathtub and the Colonel's Versailles. They strolled along the avenues in the park until evening with the children, who chattered endlessly, or never said a word. It made no difference, it was their fate. They had been unlucky. When night fell, many a husband had a hard time getting his wife to accept the terrible separation once more. It was like abandoning the son or daughter in quarantine on a distant planet.

'You're not allowed to draw on the wall,' said the dwarf in his official tone of voice. 'Obviously, I'm not going to say anything to Mademoiselle Rakoff, but she does inspect the rooms, and there are some tattletales around. Anyway, I just wanted to say goodnight.'

'It's different for me,' Ludo said spitefully. '*I'm* not crazy and I'm not staying here.'

Six days of the Centre had already made him a nervous wreck. He had spent the afternoon playing the penguin game. The penguins were badly faded celluloid toys and the game consisted of tossing rings on to their heads. At Saint Paul, however, it did not matter whether the rings reached the right place or not. They flew all over the place and the children picked them up, dozed, babbled, or wandered round in a woolly daze, blind even to their own boredom.

'That's too bad, everyone is so happy to have you here. You never know! Have you noticed that I'm still in first place in the manger?' He strutted around the room in his red jacket. 'Today you were talking again to that Lise. She's the worst of all the girls, Mademoiselle Rakoff hates her. May I sit down?' Without waiting for a reply, he sat cross-legged on the bed. 'Mind you, you draw quite well, and I ought to know! I won all the prizes, all the medals, rode in all the horse shows. I like your black flowers very much.'

'They're not flowers,' said Ludo crossly, 'it's a hand.'

'It's a black hand, that I ought to have known! Behind it there are flowers though. I like flowers very much, especially roses.'

'They're not flowers either, it's hair.'

'Yes, but it's red, like fire! That's what counts, the colour of fire.'

Ludo had gone back to his drawing, biting the tip of his tongue as he concentrated on his work.

'Where's the sea?' he asked softly.

153

The dwarf seemed thunderstruck. 'The sea? I've no idea, it must be miles away. In any case what does it matter. Think about my advice instead. You're wrong to speak to the girls and besides, it's forbidden. They're dangerous, believe me. Haven't you seen the looks they give me?'

Ludo had not noticed anything.

'Well, keep an eye out from now on. You can never be too careful with them, look at Gratien!'

'The one who hasn't a cap?'

'Or a sheep.' Odilon muffled a laugh with his fist. 'It's a scream—you've got a cow-lick!'

Maxence arrived at that moment carrying a portfolio under his arm. He blushed when he saw the dwarf. 'Good evening,' he said. 'I just wanted to show Ludovic my watercolours, but I see I'm disturbing you.'

Maxence was a blond young man and rather romantic-looking. He had a thin, weak voice, and seemed bowed down by the weight of his pyjamas.

'Not at all,' said Odilon haughtily. 'Come in, now you're here.' Then he lowered his voice: 'What about Doudou?'

'I think he's asleep, I listened carefully.'

'Perfect, I have something I want to show you later. I saw it in my apparatus.' Odilon had a marine barometer which he called his 'apparatus', and to which he ascribed prophetic powers. He gazed into it as if it were a crystal ball.

Maxence stared at Ludo's wall. 'It's a hand, isn't it? But there's someone behind it, right?'

'It's a black hand,' said Odilon, 'with flowers.'

'Not flowers,' corrected Ludo, 'hair.'

Maxence stroked the wall with his fingertips, saying in a weary, submissive voice: 'There's someone behind . . . with me, it's Saint Michael killing the dragon. I . . .'

'I paint too,' interrupted Odilon, 'my pictures are all on display in the refectory.'

Maxence had opened his portfolio on the writing-table.

The sheets of paper he was lovingly turning over were blank, or else savagely paint-splattered and slashed with furious pencil strokes. The same caption with the same mistake appeared at the bottom of each sheet: *Saint Michael slaying an dragon*. This was followed by the artist's first name in inordinately large capital letters.

'Now listen to me,' said the dwarf self-importantly. 'There are things for all three of us to see, and don't forget that I'm your guardian.'

He was holding a large key in his hand. His deep-seated fear of girls made him the most trustworthy of jailers. He was in charge of making sure that Doudou locked the hall door every evening.

'It's dangerous,' complained Maxence. 'If Mademoiselle catches us . . .'

'You're nothing but a coward, Maxence, you'll never go far!'

He jumped to his feet, peeped outside the door and waved for the other two to follow him. Distant noises could be heard in the darkness. At the end of the corridor, he slid the key into the lock, and they went into the refectory. The bowls with their silvery reflections glittered on the tables. Glowing like stained glass in the moonlight, the bay-windows shed a ghostly gleam.

Maxence had abandoned them.

'Bad luck on him,' murmured Odilon. Torch in hand, he slipped among the tables and benches like a fish swimming in the shadows. Ludo joined him by the fireplace near the manger. The ray of light swept over the paper shelter, the ox and the ass, Baby Jesus and all the sheep in a row.

'How beautiful it is!' sighed the dwarf ecstatically. 'Look I really am in first place. I'm always the first. Of course, we're neighbours . . .' He let out a cry of surprise. 'Oh no! You've lost ground since yesterday! You've fallen back six places, this is serious! It must be because you talk to Lise.' He went on looking at the manger and commenting on the ranks of sheep in a whisper: 'It's true that Antoine deserves it. But why should Miriam always be ahead of the ninepins? The girls get special treatment! Look at that! Maxence is well placed, too well, even.' He chuckled, reached for a sheep, seemed to hesitate, then picked it up delicately—as if it were a chess piece—and set it down near the back of the line.

Depressed, Ludo returned to his room and went to bed.

Micho said he'd come on Sunday that leaves two more days here with the loonies, the sheep, the penguins . . . I don't want any more of this . . . a coffee with character from beans of superior quality a distinguished and subtle blend six sardines in oil with anchovy fillets three capsules within a twenty-four hour period to be taken with a sip of water before meals promote the re-constitution of muscle fibre and blessed be Jesus the fruit of thy womb.

The first Sunday arrived. Ludo was almost drunk with insomnia. Fine appeared in his room at seven o'clock with a suit taken from a collection of used clothes donated by the children's families.

'Not brand new, but not too old. The tie's in the pocket. Don't worry about the knot, there's an elastic.'

Ludo assured her that he knew how to tie knots, even sailor's knots, and that at The Hedges he had worn ties every day.

The clothes smelled faintly of mothballs. The trousers were too short, the lapels enormous, the cut old-fashioned, but Ludo thought he looked splendid and fiddled de-lightedly with the red rosette Fine had forgotten to remove from the buttonhole. He avoided looking at his shoes, old clodhoppers that had once belonged to Micho. It was the first time he had dressed formally as a grown-up, like Tatav on holiday. He was sure that his mother would arrive and be overcome with admiration. Proudly he put the necklace in an inside pocket before leaving his room to go to the refectory.

'You certainly took your time,' Fine told him. 'It's all getting cold. The children will be coming...' Then, noticing the rosette she said: 'So you've been decorated, have you! But you've done nothing special.' Without a by-your-leave she removed the rosette.

Irritated, Ludo set the jugs of cocoa out on the trolley, swallowed half a mug of hot milk, nibbled at a slice of bread and butter, and, without telling anyone where he was going, ran off to stand watching at the entrance to the park, awaiting the arrival of the first parents.

At ten o'clock, a couple arrived in a black car and asked him his name. Hiding his cap, he replied curtly that he was not like the others, and his father was coming to take him home.

Then he caught sight of a blue *Floride* in a distant cloud of dust, recognized the sound of the engine, and felt his heart soar. *Here they are, it's them*, he thought and swore to himself that the car was turning white as it drew near, that he saw them inside smiling and waving at him, that he could reach out and touch them.

It proved to be an elderly woman in an obstinately blue *Floride*. She spoke with a strong regional accent and told him that he was going to catch cold standing around outside in the chilly air.

Until midday there was an uninterrupted flow of parents, grandparents, brothers, and sisters arriving. The children welcomed them ceremoniously on the terrace, then dragged them into the refectory where a cold buffet was laid out, presided over by Fine. Mademoiselle Rakoff moved among the guests and fussed over her charges, telling touching stories about them to their families.

First Odilon, then Doudou were sent to fetch Ludo, but he refused to come in to lunch.

That evening, when dusk fell, the visitors began to leave. The first cars began rolling slowly towards the exit, followed by the children. Ludo was still standing in the same place at the gate, obstinate and furious, like a lookout expecting to sight America any second now.

'That's the way to catch cold,' remarked Mademoiselle Rakoff.

'We've told him that twenty times,' said Doudou. 'He's *more* stubborn than a mule.'

'I'm not a mule,' said Ludo irritably. 'Besides, they're going to arrive. Maybe they had a puncture. One day my mother had a puncture and I changed the tyre for her.'

The blue *Floride* stopped in front of him. 'You've hired yourselves a semaphore tower,' joked the woman with the harsh accent. 'He's very dashing. I hope to see him again next Sunday.'

He had not the heart to eat his supper.

'You didn't eat a thing!' scolded Fine when she saw his plate still full of mashed potatoes. Then she burst out laughing: 'Is it 'cause your mother didn't come? You're not the only one, you know. It's been thirty years since I've seen my mother, and it hasn't worried me a bit. You'll see her one of these days, don't fuss about it. Sometimes they don't turn up for months. Come on, eat a little something, you'll feel better.'

'We're alike, you and I,' Odilon told him. 'Nobody visits us. What difference does it make, anyway? All these outsiders leave me exhausted.'

At the end of the meal Ludo recited the prayer mechanically and did not hear a word of Mademoiselle Rakoff's speech congratulating the children on their good behaviour. Their paths crossed as he was going back to the dormitory.

'It's a good thing your parents didn't come today; it forces you to think things over.' She spoke in a low, confidential tone of voice, looking deep into his eyes. 'You look so unhappy, poor Ludo. It's amazing how sensitive and delicate you are. Don't hesitate to come and talk to me when there's something wrong. And remember that we're your family now, your real family.'

'That's not true,' he mumbled peevishly. Feeling a hand touch his own, he turned on his heel and left.

In his room he was greeted by a roar of applause, shouting and laughter. The ninepins were lying in his bed bawling out Mass. Lucien was reciting his novel at the top of his voice, Gratien was cackling, Maxence watched without a word and Odilon, beating time with his wiry little arms, seemed to be the choirmaster of all this revelry.

'They were all waiting for you,' he shrieked, 'they want to celebrate your first Sunday at the Centre. Look how happy they are!'

Ludo gave such a loud shout that the noises stopped immediately. 'That's enough,' he pleaded, with tears in his eyes. 'You're all jealous, but I'm different, I'm not jealous, and I don't want anything. I don't even want anyone in my room when my mother's not here. I don't want to see any of you, so go.'

The children stared at him, wide-eyed with horror. Odilon jumped on to the bed, prancing furiously up and down.

'If that's what you want, since you're the brains of the outfit, I might say, we'll just leave.'

The door closed. Ludo grabbed his jacket and with a terrific effort pulled it over his head like a sweater, and tossed it at the window. He threw himself on to the unmade bed, then went over to his table to get a notebook from the drawer.

You're my mother so I'm writing to you because the lady made me do it. And also because you didn't come. Micho told me he'd come with Tatav. And you too you'd said I'll say goodbye the next time, I heard you at the door. So why didn't you come? You've got to come. I'd made a necklace with mussels and winkles and I'm the one who varnished it. But if you don't come I can't give it to you. Mademoiselle Rakoff said it's no use me being here. It's not worth me going to the doctor anymore.

There is nothing he can do. I can be an apprentice to Micho. If I know how to mend the *Floride* it'll cost less to change the tyres. I can see for myself what it's like being crazy. I'd never seen any before. I'm not like them. Not that they're bad, they're even nice. They've got eyes like the mullets when Tatav goes fishing. Today I wore a tie like Micho's I can even tie the knot.

Ludo.

Chapter Ten

One evening a month the children drew *outsiders*. The outside world was a malevolent place full of evil people who roamed round the Saint Paul Centre, an evil brood whose intentions they explored endlessly. The most imaginative works were hung up round the manger.

Uninspired by this theme, Ludo painted his usual portrait, which seemed to dazzle Mademoiselle Rakoff.

'So this is your idea of an outsider . . . very interesting . . . and what does he see behind his hand?'

'I don't know.'

'Wait a minute. He can't breathe that way, the hand is in front of the nose. Why?'

'I don't know,' repeated Ludo, as if he were seeing his drawing for the first time. 'This morning the postman had lots of letters.'

'Yes, but nothing for you. You've already asked me that.'

'My mother does write to me,' he mumbled. 'You must give me my letters, you mustn't give them to the other children.'

Mademoiselle Rakoff took his chin firmly in her hand. 'You're not really expecting an answer already, are you? And if your parents are coming on Sunday, they won't need to write. The important thing is that you've made a lovely outsider for us. I've rarely seen one like it.' She blew a brief blast on the whistle that made everyone around them look up. 'All right, children, hand in your work, it's time for your showers.' Then she added pompously:

'Ludovic has painted us a very beautiful outsider this evening.'

After the children had gone, she re-examined Ludo's allegory of misery: the hand was like a slap in a vacuum, the hair was lacquered red like real blood.

Blood.

She sent for Doudou immediately to bring Ludo back.

'I wanted to tell you that I'm going to display your work in the refectory. It's a success.'

'What?' he muttered distractedly.

'Tell me, the hair ... what is it?' She looked at the wound on his forehead, it did seem to have healed nicely.

'It's my nose. When I think very hard, it bleeds.'

She'll come on Sunday ... won't give her the necklace won't even talk to her ... all she had to do was come the time before ... all she had to do was answer my letter and if I get one today I'll give her the necklace ... I don't care if she doesn't come and I'll write her another letter and I'll tell her she doesn't have to come ... I'll tell her me I'm not asking for anything I'll tell her I'm big enough to go to The Hedges on my own ... I'll tell her to go to Peilhac to where we were in a café by the sea when you tipped your glass over in front of everybody.

'Answer me when I speak to you, instead of tearing at your eyebrows. What are you thinking about?' She had the impression that she was wasting her breath on a desert of inattention.

'Used to go after dung beetles with Tatav. My mother didn't want us taking the spoons from the sideboard.'

'In the meantime,' interrupted Mademoiselle Rakoff, 'I would appreciate it if you would not use your nosebleeds for your paintings anymore. I've heard that you ply your talents on the walls of your room. I advise you not to do it again. One more thing. I gather that you're interested in

Lise.' Clasping her hands together, she lowered her voice insinuatingly. 'Be careful of her, and be careful of girls in general.'

She was fascinated by this harem of hers, intact and untouched by conscious desires. Virgins, all of them. She thought about it day and night. The purity of their sensibilities. Virgins and condemned, like the sea, to the steady flux of menstrual blood, which broke through their wombs and set their eyes glimmering with sin.

A strange smile spread over her features.

'So you find Lise pretty? You haven't noticed that her mouth is twisted?'

'And my mother,' he interrupted brusquely, 'why don't you want to talk to her?'

'Whatever are you babbling on about? I'm quite ready to talk to your mother. All she has to do is come here.'

The following Sunday, no one arrived to visit Ludo. He wrote to The Hedges again.

My father came the other day. He's coming back next Sunday. So you should come too. He told me he wanted to talk to you so's I could be an apprentice. The lady at the Centre said too that she wanted to talk to you. I'm the one who makes the nicest drawings. And since I write letters, that means I know how to write. The cook's going to show me how to make jam, so that I can make mulberry jam at The Hedges. And I saw a Negro I didn't believe it when Tatav told me it was true.

Ludo.

Two weeks later, he still had not heard from home. Mademoiselle Rakoff kept telling him not to worry. Odilon gazed into his barometer and said that he would never see his parents again, and assured him instead of his undying friendship. Then one Friday, at dusk, Ludo was summoned to the parlour: Micho and Tatav had just arrived. He saw them at a distance through the open door and rushed over.

'All things come to those who wait,' trumpeted the nurse.

'And my mother? Where's she?' he asked Micho at once. His stepfather came forward and hugged him awkwardly.

'It's very nice to see you! Tatav and I, we're really pleased, aren't we Tatav?'

'Except for all the driving. I felt sick in the car. And we got lost in the woods.'

When Ludo tried to hug him, Tatav held out a limp hand.

'It's weird seeing you here. I didn't think they were like that, the loonies. And there's a funny smell.'

'It's really a pleasure,' insisted Micho. 'We brought you some goodies, too.' He held up a bulging shopping bag. 'You've got a rabbit pâté and some grenadine syrup . . . also some shoes. Seems that yours are worn out. It's nice to see you!' He glanced from his cousin to Ludo. 'We wanted to come last week and the week before, but your mother was ill. Nothing serious, don't worry! She just wasn't feeling well. She's better now.'

'So why didn't she come with you?' repeated Ludo.

'She's feeling better, but not one hundred per cent well yet!' Micho slapped him heartily on the shoulder. 'She'll come next time, don't worry. Anyway she said to be sure to say hello. You know, love and kisses.'

'Its not true,' mumbled Ludo. He looked at Tatav, whose clothes bore witness to the caprices of a fashion at odds with his figure: black trousers, black shirt, and matching ankle-boots. 'Who's dead?' asked Ludo uneasily.

Micho burst out laughing. 'You're right! Old Tatav looks like an undertaker. Seems the girls go for it though. Apart from that, everybody's fine.'

Mademoiselle Rakoff laughed good-humouredly at this and then excused herself for having to leave them—during the week she was busy every moment of the day. 'Ludo, why don't you show them the park while it's still light out. And your room, too. And remember not to be late for supper.'

'Where are the loonies?' sneered Tatav after she had gone.

'In the shower, and they're not loonies! There're some who know how to read and write. There's even one who's a marquis.'

'You've grown some more,' said Micho, misinterpreting his stepson's scrawniness. 'You've grown but you're rather pale. Okay, let's see the park.'

They saw no one as they went down the stairs.

Heartsick, Ludo searched in vain for the words he had been rehearsing day and night for a month. The words that would persuade them to take him back to The Hedges.

Micho studied the imposing façade of the manor house, looking larger in the advancing shadows. 'They're rolling in money here, that's obvious! Must be loaded.'

'On Sundays we have cake, but it's not very good.'

'Really beautiful trees, too, as beautiful as the ones at home. And what's your room like?'

'There's not enough space, the lady said. But now that you're here, I can come home again.'

Micho looked at him surprised. 'What do you mean you can come home?'

'I'm going home with you surely? I knew someone would come and get me.'

Micho did not answer at once. 'Listen, Ludo, my dear,' he said finally, 'it's really nice to see you, believe me! Of course we're going to come and get you, that's a promise. But you've got to wait a little bit longer. You're learning things here, you're well taken care of. There's company for you and you're not really unhappy.'

Ludo clenched his fists. 'I could be an apprentice,' he grumbled. 'The lady said that I could be an apprentice.'

'Look at that! You've got a *pétanque* pitch,' exclaimed Micho evasively, pointing to the area near their feet.

'It's to catch the penguins.' Ludo saw Tatav make a face and turn away.

'And what's to be seen over there?' continued Micho, looking towards the park.

'There's a tennis court for cars.'

'That's called a garage,' squeaked Tatav whose voice was breaking.

They followed the main avenue deep into the gloomy pine forest. The silence in the undergrowth enveloped them in an uneasy intimacy. A stinging drizzle began to fall and the air suddenly grew chilly. They came to the tennis court, rutted with tyre tracks and wreathed in mist, with the ancient car and the bathtub tilted over on its side like an old boat.

'That your bathroom?' cackled Tatav.

They stopped at the edge of the court, as though it was the shore of a lake.

'What've you been doing with yourself?' asked Micho, forcing a playful tone into his voice.

'When're you coming to take me home?'

'We'll have to see about that—have to speak to my cousin, and also to . . .' He turned the last word into a long sigh.

'Hey you two, it's freezing out here,' complained Tatav, stamping his feet.

'And why didn't anyone answer my letters?'

Micho swore he had never seen a letter. 'She must've forgotten to show them to me, she didn't do it on purpose, she just forgot. She's changed, you know!'

Night seemed to fall around them in one swoop, thickened by fog and cold. When they emerged from the undergrowth, their shoes creaked on the gravel in the court-yard. Ahead of them, the lights of the front steps and of the refectory gleamed softly.

'Before we leave we'd like to see what your room's like.'

'I don't feel like meeting the loonies,' groused Tatav.

As they were climbing the steps, Odilon appeared, in his tight red jacket, to greet them as lord of the manor.

'Welcome, gentlemen,' he exclaimed, bowing and scraping. 'Ludovic has often talked about you.'

Grouped at the entrance to the refectory, a cluster of self-conscious children peered eagerly at the visitors.

'That's the Marquis d'Aigremont,' whispered Ludo.

Tatav ignored the proffered hand.

'You're still messing up the walls,' observed Micho in Ludo's room. 'Apart from that, it's rather nice here!'

He announced noisily that the bed was comfortable, that it was just like a hotel, and that he would really enjoy spending a few days there to rest and relax. Then he asked: 'And where does Madame perform her toilette?'

It was his usual little joke about wanting the bathroom.

'It's outside. If I'm an apprentice, I can earn money, I wouldn't be a bother. So why didn't she come?'

There was the sound of running and laughter in the corridor followed by a long whistle. Sitting on the bed, Micho stared at the floor.

'Why didn't she come,' Ludo repeated, wrinkling his forehead. 'You're talking about your mother? She almost did come, you know, she almost came. In any case, we're going to tell her all about it.'

'I'm not crazy,' murmured Ludo.

Standing with his arms crossed, Tatav coughed disparagingly. Ludo was about to protest when Mademoiselle Rakoff came in.

'We're about to sit down to supper. Would you like to stay and eat with the children?'

'I wouldn't say no,' replied Micho quickly. 'How about it, Tatav, shall we stay?'

'I'm not hungry. And we told Nicole we wouldn't be long.'

'So what!' Micho blustered. 'I'm my own boss! I'm not about to start taking orders from a woman! On the other hand, she might be getting worried. She's afraid if she's left alone. And we do have more driving to do.

167

It's not important—we'll stay to supper the next time.'

Suddenly at a loss, Ludo accompanied them politely on their way out, unable to remember what he had wanted to say. He was disoriented and swept along by a current against which he no longer even tried to struggle. They crossed the refectory and the children, seated at their tables, clapped as they passed. Odilon left his seat to go and turn on the outside lights. Gusts of rain swept over the terrace. They were silent until they reached the front door. The car was parked nearby.

'That's my mother's car,' cried Ludo, rushing forward.

'You're right,' said Micho. 'It's battered, but it's fast.'

The goodbyes were brief, cut short by a heavy shower. While the other two were getting into the car, Ludo stroked the dripping coachwork and the tyres. Then Micho started the engine, and the headlights fanned out into the darkness.

'We're definitely coming back next Sunday,' he promised through the lowered window. 'It was wonderful seeing you.'

His teeth chattering with cold, Ludo hung on to the door with both hands and tried to stick his head inside the car window. 'The windscreen wipers are still making the same noise,' he pleaded. 'They need fixing. I bet I could learn to do it.'

'I'm sure you could, my boy. Now we're definitely coming next Sunday and we'll tell your mother all about our visit. Come on, Ludo, don't be so upset.' Micho slowly rolled up the window.

'Wait!' cried Ludo. 'Give her this when you get home.' He held out his necklace. 'Tell her that I made it myself, it's for her to wear to Mass on Sunday.' He did not see the look of amazement on his stepfather's face.

'I'll give it to her,' stammered Micho. 'She'll be so pleased.'

The window was closed, Tatav waved his hand vaguely. Micho was still talking, but Ludo could not hear any more. He let go of the car, which began bumping over the sand.

When he saw the red rear lights, Ludo knew that he had been abandoned. He meant to run after the car, to shout that they had forgotten him, that he wasn't crazy. But the *Floride* accelerated suddenly into another world, and its lights vanished.

'We've already nearly finished,' remarked Mademoiselle Rakoff sourly as Ludo walked in.

Without answering he went to his seat next to the dwarf, who announced arrogantly: 'It's forbidden to be late.'

'I don't give a damn,' said Ludo, so loudly that the nurse overheard.

'You're very rude and ill-bred, and you won't have any vanilla pudding because of your bad behaviour. Since seeing your family puts you in such a bad mood, I'll write to them this evening and tell them not to come again until further notice.'

An anguished silence hovered over the seated children, broken only by Gratien's slurping as he lapped up his pudding.

'It's also forbidden to answer back to Mademoiselle,' added Odilon pedantically.

Then, sticking halfway out of the red jacket pocket, Ludo noticed a photograph he recognized instinctively: the one of Nicole, the one he thought was safely hidden under his mattress. He leapt towards the dwarf, who clambered down off the bench shouting for help. Summoned by the whistle, Doudou almost had to knock Ludo unconscious to make him let go.

'Because of you,' fumed the nurse, 'I'll have to give them a double dose of sedatives. They'll be upset for months, now.'

Odilon was sobbing into a huge checked handkerchief.

'That's enough, Monsieur le Marquis! Ludo will apologize publicly and then go to bed without supper.'

'He stole my picture,' protested Ludo, somewhat hampered by the black forearm hooked round his neck.

'Let him go, Doudou. What picture?'

He unfolded a sweat-stained photograph showing Nicole, at her First Communion, holding a bouquet of flowers. 'It's my mother,' he announced proudly. 'My mother's pretty!' He glared defiantly at Mademoiselle Rakoff.

'That's all very well, but she hasn't been to visit you, and I'd like to be sure you're telling the truth.'

Still fussing over his rumpled finery, Odilon started shouting: 'It's disgraceful. It's my picture! Anyway I have the first place in the manger.'

'You're a thief,' cried Ludo, and Doudou had to grab him again.

'You know perfectly well,' the nurse murmured evenly, 'that you don't need to raise your voice here. I will therefore punish the voice that breaks the silence, and may be lying. You will not speak to anyone for six days, Ludo. And no one will speak to you. Since there is a disagreement over the photograph, I'll keep it myself.'

'But it's my mother,' he screamed, before the forearm cut off his breathing again.

She beamed angelically at the adolescent. 'The photo's all torn, and even if it was your mother, what does it matter? I hope that you carry her picture in your heart. That's all that counts.'

Ludo was not really asleep. He had thrown back his bed-clothes, taken off his pyjamas, and lay clutching the pillow, sucking one of its corners. He watched with wide-open eyes as the unknown man, walking under a black sky, held out his hand to the girl from the photograph in her First Communion dress. Both of them trod lightly over distant roads as blue as the sea, while he struggled after them trying to catch up, getting bogged down in the mud, begging them to wait for him, and always arriving too late, as the rear lights of the *Floride* disappeared at the end of the wharf. He could also hear the noise of a nail on the wall, only it was not a wall, it was the hide of a dead sheep on the beach, and the more he scraped at its flank, the more the sand flew, and the colder the night air became. Then he glued his eye to an open wound, and once more it was like a telescope showing the man and the girl wafted across the sea on steps of foam. He felt that if he closed his eyes, these apparitions would die and that he would never again see an unknown man walking, a man who had only to turn around to save his life.

My mother didn't come she said to give me a big kiss . . . she said you're sweet Ludo when I'd put heather on the tray . . . She never said who he was my father and anyway all that's not true . . . she must've even told Micho not to go there she even said don't stay too long they must've got yelled at . . . Tatav was looking at me as if I was a real loony but the loony's couldn't fix Nicole's windscreen wipers and I know you have to change the rubber scrapers but I won't tell them . . . maybe they got back to The Hedges and she asked how I was . . . most of all I hope that Micho gave her my necklace . . . she must have tried it on and she'll come and see me next time . . . but when are they coming to get me for good?

He woke up. Outside his door, real live footsteps were coming closer, barely audible, between long periods of silence. He imagined the dwarf secretly visiting the manger and blood pounded in his head. The dwarf. The thief. His mother. He leapt naked into the corridor but it was empty. The orange night-light flickered. The peaceful sounds of breathing floated through the darkness. He slipped on his pyjama trousers, went to the end of the hall, and ran his hand over the closed door that imprisoned him, hesitating to hurl himself against the panel. Then his hand touched the doorknob: it turned effortlessly and Ludo was bathed in the deeper blue night of the refectory.

It had stopped raining. Weaving among the tables, he reached the front hall, where he recognized the shadow of the staircase leading upstairs to Mademoiselle Rakoff's room, and next to it the front door with its iron grille opening on to the park. He turned the key in the lock and went outside. The brisk chill of April stung his naked chest. He had taken only a few steps towards the forest, however, when he had to stop and turn back: grating noises from the gravel underfoot were echoing through the still night. He found an old flowerbed next to the house and walked along the wall in silence, mysteriously happy to melt into the darkness like an animal in the forest.

To the north, a crescent moon was slowly finishing its course across the sky, touching the horizon with the sheen of watered silk, wreathing the pine forest in pearly mist. Ludo came to an open window and stood on tiptoe to look inside. Unable to see anything, he was about to glide away when a moonbeam shone into the room, showing Fine in her tumbled bedclothes. The shadow of a naked breast hung down over one side of the bed; on the other, Doudou lay asleep, his black skin gleaming like platinum. Shocked, Ludo turned away. He felt sad and lost. He took a short cut across the terrace and went into the woods by the main avenue. His pyjama trousers were soaking wet. His bare feet hurt; he must have scratched them, but the pain was mixed with pleasure. Arriving at the tennis court, he walked completely round the Versailles, opened the doors, and sat in front of the steering-wheel. The car smelled of mildew; the springs bruised his back. He shifted the gears, worked the pedals, imitated the horn, and fiddled with the dials on the dashboard, hoping to start the car.

She'd be really impressed if she saw me arrive in a car bigger than hers . . . anyway all my mother had to do was not have her hair cut and then sometimes she has a fever blister on her lip.

He got out of the car and went to the bathtub. Perched on slanting ground, it was full of water; oily rainbows quivered on the surface. He had never been allowed to wash in the bathtub at The Hedges. Nicole would not allow anyone else to use it. He climbed over the rim and slowly submerged himself up to his neck. He felt stifled. His muscles became petrified, icy arrows pricked his skin, tears blinded him. Then he began to feel better. Lifting his numbed arms from the rim of the bath he plunged his hands into a layer of slime at the very bottom, which felt warm to him. He gained confidence, closed his eyes and held his breath, slipping his head completely underwater. He waited, and saw red waves breaking on the red sand. Red waves, a voice shouting, blows thundering down.

Maybe she's right ... maybe I am crazy ... I never told her she was right ... that's what I should've done ... If I told her everything would work out ... I'll go back home ... and it wouldn't be so bad that I'm a loony ... never bothered Micho ... I'll send her a letter to tell her she's right ...

He was on the verge of fainting when that resolution saved his life. Light-headed, he raised his face to the sky, and the fresh air surged into his lungs.

He stood, exhausted and half-naked on the tennis court, trying to gather his wits together like mislaid clues. He almost got lost on the way back to the manor house and only fully regained consciousness when he saw a light on the second floor: Mademoiselle Rakoff was awake. He walked across the gravel with his eyes fixed on the bright window, expecting to hear shouts, to be met with terrible scenes, but nothing happened. After prudently wiping his feet on the front doormat, he got back to his room with no one any the wiser.

*

Ludo stayed in bed for six days, delirious with a raging temperature. When Fine tried to take his temperature rectally, he broke the thermometer, and babbled wildly when they asked him questions. 'He's a little fraud,' Mademoiselle Rakoff, announced, 'he must have eaten his toothpaste or a bar of soap.' When she tried to check the glands in his groin and armpits, he writhed in helpless laughter. He huddled under the covers whenever Doudou came to help him change his sweat-soaked pyjamas.

The children waved to him from outside his window. Lise pressed her hands against the glass and smiled. One evening, Maxence came, secretively, to bring him a flower, a carnation stolen from a vase in the office. Flustered, Ludo hid it under his mattress; the tattered flower reminded him of Lise's mouth.

In the afternoon Mademoiselle Rakoff, spent long hours at his bedside, holding his hand. 'Do you know the beautiful story about Saint Martin sharing his cloak with a stranger?' Poor Saint Martin had to cut his cloak in half several times a day, and Saint Blandine was kept busy taming the wild beasts, while Saint Francis—or was it Saint Anthony?—chattered on and on to the fish. Ludo was quite content with the constant drone of hagiography. It was an excellent way to avoid conversation. One evening he annoyed the nurse by nodding off while Saint Chantal was busy founding the Order of the Visitation. 'That you find the lives of the blessed saints boring, my dear boy, is definitely worrying.'

On the sixth day he got up, exhausted but cured, and had breakfast with Fine in a sort of trance.

'So, how did you sleep?' She held the bread against her chest to cut it, peasant fashion. Unbeknownst to Mademoiselle Rakoff, she saved splendid cream cheese sandwiches for Ludo. 'Answer me when I talk to you.'

'I'm not allowed to talk. I'm being punished.'

'With Fine you can always talk. So what's the matter?'

Ludo shot her a sideways look, then buried his nose in

his mug again. It was true that he was unhappy, just like when he had been in the attic, when he used to peer through the holes in the floor. 'Why isn't Mademciselle Rakoff married?' he asked.

Fine shrugged her shoulders and went on stirring the big pots of hot chocolate on the stove. 'That's the way it is, everyone in his place. To get married, you need a husband!'

'And you, why aren't you married?'

'You're pretty inquisitive for an invalid! You don't always have a choice in life. I'm old now and I know the score, backwards and forwards. Love and rats! Love for young people, rats for old age.'

He helped Fine carry the hot chocolate to the trolley.

'So you're not going to marry Doudou?'

'Why do you ask?' she said, stiffening.

'So, you're not going to have babies by Doudou?'

'You're beginning to get on my nerves with your silly questions. The boss knew what she was doing when she told you not to talk!'

A few moments later, Ludo continued in the neutral voice of a detective trying to seem casual: 'Mademoiselle Rakoff hasn't any children?'

'Absolutely not, what an idea! Except that she's got all the children in the Centre, which makes for a damned big litter!'

'Where's she go on Saturday afternoons?'

'How do you know she goes anywhere?'

'I hear the car.'

'She goes wherever it is she wants to go. She's business to do with suppliers. That's enough chitchat.'

Ludo spent the day doing nothing, still condemned to silence. The children respected his involuntary dumbness, but approached him politely and shook hands. Even Odilon showered him with slimy civilities, and Ludo forgave him for the stolen photograph.

Spring was a long time arriving, the afternoons got

longer but no warmer. Clinging shadows hugged the refectory walls, mingling their sheaves, cross-bracing the gathering dusk with gold, and changing the most ordinary bowl into an apparition. The naked eye could almost see day changing to night.

After supper, Mademoiselle Rakoff sent the dwarf, who seemed in a jubilant mood, to summon Ludo to her office. She began by letting him stand there, without a word or a glance. A steely blue reflection tinged the grey waves of her hair, which she constantly patted with her fingertips. Her polished nails gleamed. Then she seemed to notice Ludo, and brightened.

'I know that you're not allowed to speak until tomorrow evening, and I'm not going to torture you with a long speech. On the other hand, I wouldn't like to leave you in the dark about certain things. I've written to your parents. Don't worry, I didn't say anything about your wild behaviour the other evening with the poor marquis. I did ask them, however, to put off their next visit until the end of June. You're much too oriented towards the outside world, Ludovic. A bit of self-examination will help you to adjust to the Centre. In any case, we're only talking about two months. Write as much as you like, draw, learn to weave, help the children who are less intelligent than you are, but don't suffer from the delusion that your fate is unjust and that your life lies elsewhere. I watched you closely a little while ago during our music session. You seemed to be in heaven! The piece was *A Little Night Music*, by Mozart. I'd chosen it especially for you. You're very sensitive, Ludovic, but there's nothing you can do about it, you are not an outsider. You're one of the innocents, and you've found your family here. So what are you waiting for? You should rejoice. Think of those who are in psychiatric hospitals, who would give anything to be in your place.'

She smoothed his hair, smiling sweetly, and brought out what was left of Nicole's photograph.

'You say it's your mama! I know nothing about it. I

haven't any proof, after all. Besides, I wasn't invited to the wedding. If necessary, I could ask Micho the next time he comes, but she's so young in the picture, he probably wouldn't recognize her.'

She put the photograph away, then came round to the front of her desk to look squarely into the boy's eyes. Leaning against the edge, indifferent to his silence, Mademoiselle Rakoff searched his green eyes for a reassuring sign of uneasiness or confusion.

'That's all,' she said finally in a singsong voice, 'you may go.' Then, in her usual tone she added: 'Your sheep is not well placed near the manger—if my memory serves me correctly, it's at the far end. But I'm sure that during the next two months you'll be sincerely anxious to improve its position. One, last thing! Someone saw you out in the hall in the middle of the night. This is absolutely forbidden. I expect these comings and goings of yours to cease immediately.'

Odilon again, thought Ludo on the stairs.

Go and tell Mademoiselle Rakoff that it's not your photo . . . go and say it's mine anyway it's not your mother you don't need to have her picture . . . if you tell her we'll take a trip through the woods in the submarine with Tatav . . . and then your sheep will certainly stay in first place in the manger.

The tables were laid, supper would soon be ready. Going into the games room, he drew back a little: he would never be able to get used to this. All the children were there, awkward, stooped, given over to their unconscious mannerisms, moaning and whimpering, staring blissfully into thin air, standing with their backs to the wall or gathered closely round the table, whiling away God knows how many hours with bits of wool and knowing looks; one of them seemed to be consulting a picture-book on galaxies, which he traced with a quivering finger.

They had got through their day. They had tossed their rings, raked the avenues in the park, cut out cardboard figures, drawn pictures of outsiders, given thanks to heaven, listened to *A Little Night Music*—'Oh no, Benoît, Mozart isn't an outsider, he's a great musician, yes, a child, if you like.' They had swallowed everything: Mozart, the penguins, their eternal supper of mashed potatoes, the white sleeping pills, the whistle blasts, the thousands of moments that must be spent living an empty life, the thousands of steps that must be taken to go nowhere, and they would go to sleep, but find no rest. Ludo watched them turn towards him, fingers to their lips, and solemnly whisper: 'Hush.'

He answered with a long, piercing scream.

Chapter Eleven

Ludo sat in his room and started writing:

Saint Paul Centre, April
Why wait any longer to put the situation in its true per-
spective. It's just as well to clarify our difference of opinion on these things now. I was ill but I'm feeling better.
Better in my mind. You were right, but it's not really
that I'm crazy, though maybe I was just a little bit.
Micho told me you were ill too and you didn't come
and see me because of that. I gave him a present for you.
I'm the one who made it with shells and I washed
everything carefully with bleach. We're learning to
weave napkins and also to sing. Doudou said I had a
beautiful voice because I've got a big chest and
Mademoiselle Rakoff plays us Mozart records about the
little night. There's no harmonium in the little night. It's
violins she says. She showed photos of violins. There's a
shell with holes for breathing. If you want me to be a
sailor I'll do it. It's true we're not unhappy here. But
there's no view of the sea. It's not all children, there are
some old people but that's what they're called. They're
nicer than at school. I'm the strongest I carry the pans of
hot chocolate. When I'm not mad anymore I'll be able
to come home and then I'll polish the car with a chamois
leather. The windscreen wipers are broken. The weather's starting to get pleasant. We had chocolate goldfish
for April Fool's day and the dwarf swiped all mine.

We're learning the names of flowers. There's still two months left and then it's the Sunday when you're coming to get me. Thanking you in advance for your attention to this matter, please be assured, along with Tatav, you and Micho, of my sincerest best wishes.

Ludo.

He closed the *Epistolary Guide* borrowed from Maxence and reread his entire letter. He blushed with pride. And with exhaustion. It was like a book and even better. He read it out loud to himself, and again, more slowly, then put it into an envelope and took it out to enjoy once more.

Suddenly Mademoiselle Rakoff opened his door.

'Aren't you in bed yet? Do you want to make me angry?'

'I'm not tired.'

'That's enough of that, swallow this, and nighty-night!'

No sooner had she left than he slipped the white pill from under his tongue and put it away in the box where he kept his toy skeletons.

Maxence had told him about the pills they were all made to swallow. Tranquillizers. Sedatives. Mood improvers. Varying according to the time of day and the season, to impose a collective attitude and prevent the eruption of individual whims, liable to degenerate into pandemonium. Maxence had a money box, a big red apple made of plaster of Paris, that was chock full of small pills instead of change: pills he had saved up over a period of ten years.

The letter to Nicole was propped against his breakfast dish.

'Writing to your fiancée?' Fine teased him.

'No,' he replied secretively.

'So who're you writing to?'

He blushed. 'I'm not writing, I'm answering a letter.'

Seated across from him, Fine was crumbling bread into the cream floating on top of her coffee. 'If you're anwering, you can tell me who it is.'

'My mother . . . she writes to me all the time. So I have to answer her.'

'If that's true, you're quite right. And even if it's not true, for that matter. Why didn't she come the other day?'

'I'm the one who didn't want it. I gather she's pregnant. I'm not particularly pleased about it.' He stared at her. 'And for that matter, when you're sleeping with a man, you've got to watch out for pregnancy. How old is Doudou?'

'You're driving me mad with your remarks about Doudou, just ask him how old he is!' She stood up to slip on her pinafore; his eyes never left her for a second. 'What're you looking at me like that for?'

'I'm not,' he said in a tiny voice.

She burst out laughing. 'Of course not, nitwit! But it wasn't so long ago, I swear, I used to get looked at a lot! So, what d'you say to your mother?'

'I don't tell her anything.'

Fine came up behind Ludo to snatch at the letter playfully; she had not leaned up against him for more than a second.

'Give it back to me,' stammered Ludo. He seemed paralysed with shock, staring blankly at the cook as she adjusted her frock and waved the letter round with a smile. Her naked skin showed through the V-neck of the pinafore.

'What's the matter with you?' she said finally. 'Your eyes're as big as saucers. Here's your letter, I wasn't going to eat it.'

He held out a trembling hand.

In the days that followed, Ludo faithfully carried out his resolve to be a perfect innocent, melancholic but all smiles. He took his cue as a model *child* from the others and behaved so well that his sheep moved up close to the front-runners, threatening even the dwarf's favoured position. Ludo seemed satisfied. Every day he jostled with his peers round the fireplace, impatient to discover his new placing. In his two months at the Centre he had lost several kilos, and the sparkle had gone from his green eyes. He began to drool for no reason at all, to knock over plates, to stumble walking in the park. His strides were now hampered by a stiffness that he had never felt before. The rings he tossed no longer reached the penguins, he grabbed for cake as if there were no tomorrow, stuffing himself with both hands. He would go to Mademoiselle Rakoff with his shoelaces untied for the pleasure of an affectionate scolding: 'Do me a favour please and tie those up right now, you silly billy!' He who had hated his cap at first now wore it constantly.

One evening, he and Bastien quarrelled over who should wash the tiled floor in the refectory, and Doudou had to separate them. Mademoiselle explained that the upkeep of that particular area had been Bastien's responsibility for years, but that Ludo might perhaps be given maintenance tasks in the park. He raked the terrace and the avenues, raked so often and so well that he unearthed enormous roots, which he tried to rake still harder, laying bare the foundations of pine trees which, if they fell, might easily have killed someone. Ludo was taken off this task.

There were medical and dental appointments. The regular psychiatrist at the Saint Paul Centre, Doctor Waille, gave him several tests and wrote on his card: *Feeble-minded, emotionally unstable, intermittently aggressive, asocial; requires continued supervision in a specialized institution.*

Ever since his run-in with Odilon in the dining-room, the children had treated Ludo with nervous respect. They marvelled at his bedroom walls which were as colourful as an Inca sanctuary. The ninepins made off with whole plates of food to lay them at his door, still piping hot. His arrival was greeted with clapping; all eyes turned towards him when Mademoiselle Rakoff asked them questions.

This growing—and unsolicited—authority enraged

Odilon who saw his prerogatives as a leader being swept away. But no matter how much he snooped, spied, or ingratiated himself, he could not find anything in Ludo's behaviour to tell tales about. He turned up in his room every evening to sip a grenadine and water, smacking his lips as though tasting fine brandy: 'Excellent syrup, good ruby colour, and what a bouquet!' Ludo listened to his servile gossip, his interminable speeches about music, and his chaotic muddle of cultural and intellectual terms taken out of context. He no longer countered with the submarine, the harmonium, or Tatav. Sometimes Odilon stopped short: 'It's forbidden to draw on the walls. I won't say anything, but the others might. The girls . . . luckily, they're not allowed in our rooms!'

The girls. They seemed to have adopted Ludo, but he did not go and talk to them. Sometimes he caught Lise gazing pensively in his direction. She was keeping an eye on him too. She managed to follow him in the park, attracting his attention while keeping her distance. Small pebbles rained down on Ludo, who heard laughter, but saw no one. Protected by the other girls, in the chapel or in the refectory, Lise might venture a smile. Almost every day Ludo, found things under his pillow—cough drops, multicoloured ribbons, or tiny eggs made from rolled breadcrumbs. Once he found a white handkerchief like a silent love letter. On his walls, round the concealed portraits, lips and kisses drawn in red pencil appeared.

Maxence did not seem to be taken in by the change in Ludo. In the evenings he waited for Odilon to leave before he showed his face. 'You're not the same any more,' he sighed. 'I know it, you're not the same any more.'

'How was I?' asked Ludo.

Maxence spread his arms in a helpless gesture. 'Oh, I don't know. When you first arrived, I saw my home again. There was my mother, and her sister, and the avenue of hydrangeas; the kennels were on the left, and then the terrace overlooking the lake where we used to eat cinnamon toast in the afternoon. And then there was my mother.'

'Mine,' Ludo interrupted, 'makes mulberry jam. She brings me breakfast in bed and I'm the one who drives her car.'

Maxence was an only son, an orphan. He was happy to exchange with Ludo memories of a childhood neither of them had ever had.

Ludo was only really himself at night under the stars. He could tell from the voices and the creaking of bedsprings who was asleep, who was still awake, and whether the children were sleeping soundly enough for him to slip out. Often he found the door at the end of the corridor locked and had to return to his room.

But he was not the only one wandering passionately through the darkness. Nights at the Centre had their strays, their nomads, and although the curfew delivered to Morpheus those children knocked out by the sedatives, it seemed to give *carte blanche* to the private demons of the so-called normal residents. Sometimes Ludo saw Mademoiselle Rakoff, and shadowed her. She strode along as if urgently awaited somewhere, down avenues she abandoned halfway, retracing her steps, and Ludo, no longer afraid of her, and intoxicated by his own boldness, dreamed of accosting this defenceless old woman humming nursery rhymes to herself. Fine was another one who lived by night. Doudou joined her several times a week and they argued in bed together. One wanted to, the other did not. Like Nicole and Micho. Hiding at the window one evening, Ludo was astounded when Doudou jumped right over his head, fleeing from the nurse, who had come to ask Fine if she happened by any chance to have heard strange noises.

But sometimes the cook did not sleep in her own room, and Ludo wondered where she was spending the night.

Once again in the quiet of the evening, he waited. His

184

heart pounded dully. The moon traced palm trees and fins over the pictures on the walls. Ludo drew strength from the rustling forest, the distant murmur of the west wind that spoke to him of the Atlantic.

I'll be a sailor like you said anyway I'm better now . . . there's something wrong with me but it's working out and when you come to see me in June you won't even recognize me.

He took a deep breath and stepped into the corridor. This was the moment of greatest risk. He had to cross the space lit by the night-light to reach Odilon's room, two doors away, without being seen. His bare feet stuck to the linoleum as he guided himself by listening to the children's snores. The dwarf's bedroom door opened silently; and Ludo went in.

Fast asleep and sucking his thumb, Odilon was so tightly swaddled in his sheets that he looked like a mummy. Ludo went over to the armchair where clothing was carefully folded underneath a large missal. He searched the red jacket in vain. The trouser pockets were empty. He returned to the bed. Lying on his side in the moonlight with one hand under the pillow, the sleeper breathed with the shrill, furtive whine of a rodent.

It was the first time that Ludo had ventured into Odilon's room at night. Soon he would have complete faith in the sedative properties of the sleeping tablets, diluted three to a glass in the grenadine favoured by the dwarf. Ludo drew closer, knelt down, and gently grasped Odlion's closed fist, sliding it out from under the pillow. Unclenching the fingers, he was disengaging the key to the hall door when he realized that two wide-open eyes were staring straight at him, unseeing, stupefied by drugs. Ludo froze, holding his breath. With a melodious wail, Odilon closed his eyes again. Ludo snatched the key abruptly and fled.

He felt a surge of power as he opened the door to the

refectory, and almost burst into a wild cry. He was free. The entire Saint Paul Centre was nothing but a dream and he was free to go out into the living night. Making a detour by the manger, he reached into the shadowy herd to remove the dwarf's sheep, which he replaced with one of Tatav's little skeletons.

At the far end of the refectory he stared thoughtfully at the door to the girls' dormitory, wondering if he might be able to open it with his key.

Outside, a fresh breeze greeted him. A crisp chill permeated the night air like scent. Earth and sky were bathed in moonlight and the forest loomed like a windswept reef. He moved twenty paces to the north along the front of the house and crossed the terrace as if he was fording a stream, using a path he had secretly constructed from pine needles. When he felt the cold sand under his bare feet, he turned round: the buildings were black silhouetted against the bright sky. A light showed on the second floor.

He set off smartly down the avenue, swinging his arms and head, drinking in the icy air, abandoning himself to the pleasure of wandering freely: barefoot, bareheaded, and alone. He went down to the river for a swim, leaving his pyjamas and the purloined sheep on the bank. He talked to himself, splashed the alders, soaped his body with the running water, then made his way out into the main current to test his strength.

Covered with goose pimples, he lay down on the grass, and as he stared up at the stars a sensual shiver ran over his skin. He rolled round among the constellations—he had always loved those fires burning against the night without flame or smoke: he had no idea what thirst in him was quenched by the sight of them.

What's the weather like this morning . . . you're basically a good boy, Ludo . . . hand me the tray before it gets cold . . . so what would you like best . . . perhaps you're a good boy after all . . .

Ludo trotted over to the tennis court, where he examined the Versailles and thought that he would have enjoyed being some kind of a mechanic later on in life. As he hid the dwarf's sheep in the empty boot, his hand met what felt like a damp bundle of rags. It was a rolled-up pair of trousers. Turning out the pockets, he discovered a carefully folded paper.

He was still not tired. Spurred on by the memory of Fine making love to Doudou, he returned to the manor and crossed the terrace, keeping close to the walls until he reached Fine's window. There he hunched down, peeping between the slats of the shutters. Shadows intermingled, breaking up forms and colours. A jellyfish seemed to float on one of the bedposts swimming in darkness, and Ludo recognized the most famous cap in the Saint Paul Centre: Gratien's. Unable to make out anything else in the gloom, he left with a heavy heart.

Odilon was still asleep when he replaced the key under the pillow. He went into Gratien's room, found the bed unmade but empty, and returned to his own room exhausted. He wanted to be warm, to cry, to talk to someone. To go and ask Maxence if his mother put cupping glasses on him when he had a cold. Taking off his sandy pyjamas, he found the piece of paper from the car. There was handwriting on it, but only the left side was legible, dampness had destroyed the rest:

You must understand, darling Bruno, that I
where are your fine prom
for almost three years now you've been
time to tell Louisa the truth.
As an officer and a gentleman
love me to wear your uniform.
sacrifice my life taking care of the chil
you shrink from making her suffer
the ninepins, after a separation
and that you founded the Saint Paul Centre

this mutual love of ours, that we swear ev
make up your mind at last to fulfill your
her to learn the truth from someone el
are my life, my love, my pass

                         Your Hélène, who loves

He rolled up in a ball on the floor and closed his eyes. Everyone loved everybody, parents loved their children, Fine loved Doudou and Gratien, Mademoiselle Rakoff wrote love letters—he was the only one left unloved, the only one completely alone.

The next morning, the Centre was in an uproar over the mystery of the skeleton and the stolen sheep. Mademoiselle questioned the children one by one. Like the others, Ludo said nothing. He suggested to the dwarf, who was terrified by this black magic, that he must have committed some mortal sin, a lie or a theft, and that his sheep would not appear until he confessed to his crime.

The first hot weather reached the Centre at the beginning of May, setting everyone on edge. The sultry heat seemed pregnant with thunderstorms; sometimes a downpour brought relief to jangled nerves, but often the children stared up at a sky swept by weak lightning without rain. The clouds stagnated indefinitely over the motionless pines.

At meals, the girls quarrelled for no reason; petty rebellions broke out and were quelled without delay. Mademoiselle Rakoff authorized the wearing of summer clothing, and one day when the atmosphere was particularly oppressive, she tackled the heat head-on with a lecture on the Sahara, followed by a film. They saw sun-baked huts, dried-up oases, *outsiders* burnished by the endless heat ravaging a region known as the land of thirst. And, of course, they were told how lucky some children were, who never went thirsty. The speech ended with everyone enjoying a glass of cool water; it was two o'clock in the afternoon.

That evening, someone discovered that Maxence was missing. Three vaguely frightened search parties led by Mademoiselle Rakoff, Fine, and Doudou went over the house and grounds with a fine toothcomb. In vain. Fearing the worst, the nurse was about to report the supposed runaway to the police when, through the open window, she heard Ludo's shouts coming from the tennis court. She arrived soon after Doudou, who was already investigating the back seat of the Versailles. A human form lay on the car floor in the dust and the suffocating smell.

'Quick,' she cried, 'get him out of there!'

Doudou lifted out what looked like a cloth sarcophagus. It was Maxence, unconscious and rolled up in three blankets. He had put on all his winter clothes—socks, trousers, sweaters, gloves, scarf—and had masked his face with two balaclava helmets, one of them inside-out.

He regained consciousness in the refectory, after a little glass of peach brandy, and smiled sweetly at the children gathered around him. When Mademoiselle asked him what had possessed him to do such a thing, Maxence replied that he was planning on going into exile in the Sahara in the near future, but first had to familiarize himself with the climate.

Ludo had finally given up putting in an appearance on Sundays. All those parents—and not one of them his—made him sad. He stayed alone in his room, where he lay on the floor studying the joyless carnival he had painted on to the walls. He acted out stories out of his own imagination or read books Fine selected haphazardly for him from the colonel's library, a place declared out of bounds by Mademoiselle Rakoff. There were *The Little Prince*, a *Thesis of Dental Surgery: The Odontologist and his Patient*, and *Suzanne's Travels through the Sudan*. He admired all those Sibylline words. They were even more mysterious than the stars at night.

Odilon arrived to threaten him, in the guise of a friendly well-wisher: 'Reading is forbidden at Saint Paul. Except for Lucien. Encyclopaedias, yes, but not ordinary reading. Imagine if Mademoiselle Rakoff were to catch you. Or if someone were to tell her, a girl, for instance!' and he wrung his hands, as if appalled at the idea.

'And your sheep?' Ludo asked. 'Is it in hell?'

After the families had gone, he wandered in the park until nightfall, enviously savouring the scattered traces left by the visitors, the chosen people from whose ranks he was excluded.

His great day arrived. He was ready and waiting even before sunrise, and when Fine opened the hall door at dawn, there he was, parked under the night-light, holding a bouquet of flowers. 'They're for my mother,' he said almost aggressively. 'Now you'll see that it really is my photograph.'

He waited until evening, standing by the front door without a bite to eat, struggling against his fear that she would not come, unable to resist gazing longingly at the pale blue *Floride* and falling for the same mirage that had deceived him before.

Micho appeared at nine o'clock, alone. All the parents had gone home. Ludo looked at him dully; his arrival was no longer part of the magical event lovingly looked forward to for the last fifty-one days. Ludo did not even ask whether Nicole and Tatav had come. Micho was drunk.

'So here you are, you dear little devil!' he said thickly, rolling his r's. 'Well now! If ever there was a dear little devil, you're the one.'

Beaming with alcoholic goodwill, he drifted among the tables set up outdoors and was moved to tears at the sight of the children, who for their part were quite intrigued by this boisterous outsider.

'And you too, you're all dear little devils! Little sweethearts, with your caps, and your funny little ways, and all your little smiles. I've got a soft spot in my heart for all of

you, and even if you are a bit loony, so what! It's still
better than having a heartless wife who doesn't even de-
serve the splendid child she's got!' He took Ludo by the
shoulders and showed him to his audience. 'Because this
boy here, I'll tell you straight out that whoever touches a
hair on his head . . . will have to answer to me for it!'

Mademoiselle Rakoff arrived at that point to welcome
her cousin, pretending not to notice his intoxication.

'I don't recall whether you've met Fine and Doudou, my
two assistants.'

Micho shook Doudou's hand and declared that the
Senegalese infantry he had known in the army really were
the only soldiers who had not been shirkers.

'We hope we'll be seeing you more often, now,' said the
cook acidly. 'Right, Ludo?'

The boy seemed to have lost his voice.

Maxence came up behind him. 'Ah, your family has
arrived,' he said delicately. 'I was beginning to worry. Is
your mother here?'

'Shut up,' said Ludo.

Odilon was telling Micho how much progress Ludo had
made since his arrival at Saint Paul.

'Absolutely true,' agreed Micho. 'I can't put my finger
on it, but he's changed. And he's grown. Like a string
bean, long and skinny.' He grabbed Ludo round the neck.
'I can tell what you're going to ask me, you know. I'm not
crazy. You want to know why Nicole didn't come or even
Tatav! I knew you were going to ask that, but it's not
important and anyway I'm here. It's just that your mother,'
he cackled, 'well, she's got a bun in the oven, another little
devil! Got to take care of her. You'd never know it, doesn't
show yet—still got a real wasp waist. And then Tatav's
got exams, I really don't remember the whole story, they
said to give you a kiss. But you're pleased to see me,
anyway, huh? Are you glad to see Micho?'

Ludo nodded awkwardly, seeming to hesitate with a
faraway look in his eyes before blurting out: 'Holidays

191

start, in July . . . everyone'll be leaving . . . I have to go back home!'

Micho patted him kindly on the stomach and answered as though he were happy to tell him the good news: 'Well that's just it! You asked the right question. I'll tell you straight out that you'll be coming home, in less than no time!' Then, turning towards the others: 'And you too, children, you're coming to the seashore. Everybody's going to the seashore with my boy here, everybody's going swimming. And if Nicole doesn't like it, I couldn't care less!'

He had supper with Mademoiselle Rakoff and Ludo, who did not eat anything. Micho wanted to know all about the manger and swore that it was the best idea anyone had ever had. 'That's what we need at The Hedges. A manger in the fireplace. With lots of sheep lined up like racing cyclists. You know, if your mother knew I was here, she'd have a fit!' He started snoring towards the end of dinner. Fine set up a camp bed for him in a corner of the dining-room and he fell asleep promising to teach the children how to play *pétanque* the next morning. He left like a thief in the middle of the night.

The following week after this, Ludo received a letter from Nicole, signed by Micho and Tatav as well.

The Hedges, June 6

Dear Ludovic,

You don't write many letters. In any case Cousin Hélène keeps us up to date and we're pleased that you're doing better. As for me I'm quite run-down. A bad cold in April because the wind never stopped blowing. Then the doctor said I needed to rest. So you mustn't be selfish and want me to come and see you all the time. You mustn't force Micho to make all these trips because he's not so young anymore. You have to think about other people too and about all the trouble they've had. Now the hot weather's here we eat outdoors. Well, I'm sending you a package and a kiss.

Nicole

Here's a kiss from me too and it's true you ought to send us more news about yourself.

Micho

Soon I'm going to get my driving licence. My father lets me drive the *Floride* in the woods. I'm putting some bubble gum in the package for you. I don't chew it any more.

Tatav

Ludo spent two days reading the letter over and over, wearing his eyes out, and his heart.

The following Sunday, he helped Fine carry out the tables and stayed on the terrace with all the children. The air was hot and fragrant with resin. Many families had come. There was a festive atmosphere, and Mademoiselle Rakoff was in her element, strolling arm in arm with the ladies along the leafy avenues.

Ludo immersed himself in these perfumed processions, studying their gestures and their secrets. Like a solitary traveller who cannot help longing to find a familiar face in the crowd, he gazed beseechingly at every mother: he would willingly have followed the first one to take his hand.

'And who are you?' asked a pretty young woman, intrigued by his behaviour.

'Ludovic,' he answered shyly.

She laughed and touched his cheek. 'That's a charming name. You speak quite well, and you're tall . . . Are you happy?'

She had shining blonde hair, like Nicole's when she was younger. Looking down, Ludo noticed that once again he had not tied his shoe-laces. He began to cry so helplessly that she patted his shoulders, and he collapsed into her arms. It was Aliette's mother; together they went to find her daughter, a mongoloid. Watching the young woman caress her child, one would have thought it was the mother who had been abandoned.

After she had whistled the curfew that evening, Mademoiselle Rakoff went to see Ludo, who had just, crossly, turned Odilon out of his room. He was sitting on the floor, tracing the lines in his right hand with a red felt-tipped pen.

'You should be in bed. I was coming to congratulate you for once.' She closed the door and glanced fondly at the walls. 'You're going to wind up drawing on the ceiling if you keep this up! Today was a great success, everyone had a good time. One of these days that poor tennis court is going to collapse. The colonel would never have allowed it to be used as a car park.'

She spoke without haste, leaving long silences between the sentences. There was some weariness in her voice.

'I'm exhausted,' she sighed, sitting down on the edge of the bed. 'Where was I?—Oh yes, I wanted to congratulate you on your behaviour today. You were less unruly than usual. Are you beginning to like being with us?'

She went on in a pompous voice. 'Ludo dear, the Centre is one family, one big, happy family. If I say: Ludovic is our child, it means Ludovic is the child of the Saint Paul Centre, where he has his brothers and sisters and where all the parents who come to visit are his parents too.'

Raising his head, Ludo saw her knees; Mademoiselle Rakoff adjusted her skirt with a smile.

'Not true,' he snarled, 'I'm my mother's child and that's all.'

She laughed harshly. 'Let's talk about your mother! She could have tried to teach you to be polite! If you'd really like to know, I write to your parents every week and it's not my fault if they don't come. She says she's pregnant. What difference does that make? Madame Prade is pregnant and she never misses a Sunday. Madame Bernier's pregnant and she's always among the first to arrive . . .'

194

'It's not true!' he shouted, facing her squarely.

'Madame Masséna comes at least twice a month despite her asthma. Monsieur Mafiolo lives five hundred kilometres from here and he comes to see Gratien every week. Everybody has problems and obligations—but your mother never bothers to visit you! So stop making such a fuss about her . . . and . . .'

'Shut up!' shouted Ludo violently. He threw his pen across the room and stood up.

'What *has* got into you!' yelled the nurse, beside herself with rage.

Ludo looked her boldly up and down, staring at her hair and too-well-kept fingernails. 'You're the same as me,' he said, drawing quite close to her. 'You haven't got anyone to visit you. You haven't got a child, haven't got a husband, haven't got a lover. Your mother's no better than mine.'

Suddenly, as if he himself were ashamed of his discovery, he murmured with a look of disgust: 'And your hair's grey. You're an old hag!'

Chapter Twelve

Old hag! . . . The boy had reopened the wound and memories welled up like blood.

Mademoiselle Rakoff tossed and turned in her bed. The metal frame creaked. The night creaked. She closed her eyes, but her resentment and vexation were unrelenting. Her nerves were a tracery of fire, like bright-red seaweed. Her body was a dead weight. Her old body. The time was long past when the colonel used to come to her room and take her, all passion spent, without a word being spoken between them. Quickly, stealthily: his real wife was waiting for him at the other end of the manor house.

What time was it? At least three o'clock in the morning. She had not taken her make-up off and her nose was itching. She was too hot. The bed rattled and groaned. Bruno used to say it was as though they were making love in suits of armour. She had forgotten to rearrange the manger this evening, but her revenge would keep. She was sorry she had slapped Ludovic—he would think she minded.

Her hair was all grey. An old hag! He had not mentioned the wrinkles, the lines round her mouth, the dull skin, the sagging cheeks, the double chin, the drooping breasts and the thickened waist she forced into a bolero jacket so tight she could hardly breathe. The idiot did not know the half of it!

She got out of bed. Pulling on her dressing-gown over the colonel's pyjamas, which she had taken to wearing (as well as his flannel underpants and leather slippers), she took her torch and went down the darkened stairs.

The refectory was silent. Flicking the first light switch that came to hand, she lit the walls around the manger, where the garish drawings of outsiders were lined up in grimacing rows. Ludovic's picture stood out powerfully; she tore it down and crumpled it into a little ball, laughing bitterly. First of all, she would outlaw his elaborate artistic productions! And as for visits, he was going to have to wait a long, long time.

The air was even hotter on the terrace, thick with that humidity mosquitoes find so delightful. It was not an evening for strolling down to the river. She remembered the day when Bruno had taken her out in the boat, and they had almost tipped over; the skiff was probably around somewhere, rotting under the alders.

She went back inside, walked round the dining-room once more, and as she passed the door to the boys' dormitory she automatically tried the knob. The door was unlocked. It was bound to happen some day. Odilon had forgotten! But still, that idiotic black was supposed to check and make sure. Both of them would hear from her in the morning! Luckily she had her keys with her. She put the key in the lock and then changed her mind, slipping into the dark corridor instead.

She knocked for a long time on Doudou's door before he answered.

'Excuse me, I know it's late,' she said from the threshold, 'but did you know that the hall door was unlocked?'

'No, Mademoiselle Rakoff.'

'Well that's just fine! I'd like to remind you that we have runaways and sleepwalkers here.'

'Yes, Mademoiselle Rakoff.'

The room was like an oven. The heat and the smell made her gorge rise. It was impossible to see anything. She could only hear the sound of breathing and the ticking of a large alarm clock.

'We'll talk about it tomorrow. Goodnight. And give your room an airing, it smells stuffy!' She stayed where she was. 'A toothache, Doudou,' she sighed, 'it's keeping me awake. Do you happen to have some Glifanan?'

'I haven't got any Glifanan,' he grumbled after a silence. 'No, no Glifanan. I only have *aspirin*.'

He spoke reverently, as if in awe of a great divinity.

'Aspirin, for severe pain . . .'

'I have aspirin and that's all.'

They could not see each other, but their voices mingled in the darkness.

'What about a cigarette, Doudou. Have you one of those?'

'Of course not, Mademoiselle Rakoff,' he stammered, 'it's forbidden.' He sounded terrified.

'Then what smells so strongly in your room?'

'I have no cigarettes, Mademoiselle Rakoff. Smoking was forbidden by the colonel.'

'Come on, Doudou, don't be stupid. The colonel knew very well that you were smoking on the sly. And don't forget that I've twenty years of hospital experience, so turn on the light and give me a cigarette.'

There was a long sigh, and then a lamp, shaded by newspaper, was switched on. It sat on the floor and cast an intimate glow round the pillows. The first thing she saw was a big-bellied chamber pot. Doudou blinked his eyes in astonishment. He slept in the nude; she could see his woolly torso. His legs peeped out from beneath a sheepskin he had wrapped around himself like a woman surprised while dressing. He grinned foolishly.

'Of course,' she said with a touch of embarrassment, 'I'd be the first person to use aspirin.'

She was becoming irritable. Her heart was pounding too loudly, she could not think of anything to say. How old was he now? Like her, around fifty. He had always disgusted her with his smell and his colour. But all of a sudden she was cold and she wanted desperately to cling to him;

to be nice and warm under the sheepskin and to ask him if it was really true that she was already an old hag and finished.

'Well, if you haven't any cigarettes . . .'

'I've got some small cigars,' he said hurriedly, 'some Murati cigars.' He was visibly affected by the uneasiness she seemed to radiate as she spoke. He pointed to the chest of drawers and started to get up, but Mademoiselle Rakoff had already pushed aside the packet of biscuits that hid the cigars.

'May I offer you one?' she asked.

'I don't really smoke on the sly. One now and then maybe.' He held out his hand palm up, like a beggar. Looking at that huge pink and brown paw, she felt the urge to plant a kiss in the centre of it.

'Matches?'

He picked up a box of kitchen matches lying on the floor.

'Well look at this!' she said, taking them from him. 'These are the Centre's matches. If you need them, ask for them.' She sat down on a stool near the sink, brought the small cigar to her lips, and puffed out a grey cloud of smoke, which she smoothly inhaled up her nostrils. Feeling better, she saw that Doudou had tucked a cigar into his mouth without lighting it, not daring to ask her for the matches.

'Excuse me, Doudou!' With a conspiratorial laugh, she crossed to him. The bed was simply a mattress on the floor; she started to bend over, but finally had to sit down to hold out the match. His hand brushed hers as he guided the flame to his cigar.

'When you have a toothache,' she mumbled in a different tone of voice, 'there's nothing better than tobacco. The colonel was a great smoker in spite of his rule against it, but a pipe is less harmful. Did you love Colonel de Moissac? I mean, were you fond of him?'

She felt great relief at saying the word 'love'.

'Yes, Mademoiselle Rakoff.'

'You know, Doudou, now that I'm old and I think back on all that, I see things differently. With hindsight and maturity one becomes, how shall I put it? Lucid?'

He was sitting up against the pillow, more sure of himself now. His eyes sought those of Mademoiselle Rakoff, who lowered her eyelids prudishly.

'Am I old, by the way?'

The question was addressed to no one in particular, and he ignored it.

'No, really, Doudou, be frank. Am I old?'

'No, Mademoiselle Rakoff.'

He did not sound very convincing, the beast!

'So you were fond of him?'

'Yes, Mademoiselle Rakoff.'

That terrible accent . . . The colonel's voice had been so distinguished. Just look at him, that big monkey flopped down there in his sheepskin, smoking a foul-smelling cigar. It looked as though he were smoking one of his own fingers!

She returned to the stool. 'I loved him too, that is to say, I too was fond of him. You see, he was a man, a real man. Devotion to duty, a sense of values, and so loyal, so pious, and yet adorably selfish, like all men! It was his wife who ruined him.'

She no longer spoke to Doudou, but through him, to her own memories. 'I'll never forget the look on her face when I arrived. She put on airs. She never let him out of her sight. She was jealous, you know. She imagined that there was something going on between the colonel and me. It's true that we were friends, that we respected each other. Of course the colonel was attractive and I was young . . .'

Why was he looking at her like that. He seemed dumb-founded. They must look a pretty picture, the two of them with their cigars! He was wild-eyed and naked in his bed, and she was in her dressing-gown on a rickety stool, wearing the colonel's slippers.

'What about you, Doudou, what did you do when you were young?'

'The colonel knew all about that. I was working in the sugar factory, and another man came for me with a knife and then I . . .'

'That's right, that's right, I remember him telling me about that unfortunate business. Let's not talk about it. Don't you ever feel lonely? You haven't ever thought of getting married?'

'Oh, no! No. To get married you have to be in love.'

The dimwit, what did he know about love? How had he managed all these years? Desire must have slowed to a stop under the black skin, disappearing at last. She had thought it would abandon her one day, that she might finally go to sleep without wanting to touch another body, somebody, anybody.

'Well, I'll leave you now,' she sighed as she got unwillingly to her feet. Then she noticed the brightly coloured pictures painted on towels hanging on the walls.

'It's me who did them,' said Doudou proudly. 'I paint at night.'

'And where do you get the towels?'

'From the kitchen, Mademoiselle Rakoff. But they're old ones. Used-up towels . . .'

'A towel, my dear Doudou, gets better as it gets older. So I would appreciate it if you would give up your painting.'

'But I just paint outsiders, Mademoiselle Rakoff, like the children!'

She seemed to lose her patience. 'They're blacks, your outsiders, and of no interest to me. You had better spend your time keeping doors safely locked. But thank you all the same for the cigar.'

After she had gone, Doudou scratched his chest hard, then his right calf; they had been itching terribly for some time. He wondered if he had just been visited by a ghost.

*

The week went by. Mademoiselle Rakoff was frosty with Doudou, cold with the girls, and cuttingly affable to Ludo.

The boy wrote separately to his mother, to Micho, and to Tatav. When the nurse refused to send the letters unless he paid for the stamps, he fetched three five-franc pieces from the sock under his mattress and brought them to her office. She called him a thief, confiscated the money, and said that, he could not possibly imagine she was going to send the letters under these circumstances.

'And my photo?' he asked suddenly.

'What photo?'

'My mother's. Odilon told me it was mine. And that he'd told you that it was mine.'

A nasty, sly expression came over her face. 'Do you really think I'm going to give it back to you? Let's talk about the stolen sheep instead. Perhaps it returned to the fireplace all by itself! So if you want your photo, you'll have to tell me everything. First of all you can tell me where you got this money.'

'My mother gave it to me.'

'Liar! Your mother wouldn't have given you a single sou. In any case it's quite easy to verify, now that there's a telephone at your house.' She leafed through a thick notebook and dialled a number, smiling at Ludo when someone answered.

'Hello? Madame Bossard, please . . . Oh, it's you, Nicole —this is your cousin Hélène Rakoff speaking, from the Saint Paul Centre . . . Yes . . . No, nothing important, I assure you . . . No, I just wanted to clear up a little matter about Ludovic . . . Oh no, not at all . . . Is it true that you gave him a small sum of money? . . . No! . . . I thought so too . . . We don't allow money at the Centre and . . . What? Your five-franc pieces disappeared before he left? No, it's a question of a small bill, but still! Perhaps after all it was Micho who gave it to him . . . Well, thank you very much . . . Perhaps you would like to speak to him, he's standing here . . . Yes, I understand . . . But of course I understand . . . Well, goodbye then . . . And I hope to see you soon.'

She hung up, looked at Ludo, and threw the coins on her desk as though they were dice.

'A fine thing! How old is your mother?'

'I don't know,' Ludo mumbled.

'She has a young voice, in any case. Could you hear her?'

'When's she coming to get me?' he whispered.

Mademoiselle Rakoff clasped her hands and smiled encouragingly. 'Very soon, surely. Holidays start next week. If, of course, I allow you to leave. But you can already count yourself lucky that I didn't say anything about the five-franc pieces. Is she blonde or brunette?'

'Her hair's cut, now. In the photo it's not cut.'

'She's not an old lady, if I understand you correctly! Anyway, I haven't finished with the other matter. I'm keeping the stolen money, and naturally I must ask you to hand over the rest of it. I shall arrange to have it put towards your account.'

Later that evening Ludo gave one quarter of his remaining coins to Mademoiselle Rakoff. That left him with a hundred francs in the sock.

The following Sunday most of the children went home. They did not seem particularly thrilled to be leaving the Saint Paul Centre and said goodbye to Ludo rather gloomily. Antoine hid in a tree with his sheep to prevent his parents from taking him away. A liveried chauffeur came to get Miriam at the wheel of a luxurious American car; the girl had to be almost forced to get in.

By mid-July, only ten of them were left: ten children frightened by their vulnerability, shamed by the loss of their companions. Time hung heavily for them, like clothes a size too big.

Every day Ludo expected his family to arrive and every day Mademoiselle Rakoff told him to get ready to leave.

Activities proceeded at a slower pace. The whistle blew less often, the penguins enjoyed a brief respite and the nurse went around in a sleeveless dress. She kept the children busy with light gardening and picking wild flowers from the ditches by the road. The deserted dining-hall echoed with a hollow sound; there was orangeade at meals and special treats for pudding. The sheep, becalmed in their manger, were all on an equal footing. There were no more music sessions, except if it rained. Ludo longed for bad weather.

His eyes often met those of Lise. The walls of his room still displayed little messages meant for her: a black hair wound round a white pebble, two intertwined grass blades forming twin rings.

A letter from Micho arrived.

Dear Ludovic,

I'm very upset by what I've heard. Cousin Hélène wrote that it was you who took the five-franc pieces out of the kitty. Your mother suspected you at the time but I wasn't sure. It was a rotten thing to do. Apparently you're also a troublemaker and you're not polite. She says if you go on like this she won't be able to keep you and you'll have to be sent somewhere else. I know it's not always easy for you. It's not easy for me either. Now your mother, who was pregnant, has lost the child and she says it is because she had too many worries about you. The doctor says she is supposed to keep quiet above all. So don't be surprised if I can't come right away. I will come but you'll have to wait until August to come home to The Hedges. Everyone sends their love.

Micho

I'm sending you fifty francs so there won't be any more foolishness by you.

One morning Ludo did not shave. It was not a conscious decision on his part, he simply did not shave. At first

Mademoiselle Rakoff thought it was an oversight and told him he looked like an old goat. At the end of a week he was still avoiding the razor, and the more his beard gained ground, the more he hid behind it. He had long been in the habit of plucking at his eyebrows; now they began to grow back thickly. The children touched their cheeks when he went by.

This retreat into hairiness changed his behaviour. He seemed sly. He knew how to stay still and unseen; they thought he was absent even when he was there, and they ended up forgetting him. He still had breakfast with Fine, but asked her no more questions. His eyes, glazed by insomnia, followed her everywhere, the eyes of a judge or a suspicious lover consumed by bitterness. He became aggressive even with Maxence. When the latter attempted to draw off a few of the false memories of maternal tenderness he always kept on tap, Ludo snapped at him: 'Don't know anything about it. I don't know who my mother is. It was my father who brought me up.'

He was bothered by crazy nightmares, in which he was accused of having put fish innards into his mother's chest of drawers; the sheets were smeared with mounds of whitish intestines. Or else Nicole, bending lovingly over his bed as he slept, smiled at him as she had never smiled before. But then her teeth and hair would begin to fall out, little holes dripping with blood appeared in her open mouth until her smile was no more than a black hole in a death's-head.

During the day he killed time with excavations. He had inspected all the hidden corners of the park, explored every thicket. His findings included forks, broken bowls, a chewed-up rubber bone, and Colonel de Moissac's flat-bottomed boat, submerged and invisible beneath the alders.

He wrote to his mother but no longer sent the letters. He used his catechism notebook for this purpose: a log-book, undated, in which he wrote imaginary replies to himself, writing about feelings nobody cared enough to have for him.

He had set his heart on August. The month passed, day by day without bringing any message from The Hedges. Reality seemed to slip by at his own pace. He heard words beating inside himself but refused to listen to them:

They were abandoning him. He contemplated the evidence in his idle hands: *they were abandoning him.* He saw his absent mother in his own eyes and fled from mirrors, from his memory—and overcome at last, he fled from the certainty he had harboured since birth: *they were abandoning him.*

A forest fire broke out. Red fire-engines with their shrieking sirens invaded the terrace one afternoon. Menaced by flames, the Centre was evacuated. To the south, blackish plumes of smoke billowed over the pines as a light wind brought the smell of burning. Lise sat down next to Ludo in the van. Clutching his barometer, Odilon begged the driver to get going. Then the wind shifted suddenly, and the fire was quickly brought under control.

Two hours later, Mademoiselle Rakoff signalled the end of the alert, and the children climbed out of the van. A prayer of thanksgiving was launched heavenward from the terrace, where the air smelled slightly scorched. That evening, a film about the world's great rivers preceded the distribution of sedatives.

The next day, Saturday, as he was crossing the empty hall shortly after lunch, Ludo found the door to the girls' rooms wide open and ventured into their forbidden world. A sweetish smell permeated the seemingly deserted wing. In a room similar to his own he saw walls covered with coloured pictures, the faces of handsome men wearing cowboy hats. He opened a desk drawer and leafed through a notebook tied with a pink ribbon. The unruly handwriting endlessly repeated the same name: 'Lise.' There were kilometres of 'Lise' galloping close together along the lines all the way through the notebook, even the inside back cover had been subjected to the same incantation.

He stretched out on the bed, and his mother appeared. He had only to close his eyes to see her. A face from the past, in the gentle world of memory where voices, now silent, still lingered.

Sudden laughter startled him, but he was alone. In the empty corridor, the tranquillity was undisturbed. He returned to the entrance hall in a pensive mood. Out on the terrace, the muffled collisions of a game of *pétanque* popped softly in the drowsy air. It was then that he noticed a black hole under the staircase, a gaping trapdoor with steps going down into the darkness. Mademoiselle Rakoff was out in her car. Fine and Doudou were outside playing with the children. Ludo grasped the rope bannister and went down the stairs.

He found himself in the cellar. He had never suspected that the manor would have such an underground vault. He could feel the cool air on his neck, smell the rancid humidity, hear the plop plop of dripping water. Groping his way along the gritty walls, he came upon a dark tunnel, where faint, unidentifiable noises grated on the silence. He was about to turn back when his fingers closed on a knob: the door creaked open.

At first he could see only a small, crescent-shaped basement window. He took a few steps into the gloom, walking on a litter of old papers and folders scattered across the floor. As he drew back to leave the room, he was startled by a silhouette moving towards the window; a face emerged from the darkness, and Ludo murmured in amazement: 'Lise . . .' Covering her mouth with her fist, she laughed in that childish way that seals a forbidden complicity. As she approached him in the dirty, ashen half-light, he was at first frightened by the vague realization that he was alone with Lise, that they were alone in the cellar. He could hear the sea—it was the emotion pounding freely with their every breath. They were already locked in each other's gaze, their hands clasped together, and Ludo never even knew they were sinking down among the photographs, lying entwined among the hundreds of photographs where dead people laughed their heads off.

Chapter Thirteen

When the holidaymakers returned to Saint Paul at the beginning of September, a small celebration was held. Mademoiselle Rakoff gave the speech of welcome, the one Colonel de Moissac had written for the inauguration of the Centre. God's blessing was asked on the year ahead.

Mademoiselle Rakoff made Ludo repaint his room, because the walls, as she put it, would have frightened even a lunatic. Ludo used to leave the tins of paint open at night; light-headed from the noxious fumes, he fell into the deepest sleep he had ever known. During the evenings, the banished drawings came back to life under the electric light, and dribbles of paint traced big teardrops coursing down between the fingers.

Odilon was still spying on him. That honey-tongued malice, disguised as good intentions, always alert and snooping about, presented a threat suddenly, made real by the turn of events. Mademoiselle Rakoff regularly urged Ludo to admit he was spreading outrageous stories about her. Where did these accusations come from? She replied evasively that it was part of her job to know everything. 'I bet you call me "the old hag",' she said.

When Ludo thought about Lise, his strongest feeling was one of anxiety. He met her in the cellar on Saturday afternoons with the help of the other girls, who were delighted to share in this conspiracy of love. The moment after Mademoiselle Rakoff left, they gathered at the entrance hall to keep watch and discourage the dwarf from coming too close.

Ludo and Lise spread old rags destined for the shredder on the floor where they lay down. The caresses they lavished on each other did not end in physical intimacy. They spoke very little, kissed one another completely clothed and lay dozing in each other's arms. Ludo could not see Lise's mouth clearly, but he could touch it. The mutilated lip seemed whole again in the darkness.

One day she wanted to see him naked. She lit the candle-end they had brought, undressed him solemnly and moved the flame along the entire length of his body, without a word.

At night, in his room, Ludo contemplated his aching penis, imagining Lise, desiring her. Then he went to knock on her darkened window, covering the glass separating them with kisses. He continued to spy on the love-making of Fine and Doudou, trying to find out what sorcery it was that transformed shared pleasure into sleep.

When he chanced to meet his girlfriend during the day, he saw a sloppy girl hiding her femininity behind a mask of petulance and grumbling.

Micho wrote to him in October.

Dear Ludovic,

Some people say life is just a bowl of you-know-what and every day we get to eat a bit. As for crap, there's certainly a lot of it around here! Not that I'm one to speak ill of anybody. And it's true if you look at things from your mother's point of view it's no joke to be expecting a baby that goes and dies on you. That was a tough blow even for me. But it's no use complaining, you can't have everything in life. All I can say is, your mother and I aren't getting along too well. Since the accident things have been going badly. It's true I didn't tell you about it, but she drove that damned car into a ditch, just what we needed! Your mother wasn't hurt, but the man on the little motor bike lost an eye. And since she'd had a touch too much to drink, you can imagine the mess we're in. This'll be the first time I've ever seen the inside of a courtroom, and who knows how it will all turn out. She says it's my fault, which stumps me completely because I was waiting to have supper with her when it happened. Tatav said he wasn't writing to you anymore because you don't write back. And your mother says the same thing, you never answer. Well anyway when I have a moment I'll pop over and also I'm sending you a parcel. Love from everyone.

Micho

Ludo calculated that he had been at the Saint Paul Centre for ten months, almost a year. His mother had never come to see him. He had never left the Centre, Tatav did not love him anymore, and Micho was waving around promises of a return to The Hedges that were just hot air. He was physically overcome by nostalgia. He smelled, once again, the scents that wafted to his attic on the evening air. He relived the nights spent hovering outside his mother's door, the afternoons at the beach, the breakfasts, the humiliations, the good and bad memories came flooding back together in a golden haze and the bitterness he felt overflowed on to the children.

Looking out through the front door, he could see the future, but did not know how to change his destiny. Perhaps he might succeed in improving his luck if he were somewhere else? Perhaps Nicole and Micho would welcome him with open arms if he simply arrived at The Hedges one fine day? How could they keep him from going into his house, his nigloo, or keep him from listening to the harmonium and taking up his life again, a life that began there, in that open forest leading to where outsiders lived? But he always hesitated at the last minute, afraid of the truth awaiting him in the outside world.

He stayed away from the cellar for two weeks and then gave in to curiosity. Lise was there, silent and grave, her face lacquered with shadows. They had not been together for more than a minute when Ludo jumped up.

'What is it?' she murmured.

'I heard a noise.' He did not dare to light the candle for fear someone might notice the flame through the window. 'I heard a noise,' he repeated.

They listened, but heard nothing. Blinded by darkness, Ludo could not see Lise anymore.

He was oppressed by foreboding. The noise was out there somewhere, silent and concealed but still threatening. Taking the candle and the matches, Ludo left the room, moving slowly down the narrow passageway. His teeth chattered. He had some difficulty lighting the candle; the floor and ceiling seemed to tremble in the yellow glimmer as limp shadows scuttled for cover. In a sudden panic, he searched through this crushing mass of icy darkness and discovered the sound of someone breathing, very near; looking down, he found Odilon, clamped against the wall like a toad in his ancient red jacket. His eyes wide with ecstasy, the dwarf was straining every fibre of his being to spy on Ludo. Then a nasty laugh shook his electric little body and he bolted for the cellar door.

Ludo never felt the candle burn his hand when the flame went out. He did not react when Lise came up behind him.

'What was it?' Lise asked, touching his arm.

'I knew it,' he answered sadly. 'There was a noise.'

From that moment on Ludo was constantly on his guard. He was afraid the dwarf would denounce him, terrified whenever Mademoiselle Rakoff appeared, and too frightened to go near Lise. Her pleading looks could not persuade him to return to the cellar. All the same he was in anguish, tormented each Saturday by the thought of her waiting for him in vain.

Although Christmas was a month away, the entire

Centre was already busy with preparations. Fine was teaching the children carols, while Mademoiselle Rakoff tried to sensitize them to the issue at hand with edifying lectures on the Nativity. The children were thrilled by the pine trees, silver with frost. Mademoiselle Rakoff distributed scarves, and in the evening, showed films about glaciers and the eternal snows.

Christmas was the big day, the birthday of Jesus, the Divine Champion of Innocents. Each year Doudou set up a tree in the refectory, while the children decorated the manger and walls with garlands and little lights, handmade in the workshops. Parents came for the day; Father Ménard said Midnight Mass at about seven o'clock, followed by the Christmas Eve party.

One Saturday, Mademoiselle Rakoff had a surprise for her charges: 'I shouldn't say anything, since it's a secret . . . but I'll tell you anyway: There's going to be a piano concert on Christmas Eve.'

Odilon, who considered himself a connoisseur, asked who the performer would be and whether by any chance it was Cortot.

'Our pianist is Madame Alice Tournache, Aliette's mama. She's a great artist. She gives recitals throughout the region and was awarded first prize at the conservatory in Angoulême, where I was born, by the way. I should like you to look your very best in her honour. Any questions?'

Maxence asked if there would be a piano.

'Of course. Antoine's mother has agreed to lend us hers.'

Antoine stood up proudly to take a bow.

'You heard,' said Odilon to Ludo. 'A concert! I used to go to all the concerts.'

'What's a concert?'

'Oh, you know, it's a performer playing an instrument. Concerts are wonderful!'

'My father's a concert, too. He plays the harmonium.'

Odilon accompanied him back to his room, where he

213

asked in an artificial voice: 'Tell me, are you coming on our walk this afternoon?'

'Why not?'

'But you never come, as a rule.'

Ludo scowled. 'That's not true. I came last time, and the time before.'

Odilon smiled shrewdly and moved out of reach. 'It's all the same to me, do as you like. In any case, I never said a word to Mademoiselle Rakoff.'

That afternoon Ludo resolved once more not to join Lise. He was drawing in the games room when Odilon appeared.

'So here you are! We're leaving for a walk in the wood with Doudou. Coming along?'

Ludo began by stammering that he would join them right away, then suddenly decided to claim a prior engagement making figures for a Nativity scene. 'It's in the chapel with Fine . . . I promised.'

Odilon made him a sweeping bow, smiled broadly, and left.

Ludo did not budge. Through the open window he watched them all trot off after Doudou, and was surprised when he saw the dwarf's red jacket in the crowd. Sunk in thought, he waited another few minutes before venturing out into the hall. No one was there. The refectory was deserted, the hall door was bolted. It seemed the manor house was completely empty except for him, locked in by mistake. He called Fine, but heard no answer. He knew she was busy in the chapel at that time. The trapdoor under the staircase was closed. He lifted the cover, stared at the black hole, and went down. He listened to the silence underground. This was not the first time he had had this feeling of absolute solitude as he went to join Lise, a solitude, so profound that it swallowed him up like a dream.

He opened the door with a pounding heart and froze, terror-stricken, at the sight of a man standing with his back to him in the half-light of the basement window. He was in uniform, with boots and a *képi*, holding a sabre. Slowly he turned towards Ludo. His eyes were hidden by the visor, and his features distorted by a fixed smile. Doffing his *képi* with a ceremonious gesture, he spread his arms slightly, showing off the uniform. He removed his white gloves as though he were on stage, pulling at the fingers one by one, then held both gloves in one hand and slapped them against the naked palm of the other. Two dark eyes stared at Ludo, holding him spellbound. The muffled noise of the sabre falling on to the clutter of papers underfoot made Ludo jump. In that moment of panic, he saw a pale, painted face with a scarlet mouth trembling under a moustache as tapered as an eyebrow. The teeth looked yellow against the bright red of the lips. Ludo could smell camphor and cologne. A dry finger brushed his cheek.

'Poor little Ludo who never says a word,' murmured the apparition. 'So unhappy because he hasn't got his mama ... because he doesn't get kisses from his mama ...'

Ludo stood there, aghast, unable to reconcile the sugary voice of Mademoiselle Rakoff with this old soldier made up like a clown.

'It's true your mama's not very nice to you,' she continued, carefully peeling off her moustache and delicately applying it to Ludo's upper lip. 'Poor little darling ... who doesn't even see how we love him at Saint Paul ... You know I feel sorry for you, dear, very sorry indeed.' She spoke as if in a trance, and purred softly into his ear, cheek to cheek: 'I'm your mama here, in a way. I can give you all the love you need, you know.'

'It's not true!' he cried, pushing her back so violently that she went sprawling on to the papers. 'You're not my mother, my mother's beautiful! I don't want you to be my mother!'

She was already getting to her feet, unrecognizable, her voice low and quivering with hysteria: 'What's going on in that head of yours, you poor little maniac? What are you

215

thinking about, your mother and your filthy ideas!'

She had turned on the light. A harsh glare from the ceiling washed away the shadows. He shrank back from this gaudily painted vision in an officer's tunic unbuttoned to the navel.

'Odilon told me everything, just imagine! Did you think that I was here by accident? That I was taking a stroll? He saw you completely naked in the cellar, with a girl! And you're going to tell me her name! The name of your female accomplice!'

The smiles and sweetness had vanished, leaving a voice screeching with hatred that came straight from the heart.

'If you don't tell me straight away, they'll all pay! And the others will denounce her.'

'I was alone,' whispered Ludo.

'You expect me to believe that? An old woman like me? You were naked with a girl!'

'It's not true,' he murmured.

Laughing at him, she rubbed off her make-up with her forearm, as though it were dirt. 'I'd like to have seen that,' she spluttered. 'You've probably forgotten that I took you in out of charity, yes, charity, and I was too kind! With a mother like yours, I should have been more careful. They have lovely children, sluts—they make marvellous mothers, sluts do!'

Bringing her face close to his she whispered: 'Tell me what the two of you were doing in the cellar, like the animal that you are. Go on. Tell me! You're finished here in any case, completely finished . . . I'm throwing you out!'

'I'm going home anyway,' stammered Ludo, his mind reeling.

'Home? You haven't got a home, you cretin! You're going to an insane asylum! A mental hospital, and sooner than you think!'

'I won't go.'

She froze. 'You won't go?'

'My mother's going to come and get me.'

'You've gone completely barmy about your mother! If there's anyone who isn't about to fetch you, it's her. You're going to regret this where you're going! You won't get a chance to play your usual tricks there. They've straitjackets for the likes of you! It's too bad I haven't got time to arrange for you to leave before Christmas. But if you start misbehaving between now and then, I'll get the police to . . .'

'She's coming at Christmas,' he interrupted, now as angry as she was. 'At Christmas! Christmas! Christmas!' He shouted as he ran like a drunken man down the tunnel.

At the foot of the stairs he heard a peal of laughter, and looked back to see Mademoiselle Rakoff grab the sabre and hurl it at him like a javelin.

He ran to his room, where he could not stop muttering in a shattered voice: 'Christmas, she's coming at Christmas, that's definite!' He was shivering. His mother was everywhere, on the wall, the bed, the table, and her reflection crackled like flying sparks. Tearing a page from his catechism notebook, he scrawled out a letter.

Now I'm grown-up, I want to know what's going to happen to me. Tell me what's going to happen to me. You've never told me anything. You made me leave the attic. You made me leave the house. You made Nanette leave and you've never come to see me here. Now the woman wants to throw me out. She wants to send me to a proper lunatic asylum. I'm not going. I'm not really mad. I'm not. I'm your child. You never told me about my father and I know nothing. I want to come home to The Hedges. I want to stay with you. You have to come at Christmas. You must come and get me, if you don't she's sending me to an asylum. All the parents come to the Christmas Eve party, if you don't come I haven't anything left, I'm all alone if you don't come, none of the other children are all alone. You're going to come at Christmas, that's definite, and also I apologize to you.

Ludo

The letter was posted that very day. Mademoiselle Rakoff, who was no longer speaking to Ludo, sent him a message through Doudou, informing him of his future address: the mental hospital in Valmignac. In case he wanted to let his parents know himself.

Ludo spent the next few days in a state of collapse. He made no contact with the other children, avoiding the workshops and collective activities, barely showing up for meals, ignoring Mademoiselle Rakoff's whistle—and yet the nurse seemed indifferent to his solitary rebellion: no longer a part of the children's circle, he had been cast into the temporary refuge of banishment.

Fine told him that an ambulance from the hospital had been hired for the following Monday, right after Christmas. 'Seems you were with a girl. Should've spoken to me about it, I would've fixed things up. We're not monsters after all. Doudou would've helped you too . . .'

Ludo watched the party decorations go up with a feeling of terror. He remembered fir trees discarded by the road-side, booby-trapped presents, arguments, and wondered what disaster was creeping up on him this time. Odilon was too afraid of reprisals to sleep in his room: he and his barometer took refuge every night in the boiler-room near the workshops, where he fell asleep, drenched in sweat, in a space between the boiler and the wall. Ludo took revenge by urinating all over his enemy's walls in the dead of night. He sometimes caught sight of the dwarf during the day, but at a distance, like a wild animal that cannot be approached.

The day before Christmas began with carols at the Saint Paul Centre. A record-player was set up in the hall. Garlands were hung round the dining-room, frosted silver and gold balls were tied to the tree, figurines were arranged in the manger and the children rehearsed their hymns for Mass, boys and girls together in honour of the Redeemer. As he did every year, Doudou put on his Father Christmas outfit and attached a white beard to his chin, while Fine showed off the cakes and chickens she had cooked in advance. The children spent the day marvelling impatiently at the finishing touches.

Ludo raked the gravel round the manor house.

The piano borrowed for the concert was delivered during the afternoon. Mademoiselle Rakoff had it installed in the chapel, which was re-arranged for the occasion as a theatre, with a dais surrounded by chairs. Ludo had never seen a grand piano. He was dazzled by this great deep-sea beast with shining black skin, its shape seemed to suit it for a sudden flight. It was even more beautiful than Micho's harmonium.

His heart leapt when he saw the pianist's photograph tacked up on the door: gleaming long hair framed a face with almond eyes. It was the young woman who had been so kind to him one Sunday.

When night fell, the children put on their finest clothes, carefully laid out the evening before.

The parents arrived more or less at the same time, about twenty people dressed in their Sunday best, making a great show of trying to conceal mysterious packages until they had been hidden away in Mademoiselle Rakoff's office.

Alone in the darkness, stamping his feet to keep warm next to the open front door and freshly shaved, Ludo watched headlights appear far down the road and followed their approach, trembling with hope, until his inevitable disappointment.

'Hasn't your mama arrived yet?' snapped Mademoiselle Rakoff when all the guests had assembled.

'I'm not going to the asylum!' growled Ludo.

'Oh yes you are, my boy. But Merry Christmas anyway!'

Nobody came. Ludo went through the whole celebration with his teeth clenched. At Mass, he joined the line of communicants and swore under his breath when he received the Host. Next came the concert. He glared at Mademoiselle Rakoff while she announced the selections by Bach and Mozart to be played by Alice Tournache. Then the concert worked its magic: the hush, the opening of the piano, and then it was as though the music had come alive from the depths of its own blackness to console him. He gazed at the pianist, unseeing. He floated, serenely within himself, carried along on a wave in close harmony with his longing for the past, carried back over the years until he could hear his earliest memories quivering in the music. Ludo did not clap at the end, which brought disapproving looks from his neighbours. He rose from his seat with a feeling of deep sadness and with tears in his eyes. On leaving the chapel, he surreptitiously took the pianist's photograph from the door and stuffed it inside his shirt.

Afraid of arousing suspicion, Ludo did not look at Lise at all during dinner. Although he was hungry, he ate nothing. People spoke to him, but he did not answer. The bustle and excitement of the meal were endured by him in a deathly silence — the faces seemed cadaverous, the shouting and laughter sounded like the splashing of foetid water. Finally, when Mademoiselle Rakoff asked him to cut the yule log cake, he suddenly stood up and announced, staring at the ceiling: 'I DON'T WANT TO GO TO THE LUNATIC ASYLUM!' The silence lasted as long as a sharp intake of breath, and then the parents looked away in embarrassment. The conversation picked up again, louder this time. At a sign from Mademoiselle Rakoff, Doudou, still dressed as Father Christmas, came to take Ludo back to his room.

The sedated darkness spread round Ludo like a lake. The Centre was finally asleep; Father Christmas had ceased his drunken babbling. Ludo got quietly out of bed, put on his two pairs of trousers, one over the other, and rolled up his few belongings in a blanket, which he tied with string. Then he knotted his money-sock round his waist, slipped on his lumberjacket, and left the room. The hall door was locked, but Doudou had forgotten to remove the key. He would not need to use the dwarf for his escape.

A smell of stale tobacco lingered in the refectory. At the far end, in the faint gleam of the Christmas lights, the manger flickered like a bivouac round a camp-fire. Wind howled through the pines.

The night was so dark that it blotted out the walls, leaving the windows standing upright in the darkness. Weaving between the tables, Ludo reached the fireplace, where he bumped into an invisible obstacle. The light of a match revealed a pile of golden packages: the children's presents. He struck another match and sneered. Shoes were lined up along the edge of the manger, twenty lovely shoes like twenty little canoes heading into the wind from the shelter of a harbour. All the sheep, all the fake sheep, in their fake stable, round a fake Nativity looked profoundly bogus. He snatched up the pink cradle with its smiling infant, arms outstretched, and hid it inside a shoe. That was better. Tonight Baby Jesus was not going to lord it over him.

His matchstick fell into the straw, and suddenly in the darkness a pink flush bloomed like a glow-worm. The smell of smoke drifted upwards as the light quietly re-kindled itself. A surge of red awakened shapes in the blackness and shadows began to leap and flutter. Ludo watched the tiny tongues of flame grow bold enough to lick at the nearest sheep. He said to himself, 'I'm going to put it out,' but did nothing. Paper ignited in the spreading embers throwing off bitter fumes and sparks like confetti. 'Too late,' he exulted, 'everything's going to go up in flames.' He admired the speed with which the blaze spread along the walls of the manger with a faint roaring sound, darting shafts of brightness out into the dining-hall. 'You're all jealous!' he growled between his teeth, imagining that

221

Mademoiselle Rakoff, his mother, and the others were going to breathe in the flames and go up in smoke.

He moved unwillingly towards the exit, looked back once more at the fire, his fire, and then, proud of the Christmas present he had finally managed to give himself, disappeared into the night.

He trembled so hard as he climbed over the outside fence that he had to rest for a minute on top of it. Then he dropped down on the other side. Ludo could not see a thing, but he was free; the black road stretched out before him like a tunnel.

Part Three

Part Three

Chapter Fourteen

Ludo walked all night. Normally he did not feel the cold: now he was shivering, as he tried in vain to forget about his mother. The falling snow brushed him silently, like feathers. He was afraid of the dark! He looked back time and again, thinking he heard the dwarf laughing from a hiding-place in the trees, or else he imagined the entire manor house, with its children and its manger ablaze, close at his heels like an ogre sent to hunt him down.

He arrived at the metalled road and followed that for a while, but when he saw distant beacons in the night sky, he prudently returned to the trees, making his way through the pathless woods.

At dawn he came to a sleeping village. The sight of an electric shop sign alerted him to the surrounding houses and stopped him dead in his tracks. The snow had stopped. Silence lay thick and unechoing, like drifts piled up against the walls just emerging from the shadows in the thin light of early morning. He hesitated in front of a café with its telltale red tobacco monopoly sign; his hunger drove him inside to a dimly lighted room. Three men were standing at the counter. An old man sat daydreaming in an arm-chair, his mouth hanging open, hands folded in his lap. Not a word was being spoken or a sound made. Their eyes stared blankly at Ludo.

'Ah, you've come in from the cold!' said the proprietor, eventually, from behind the bar. 'If you shut the door, it'll be even warmer.'

Ludo sat down at a table. He was on the verge of fainting, and stared at his chapped fingers as though he had just found them there, near the ashtray, forgotten by a customer. A thousand fingers crawling with chilblains and waiting to be tossed into the dustbin.

'Seasonal worker?' asked the man, glancing towards Ludo's bundle.

He nodded. Nicole was wearing dark glasses and she was crying, at the Fairway Café that time. She would need her dark glasses and some Sauternes, when they told her that her son was dead.

The proprietor had come over to his table. He sported enormous brown side-whiskers on a hatchet face. 'It's not really the right time of year for seasonal workers. What'll you have?'

'A Sauternes,' stammered Ludo. 'With some bread and butter.' A large floppy dog sniffed at his feet, then lay down on them, sharing his warmth. A clock struck eight with a twang and the big hand clicked loudly as it marked off the minutes. Ludo kept his eyes lowered, afraid of betraying through a word or movement that he was crazy and a recent escapee from a lunatic asylum.

'That's five francs exactly', said the man, setting a plate down in front of him.

He paid. A tiny publicity calendar with nude pictures had been put between the glass and the saucer. The proprietor winked at him from across the room.

The wine loosened his ideas a little and made him feel better. The other three customers were still glued to the bar, and the old man in the armchair seemed part of the scenery: stuffed animal heads, trophies, and athletic jerseys.

Ludo had another Sauternes and a glass of hot milk. Now that the sun was up, the window let in the outside world; he could see people, and short trees, like stumps. The man with the side-whiskers turned on a radio that began reeling off the international news of the day. Was it possible that out of all these events, all these misfortunes, his could be the only one missing? Suddenly ill at ease, he gathered up his things, put the publicity calendar in his pocket, pushed the dog away, and left without saying goodbye.

He found himself on an esplanade ringed with squat little shops, their metal shutters closed. There was a church at the far side; its bells were ringing for Christmas Mass, summoning latecomers who hurried towards the porch. And then it was silent once more. Ludo gritted his teeth to keep from crying. He was crossing a phantom city. He was nowhere, going nowhere. He was no one. All alone in the strange village, without home or identity papers, he began to miss the peace and quiet of Saint Paul, Fine and Lise, and felt like asking anyone he thought of to forgive him.

It was then that he saw an arrow-shaped sign that made his heart leap: ATLANTIC SHORE 6 km. He had returned to the sea, his most secret memory, still pure and inviolate after all this time. Ludo set out once again. Laughter echoed through his head. He was haunted by the burning manger. Nicole, holding a sabre, naked under the uniform. She was kissing Doudou, up in the attic. The dwarf sneered, wearing a dress with torn flounces. Mademoiselle Rakoff came in disguised as Father Christmas. Her lipstick melted in the flames.

When a car came by, he lay down in the ditch. People were probably looking for him everywhere. Policemen, orderlies, ready to beat him and shut him up inside a white van like a real lunatic. His stomach in knots, he swore to himself that they would never catch him. He would hide. They would think he was dead, frozen stiff. The police would telephone his mother: your child is dead . . . How he would have loved to see her face when she heard! Leaving the road, he tramped across the frosty, rutted fields towards the forest.

The tree trunks were streaked with frozen drops of water, like candlewax. The silent, silvery half-light comforted Ludo. He began to feel soft gusts of salt air on his tongue. Pine needles in meringue shells of hoar frost crunched underfoot. The wine he had drunk started him wondering whether the shoes had burned along with the sheep, whether the children were walking around in their stockinged feet on Christmas Day, whether they were unwrapping toys fried to a crisp, or making snowballs from the ashes.

He had not wanted to hurt the children, nor to set the manger on fire, for that matter. The match had fallen by itself, like a drop of water or a crumb and the flames had sprung up spontaneously.

And yet, it was true that he had wanted to set the place on fire. He remembered it clearly. The match had not fallen by chance. It was crumpling up in his hand, a black thing with a little red tooth. He had spread his fingers to avoid being burned, but held the match just above the straw, without putting it out. And he had set the flame down in the thick of the sheep, hoping to send them all to blazes.

No, it was not true after all. The fire had started before he even knew what was happening. Perhaps the manor house had burned as well? Perhaps there were no more children at the Saint Paul Centre, no more Centre, no more Mademoiselle Rakoff, no more anything? Perhaps he had never been born?

Ludo found a path covered with rotting bark and followed it.

Odilon was the one he would have liked to see go up in smoke with his barometer and his red jacket. He had looked for him everywhere, in the cellar, the infirmary, the other bedrooms and at the far end of the park. He had looked for him without any premeditation or desire for vengeance, blindly. If he had found him, he would have killed him.

A powerful, low rumble reverberated from the ground, like an earthquake. Oblique shafts of daylight began to brighten the forest gloom, slanting between the tree trunks from a clear sky.

Ludo came out of the woods onto a lake of sand with a scattered growth of tall grass in a delicate shade of pink. Ahead he saw a gentle upward slope of bare ground, a hill battered by salt spray.

He ran to the crest of a dune and gazed, breathless, at the overwhelming spectacle of the waves. The blue of the sky was deepening, its serenity mirrored in the glittering sea below. Surf flecked with foam broke on the shore. In the distance, a ship was passing. Dropping his bundle, Ludo took off his shoes and sat down, drunk from the resin and the ozone in the air. He turned round to look at the other ocean, the pine forest, reaching as far as the eye could see, on which no ship would ever sail. On either side stretched a beach so long and straight that it melted into a bluish haze on the horizon. Silence was everywhere, a sovereign, supernatural silence that cushioned the veiled rhythm of the surf. The sky was streaked with pearly grey and the glimmerings of a distant storm. To the south a squall bathed the horizon in a leaden column, while to the west the open sea moved freely, its sharply etched waves swept by a crisp breeze.

The air was mild. Although he had never been there before, Ludo felt as though he had returned to his birthplace: the same Atlantic, the same sun, the same empty vastness; only the wharf was missing. On the dune to his left, a pillbox had toppled down the slope, lying abandoned like a giant's toy smashed to pieces. Ludo walked over for a closer look. Sand had invaded the edifice, plugging all its openings. There was a machine-gun mount, dotted with hunks of corroded steel. Clambering up on it for a better view, he gasped with surprise: there was a boat stranded on the beach, practically at his feet. It was some kind of a freighter, a blackish hulk, dug prow-first into the shallows, with its stern reaching into the pounding breakers.

Ludo collected his belongings, then stumbled and slid

his way down to the shore. He tried to run but could not. He had no breath left and the ship was much further away than it seemed. The bow lay in an enormous translucent pool that gathered in the dying eddies from the foaming surf. Ludo waded in up to his knees, but gave up trying to reach the stern, as the sea was becoming rougher and more dangerous with every step. The surf banged noisily on the aft section, occasionally revealing part of the propeller in the trough between two waves.

Ludo went back to the beach. He had never seen a boat that big before; it was at least fifty metres long, he guessed. Now he noticed how damaged it was, a rusty derelict, an old sphinx of pitted, twisted metal. Scattered traces of blue paint lingered, pock-marked by wear and tear. The original Plimsoll line had disappeared, overlaid by green streaks neatly traced along the hull by the tides. A cable dangled from the hawsehole, a long dribble of black steel that hummed and twanged in the slightest breeze. The name was barely legible: SANAGA. The scrap heap was alive with the noise of running water, muffled sounds and cataracts gushed from its inside—the old wreck had more holes than a watering-can, and Ludo felt real sympathy for it, pitying its decrepitude.

At low tide he was finally able to wade round the boat without losing his footing. The stern was tufted with slimy seaweed. 'You're mine,' he murmured, stroking the propeller, impressed by the huge steel trefoil encrusted with limpets. A piece of sheet metal was missing at just above eye level, probably a hole made by looters. Throwing his bundle inside, Ludo hoisted himself up. In the murky light, he could just make out the tangled spine of an engine lying three-quarters underwater. The air reeked. Ludo could barely see enough to move about. Groping his way up a ladder, he emerged into a dark mess-room where the tables were bolted to the floor. A door at the far end led to a cabin which was green with moss. He could see the Atlantic through a grimy porthole. A wave of nostalgia swept over him, and he imagined he had come home to his attic, breathing in the mouldy, rancid smells of his dripping surroundings: the blackened mirror, the stove, the washbasin, a room full of junk that seemed a treasure trove to him. Exhausted, he collapsed on to the berth, his head spinning. Enormous rocks started tumbling silently towards him, but they were really faces. He had fallen asleep.

Chapter Fifteen

Ludo stayed buried in the wreck for several days, insensitive to cold or hunger. Although he had unrolled his blanket, he did not use it. The sea rose and fell, swabbing out the holds. He felt as though it were forcing its way inside him to engulf his past life.

Thousands of mirrors danced before his eyes, square, or round like little suns. They crumpled, plunged into darkness, blazed up again in a red glare, all of them showing the same night-black hand reaching out to kill him.

A distant whistle crossed the open sea, like a dog howling in despair.

He nibbled without interest at the biscuits Micho had brought on his visits to the Saint Paul Centre; he munched Valium pills, his secret hoard accumulated over months. Stretched out on the ground, Ludo told himself, over and over again, that he had discovered a beautiful ship and that it was time to explore his wonderful find, but he did not move. He recited his *Hail Mary* just to feel words were in his mouth.

The future no longer preyed on his mind. He was going to live there, on the *Sanaga*. Already he saw himself refloating the wreck and sailing it to Peilhac by himself, tying up under the windows of the Fairway Café where his mother might see him. She would come out to the quay. He would let her weep and beg. When she called to him, he would not hear her. She could plead for forgiveness for as long as she liked, he would remain unmoved and sail away without noticing her.

The rollers slamming against the stern often disturbed his sleep; he woke up disoriented, not knowing where he was. Ludo saw the manor house on the shore and the ship beached on the terrace in the middle of the pine forest. The Atlantic was catching fire; the dwarf jumped at him; long white cars were closing in on the wreck—*they* had found the madman.

One afternoon, investigating a tickling feeling on his stomach, he unbuttoned his shirt to discover a tiny green crab strolling across his bare skin. Their eyes met, and the baby crustacean raised its weapon: a single claw, into which Ludo slipped his index finger. The crab drew blood. Ludo ate it alive.

It was hunger that got him moving again; almost a week later. There was nothing left to eat, and he had not had anything to drink since Christmas.

Everywhere inside the ship he met the same litter of abandonment that reminded him of the attic. There was a stove in the galley, along with a full bottle of dishwashing liquid. Next-door was the pilot-house, where the wheel was still at its post and the magnetic variation tables were glued to a partition glazed with damp. Pieces of electrical equipment had vomited their entrails. The shore was almost invisible through portholes flecked with salt.

Ludo stepped shakily out on to the deck, which sloped slightly to the right and seemed thoroughly limewashed with bird droppings. The sun was shining. He bent to drink from the channels of water glistening among the rotting coils of rope. Farther along, under a tattered canvas cover, a longboat sat overturned, its lines missing. Calor gas bottles were stowed away in the bulwarks. He had to clamber up an iron ladder to reach the forecastle which was strewn with broken seashells. A greasy work-glove lay on a sheet of metal where the links of a chain had wept sallow tears. Overboard dangled a severed cable, clanking in the breeze. The pines and the sea were masters of all he surveyed.

Neither Mademoiselle Rakoff nor the orderlies would ever turn him out of this palace of rust. They would never find him again. Ludo went down to the engine-room, where the lapping of the waves echoed with a hollow sound. Opening cupboards, he saw mildewed dungarees still moulded to a human shape. Near the exit, a blackboard faithfully recorded the last watch at midnight on the sixth of June, 1960: names like 'Abdul' and 'Guizem' were slowly fading away.

The tide was going out, and the waves were breaking far behind the rudder; Ludo jumped down, landing knee-deep in the pool surrounding the wreck. The floury white sand shifted delicately as a gust of wind shivered across the beach: the seagulls silently took flight. At the pillbox Ludo turned to make sure that his dream was real. The *Sanaga* was right where he had left it. He was saddened by the thought that his footprints would disappear at the next high tide; soon he would find a way to let everyone know that this was his home.

As he reached the forest path once again he heard the whistle that tormented him at night.

It took him an hour to reach the outskirts of the village, where he saw a signpost marked: LE FORGE. It might have been close to midday but the houses were asleep with their shutters closed. A thin, chalky light made the silence seem bitter. Ludo walked up the empty street, gripped by the air of solitude and desertion. He found the small square with the church and the café where he had stopped on Christmas Day. When he opened the door, it made a sound like a bicycle's bell. The old man was still in the armchair to the left of the entrance, sitting amid the mounted stag's heads and sporting trophies. There were no other customers; the man with the side-whiskers was playing the fruit machine.

'Just a sec,' he said grumpily. It was a good five minutes before he came over, looking put out. 'I had all the bonus points lit up, all of them!' he complained. 'If you hadn't come in, I'm sure I would've beaten my record and raked in three free balls. Well, it's not the end of the world. What'll you have?'

'Some bread and pâté,' replied Ludo.

'Next door for groceries, sonny. My wife takes care of that. Don't bother to go outside, it's the same address, just go through there.'

Ludo followed him through a curtain of coloured ribbons into a shop so full of household goods that there was hardly room to move.

'Marie-Louise,' shouted the man at the top of his voice. 'She's coming,' he assured Ludo. 'I bet she was dozing. She does the food and the odds and ends, while I run the bistro. And I also cut hair. They say the shoemaker wears the worst shoes, well, there's nobody round here to give yours truly a haircut.'

A woman appeared, smiling at Ludo as if he were an old and valued customer. Her hair was going grey, which made her look a good twenty years older than her husband.

'Caught you dozing, didn't I! You've got a customer wanting pâté. He's a seasonal worker.'

'Pâté,' said the lady sweetly, 'we've got plenty of that. What else do you need?'

The bicycle bell next door pealed.

'Now there's someone else!' groaned the man as he disappeared, 'I can tell I'm not going to get a moment's peace today.'

Ludo bought food, matches, a pocket mirror and a bag of charcoal. The shopkeeper laughed when he untied his sock to pay. 'You're quite early for a seasonal. And probably low on money.' She offered him credit, but he refused, not knowing what she meant.

As he was leaving the village, he met a small woman in black and turned round to look at her. She had stopped in the street to stare in his direction. A hundred metres further along his way, she still had not moved. At the edge of the wood, Ludo wondered if she was following him, but saw only the orange glow of twilight in the deserted fields.

Patches of sunlight still gleamed like gold on the forest floor, but it was getting cooler. Ludo walked quickly, dodging his memories and his mother by listing his impressions out loud: pain in his feet, cold, silence, dampness, fatigue, sleepiness. When he reached the sandy clearing he noticed a warning posted on a pine: DANGER NO SWIMMING. He studied the horizon carefully, but could see no reason for alarm.

A soft light played drowsily over the thin strip of beach left at high tide. The air was completely still, and the water so smooth and shiny that the sun setting on its western rim looked like a red ball on a polished table. Downy clouds filled the sky. The *Sanaga* looked as if she was made of solid gold.

Ludo was walking down the beach but stopped short, panic-stricken. There in the fresh sand were huge boot-prints running parallel to his trail and heading straight for the boat. The sadness and hostility of the world closed in on him. Boots. Nicole with boots. Mademoiselle Rakoff with boots, Tatav, Odilon, all his bad memories, booted like ogres, had invaded his hiding-place in his absence and were planning to capture him.

With clenched fists and teeth he cursed the universe, quaking with fear in front of the ship encircled by waves, imagining the intruder still on board and wondering how he had managed to get there despite the high tide. He did not want to run away before satisfying himself that he really was being hunted. Maybe it was only a vagabond like himself. After all, who could possibly know that he was there?

Nightfall slowly turned sky and sea the colour of ashes. The mournful whistle still echoed across the water, dying away, then returning: two notes endlessly repeated.

Suddenly the quiet evening was shattered by the distant crash of a single wave, its whiteness looming up on the horizon for a moment before vanishing.

Ludo sprang to his feet shivering. It was quite dark now and calm once more. He was so dazed that he did not notice a dinghy move away from the ship and scull in to shore.

'What the fuck are you doing here?' asked a man as he leaped out on to the sand.

Ludo yelped and dashed out of reach. 'And you?' he replied.

The man pulled the skiff on to dry land and came towards him. He was short, but broad-shouldered, with a big, round, bald head, a moonscape without a single hair.

'You've no business to be here,' he continued in a nasty voice. 'This here's my place. How old are you, anyway?'

'Sixteen.'

'I don't want to see you round here any more, got that? I had my eye on you when you first showed up. Little sneaks like you don't scare me one bit. This wreck's mine and no one comes here. Where'd you come from anyway?'

'Dunno.'

'If I find you here tomorrow, I'll throw you out. And don't bother looking at me like that.' He turned the dinghy over, then heaved it effortlessly up on to his back. 'What the hell are you sleeping on that wreck for? Never seen the like . . . It's a pile of rust, a rubbish bin. The scrap merchants'll be here to cut it up before the end of . . .'

Out of the heart of the night, a thunderous wave cut him off.

'A bitch of a reef,' he fumed, turning towards the sea. 'Got a nerve, you have.' He disappeared in the direction of the forest.

When the tide had ebbed enough for him to reach the ship, Ludo climbed back on board. He tried to light a kerosene lamp in the dark, but the wick would not catch. He stretched out on the floor, forgetting his hunger. He would never go back to Saint Paul. He would never go to a lunatic asylum, never. He would stay here in spite of the man's threats: he was not doing anybody any harm. Sleep crept over him. Lise was undressing behind a red windowpane. He imagined a concert just for him in this wreck where the universe spun off balance. Sometimes he saw his mother at the piano and sometimes it was himself. Ludo, playing before an audience of adoring women. He was dreaming. He caught sight of the walking man, striding along the forest path, but when he overtook him he turned around laughing because it was himself—it was Ludo he had been following and fleeing from all these years.

The silence awakened him around midnight, a lived-in nourishing silence, in which sounds formed softly but distinctly, like droplets. He returned to the beach, entranced by the whispering of low tide. He watched a little red flame dance about close to shore, breathed in the ivory-coloured night, studied the murmurings of the stars languidly glittering in the darkness. The infinite medley of light and shadow revived his old wanderlust. Ludo walked off into the night.

Chapter Sixteen

He had been living on the *Sanaga* for a month, experiencing a purifying feeling of oblivion unknown to him since the days of his hiding-place in the attic. In his small mirror he followed the progress of his first white hairs as they threaded their way into his beard. He decided he looked old, as decrepit, in his own strange way as the ship. He had lost weight and was bony, with a spider's web of fine wrinkles drawn across his face, and dark circles round his eyes. As his features became pinched and wan, his eyes looked greener and more lost.

He became accustomed to the tides sweeping through the wreck as if it were breathing, water rushing through countless nostrils in walls peppered with broken rivets. Only an occasional brief groan from the steel hulk betrayed the ancient dream of sailing the seas still alive within it.

Ludo believed that he had forgotten his mother, but he spent his nights in a restless sleep, his memory of her fading with the first light of dawn. Every morning the same fleeting anguish overwhelmed his awakening: *they* were coming to get him. *They* were there but not making a sound. *They* were drugging him and taking him back to Saint Paul. *They* persuaded him day after day that he had never escaped. There was no *Sanaga*, no piano, no Hedges, no one at all: he emerged from the spell of a long coma and was cured.

His worst fear was that *they* would find the boat. How many of *them* would there be, with their white cars and their curses? Smiling at him, at first, and saying: 'It's for your own good, Ludo.' At such moments he grabbed a signal flare, clasping it so tightly that it hurt, and aimed it at the indifferent night. Maybe if I see them with my own eyes, maybe I really am going mad.

The beach was empty during the day, and at high tide or low, Ludo had no other company than the Atlantic and the gulls. Even the man who had threatened him stayed away.

Once he saw four horsemen in a distant cloud of sand, and kept out of sight. It was a mounted shore patrol, four policemen who tried to reach the *Sanaga* but gave up and trotted briskly away when their horses baulked at the waves.

Ludo had found marvellous things on the ship: a fire extinguisher, some boots, a torn sou'wester, some cutlery engraved with the initials 'B.E.,' a bottle of rum, a locker with a brass Colt for shooting off flares.

Some old life-jackets served as floats for a raft he used to come and go between the wreck and the shore. The day he launched the raft was almost his last. Unaware of danger, he had left the beach far behind when the ebb suddenly carried him over an invisible reef. A sound-buoy tilted one side in the white water, straining against the force of the current. And then the tide had turned, providentially, saving his life. Ludo had finally found the source of the moaning noise that woke him in the night.

He had to light the briquettes with rum to build up the charcoal stove. When his fuel ran out at the end of the week, he abandoned all attempts at heating, but continued to use the kerosene lamps and the Calor gas oven.

He caught fish and ate them, using a bent nail for a hook. Ludo set a line baited with bacon off the stern and caught little stone-coloured fish with fiendish faces that he loved to watch suffer. One evening he caught a seagull. While he was casting the line, it had swallowed the nail and tried to fly away. Ludo pulled it in like a kite, struggling with the bird as it pecked and flapped furiously at him, while vomiting tiny crabs and bloody sandhoppers from its recent meal on to the beach. He fricasseed the gull with limpets collected from beneath the wreck and went to bed almost proudly, filled with the bourgeois satisfaction of having treated himself to an especially good meal.

Some days he was brimming with enthusiasm, scrubbing the inside of the ship, grooming the steel carcass as if he could bring it back to life. He had painted his eternal portrait on the mess-room walls, the face more and more hidden behind the hand. But on other days he woke up listless and deathly afraid, torn apart by the cry that had echoed through his being ever since he was old enough to suffer and from which he had never managed to escape. Then he would wander from cabin to cabin until he simply sprawled on the floor in utter hopelessness.

The shopkeeper and her husband in the village of Le Forge seemed to have taken a liking to him. In fact, they were not married. His name was Bernard and hers Marie-Louise, but he usually called her Little Miss Muffet. Ludo had told them that he was staying at The Hedges, a private house outside the village, but they had not taken offence at his lie. Seeing that he had very little money, they hired him to stack crates and bottles in the courtyard, paying him with food. Ludo came to the village very seldom, however. No matter how deserted or how placid Le Forge appeared to be, he always had the feeling that someone was spying on him and that the windows were not innocently empty. The few passers-by he met as he slunk along, hugging the walls, never failed to turn round and stare at him.

Bernard had offered to give him a 'stylish' haircut, trimming his temples and the nape of his neck with electric clippers. Finally he had stuck the whole comb into a jar of brilliantine and plastered down Ludo's hair, revealing his jug ears in all their glory, much to the poor boy's dismay.

Ludo was jolted awake one night by a series of loud, crackling explosions. He dashed to the wheel-house, afraid that the ambulances with their hunters in white had come to take him away. There were at least ten motor cyles waltzing around on the sand by the wreck, their headlights slicing through the darkness, the noise of the racing engines competing with bursts of demented laughter. After a few more minutes of this rodeo, the bikes drew up about twenty metres away on the port side of the ship, which loomed in the glare of their headlights. The silence was broken only by the sighing of the sea and the buoy's plaintive cry.

A tall man stepped forward: 'Don't pretend you're asleep,' he shouted drunkenly, 'we know you're in there . . .' The others backed him up with jeering and catcalls. 'C'mon out! Let's have a look—we just want to see your face. We're not going to eat you alive, we just want to have some fun with you. So c'mon out, stupid.'

Silence again. Ludo was sure they could not see him.

'Scared?' shouted the tall man, holding his arms away from his hips like a cowboy ready for a shoot-out. 'If you've got the nerve, all you have to do is come down here and let us have a look!'

General hilarity.

'Hasn't the nerve,' suggested a drink-sodden voice.

'If he won't come down,' said another to the tall man, 'you go up and get him.'

'You hear what my friend said? I'm going to come and get you! We'll all come up and give you a little kiss. And then you'll be in trouble!'

After a brief consultation with the others, the leader walked unsteadily towards the stern, obviously familiar with the entry-hole.

Ludo ran off desperately to get his flare-pistol, loaded it as best he could and hurried down to the engine room. No sooner had he hidden himself by lying flat against the dripping steel than a shadow appeared in the entrance. His visitor seemed to have lost some of his jauntiness. 'Can't see a thing,' he muttered into his beard. Trying to reassure himself, he straightened up with his hands on his hips and shouted: 'Where're you hiding, you sonovabitch?' His hob-nailed boots made the bridge ring. Motionless, drenched in sweat, Ludo gripped the Colt at arm's length, keeping his eye on the dark shape coming towards him. He lost sight of it when it was quite close but could smell the man's breath, and he fired blindly, closing his eyes and squeezing the trigger with all his strength. The smoke shell hit the man full in the chest, setting his jacket on fire. A flood of greenish vapour filled the hold, and Ludo saw his would-be attacker turn tail and run screaming back where he came from. Shaking, Ludo climbed up to the wheel-house in time to see a silhouette in flames racing for the sea, escorted by the bikes. The fire died out. 'They're going to kill me,' murmured Ludo sadly, watching the black squadron slowly return to the *Sanaga*. That night he would have done anything at all to save that worthless treasure, his life.

At the base of the ship, the bikers were making Molotov cocktails from bottles and rags soaked in petrol. The first one landed on the deck, rolled into a puddle and went out. The second scored a hit when it broke a window in the wheel-house, brushing against Ludo before exploding on the card table and spraying all the varnished wood with stinking flames. He grabbed the extinguisher and worked feverishly, managing to put out the fire, but between the green smoke billowing up from the engine room and the blackish fumes from the burned walls, he was suffocating and decided to go out and die in the open air instead of trapped in a smoke-hole like a snake.

He dropped to the deck when he heard the whine of a gunshot, held his head in his hands, and howled out his anguish. There were more gunshots, but, strangely, they chased the noise of the motor cycles far away and then there was silence. Ludo lay there without moving, fluttering his eyelids, convinced that if he opened his eyes, the shouting and monstrous horrors would return.

There were footsteps on the deck.

'You get beaten up?' asked a gruff voice.

Ludo turned to look at him. 'No,' he said softly.

'Any more of that and they would've torched this old tub for me, the bastards!'

Ludo recognized the impressive build of the man who had warned him off the ship a month before.

'You've got good aim, boy! He was sporting a heck of a black eye, that silly clown!'

'I didn't do anything,' said Ludo. 'They attacked me first. I don't even know them.'

'Calm down and don't worry about it, they're scum. Friday night to Monday morning, all they do is drink beer and ride around on their bikes. They won't tell anyone about you, they're too scared of the pigs. Come and have a drink.'

They went below to the wardroom, where Ludo lighted a lantern and opened portholes to let out the smoke.

'That's quite a job you did on the walls,' remarked the man as he looked at Ludo's paintings. 'And you've set up housekeeping, too . . .' Sitting at a table, he examined the bottle of rum Ludo had just brought out. 'That's very nice, but something's missing. We need glasses to drink properly. If I was you I'd check out the rubbish dump, a bit to the south of here. You'll find everything you want there. If the scrap dealers leave you enough time to move all your stuff in! What's your name?'

'Ludo.'

'Mine's Francis. Francis Couélan.' The man was completely bald, without eyelashes or eyebrows. 'It's from when I was a child,' he said, touching his forehead. 'I fell into a lobster swimming-pool, you know, a pond, like a big holding tank! Didn't know how to swim. Just like I'd dived into a toolbox, with live tools! They fished me out straight away, hadn't even been pinched. Not by the lobsters, anyway, but the fright certainly affected me! That night all my hair fell out and I was left as smooth as an egg. And it never did grow back. But it never stopped me from becoming a sailor.'

He had also put in twenty years in Cayenne for raping an old woman, the village centenarian, in the course of one evening's entertainment; the old woman had died. At sixty he was still a Goliath, his arms and torso tattooed to the greater glory of womankind. He lived like a hermit in a gypsy's caravan at the edge of the forest, not far from the *Sanaga*. No one had ever been inside, no one ever dared to go near it.

One day a small circus had camped on a nearby dune. When the roaring of an old lion kept him awake, he had burst into the cage and broken the offender's shoulder with a broomstick, before the weeping eyes of its trainer.

'Could've been worse, at least he didn't rape the animal!' they all laughed in Le Forge. And the neighbourhood got up a subscription to pay for the damaged king of the beasts.

'Bloody idiots! Real stinkers. But don't worry, I'm here. I know how to deal with the silly bastards! In fact, that's all I do know. So, you like it here?'

'It's all right,' replied Ludo.

'I've got ships and sailing in my veins, too, you never get rid of it. Wakes you up at night, eats at you. And I've got to tell you, the scrap dealers will be coming soon.' He was almost whispering to Ludo, like a wise old pirate privy to the most extraordinary secrets. 'They're all crooked, those scrap merchants, you never know when they'll come, but they always do. Don't know why they like to break up boats, but they won't get the copper this time,' he added with a sly wink, leaning towards Ludo. 'The pipes, taps, all the copper, I'm the one that has it. Property of yours truly. I've got everything here—I'm not that stupid!— right on the boat, stashed down there in the bilge. I sell it off as I go along.'

Ludo was startled by a sudden bleating sound from somewhere near by. 'What's that?' he asked apprehensively.

'That's my sheep,' laughed Couélan, 'don't be afraid. The only survivor when the *Sanaga* went down. It was full of sheep, all over the deck. He's the only one that didn't drown.' He took another swig. 'All carried off into the shoals. Damned reef! You've seen it out there at spring tide? Nothing but white water. That's where I went to get him, in my dinghy! Didn't think I was going to get back. Listen now how he looks after me.' Going over to a porthole, he began to bleat into the night, making the veins on his neck stand out like ropes; there was an answering echo. 'He's waiting for me on the beach. He'll certainly be pleased to meet you.'

Ludo went with his visitor to the hole in the ship's side, where his lantern shone on a big black sheep.

'That's Panurge!' announced Couélan. 'They killed off my dog, so I adopted this ram.'

Ludo buried his fingers in the rough, curly wool, happy to meet a live sheep, all warm and tufty, not one of those hideous fetishes he had sent to their deaths on Christmas Eve.

'I tried hard to make him bark, but it didn't work. So I talk to him like another sheep. Know why I call him Panurge? Because of the Bible, with Moses, when he crossed the River Jordan. They all followed like sheep. Well, good night! And don't worry about that gang, they won't be back again.'

Ludo watched him walk away.

All night long, in his sleep, he followed a sheep as it guided him through his memories, leading him to the attic, The Hedges, Saint Paul, and whenever he caught up with it, it was always himself he was following: Ludo.

He took Couélan's advice. The next day he visited the seaside rubbish dump, a vast tip where mounds of refuse rose and fell in their own natural cycle. Columns of vapour

246

threaded upwards through air saturated with the smell of rotting food, profaning the scent of resin and ozone. Ludo entered this labyrinth with relish, as though he had found another wreck, another delightful treat; he marvelled at this petrified typhoon that collected all things here below, a powerful object lesson in the breakdown of matter into its constituent elements. A raucous crowd of gulls and crows huddled over the filth, moving a few metres away as he approached. Here and there were eruptions of stoves, gutted cars, armchairs, baby's prams, dogs, rails, melded together into a silent charivari. Ludo saw a horse completely covered with sucking flies. To dig up six unbroken plates, he had to untangle them from a net of roots beneath a clump of nettles. He found the second half of *Quo Vadis*, which he skimmed where he was, sitting behind the wheel of a burned-out lorry. He picked up knives without blades, pots without handles, clothes he packed into a caved-in suitcase. There was nothing the dump did not offer to its guests. Ludo would not have been surprised to unearth the impossible, a church, a submarine, his childhood years in Peilhac. He even began to wonder if the Saint Paul Centre and all its innocents might not be lying around somewhere under all the sludge.

He found his most beautiful treasure towards the evening: a musical box shaped like a grand piano, worthy of belonging to an aristocrat. He wound it up, then stood there awkwardly, holding *Forbidden Games* in the palm of his hand, a tune he had never heard before. And that was how his memory caught up with him, quietly, in the middle of a rubbish dump, his grudge against fate melted away. He could feel the pulse which music revives deep in the heart of years long past. Ludo rewound the toy and, felt as though he were rewinding his life, going back through time to his birth and his truth. He saw his mother again, wanted to touch her, talk to her . . . Purged of all resentment, it was almost with remorse that he recalled his life at The Hedges.

Back at the wreck, he lay down on the floor in darkness and listened to *Forbidden Games* several times. Then he lit the lamp to write a letter to Nicole.

You know I left but I'm doing fine. I left because you didn't come at Christmas. But I didn't freeze. Now you can come and see me on my boat. There's a village called Le Forge and if you follow the road as you leave you come to the sea and you'll see my boat on the beach. That's where I am. That's my home. I can even entertain you if you come. I even have a profession it's that I'm a seasonal worker. It would be nice if you came. You can write to me at the café in Le Forge.

Ludo

He went up on deck, looked thoughtfully out at the open sea, and tore his letter to bits, scattering them overboard.

Chapter Seventeen

Once again he was overcome by nostalgia. He had finally escaped from insults and shame, there being no one around to tell him over and over again that he was an idiot, low-born and dangerous. He was alone. He wandered endlessly through his memory and forgot all about the wreck. Instead, he heard the stairs creak, the key turning in the lock, and he would hide in the aerie with his collection of mullet heads. On certain days, looking out of the porthole, he saw the courtyard at the bakery, the walls of the house, the misty fields, he smelled the warm bread, and these memories, rising naked from his past, became tinged with bitterness. He strayed in his thoughts from Lise to Nicole, imagining his mother with a hare-lip, and reflecting for the first time that she had never kissed him. Closing his eyes to the lie, he passionately kissed his own hands, dreaming of her skin. Nanette was there, he heard her voice. It was a song without words, faceless, colourless, a soft continuous humming.

He was haunted by images he could not connect to anything. A little boy was walking barefoot at night. A little boy was going up the stairs. A red hand swam before his eyes.

Then the questions flooded in on him: who was the child? Whose hand was it? Why had the baker and his wife treated him so badly? Had he already seen his father without knowing it?

He cried for hours one day and watched himself cry in

the mirror, feeling nothing, neither pain nor sadness. He was bleeding, like a dead star, without any visible wound. His sexual instincts tormented him at night. He remembered Fine's heavy, compact breasts, with their black nuggets at the tips. Hiding his penis between his legs, looking down at his body thus deformed, he wondered if he might not have liked to be born female, with beautiful breasts like Fine or his mother. The hallucination prolonged itself into sleep; Nicole, Fine, and Lise were transformed into chimaeras he had to slice open on a table in the refectory—and suddenly the table became the wharf, tossed about in the open sea.

He dreamed too, of a profession, of a place in society. He had made himself a letter-box with his name on it from an old Californian champagne crate salvaged at low tide, which he lashed to a broom handle, and planted in the sand near the wreck, above the high-tide line.

He ate without appetite, nibbling nervously and at random on barely cooked fish, seaweed, and limpets with the supple consistency of Tatav's chewing gum. He drank indifferently from the sea or from puddles of rainwater on the bridge. The only thing he really missed was his hot milk in the morning, and sometimes he went to Le Forge just to bring back a few precious milk cartons.

Francis Couélan visited Ludo regularly. He had carved a knife especially for him: a big one on a leather thong, with a wooden handle in the shape of a mermaid arched like a phallus. He also gave him rabbits from his poaching snares. Ludo hated the rabbits, which looked like newborn babies once they had been cut into pieces. After Couélan left, he got rid of them beneath the trapdoors in the engine room. There were about ten of them down there, marinating in the brine like so many embryos in a dead womb.

Seated in the mess-room, Ludo and the ex-convict barely spoke to each other, silently drinking a concoction of rum and strong tea that made the adolescent's head spin. But sometimes Couélan burst out with an impromptu tirade, going on and on about shoals, stars, or the influence of the moon and winds on the size of the breakers at the reef.

Seeing Ludo splashing around naked in the waves, Couélan taught him the breaststroke. Then the boy who had never learned to swim began paddling round the ship in mid-winter, blithely ignoring the warning notice.

It was the tides that determined how he spent his time. When the tide was high, he brought out a lopsided arm-chair and sat at the stern, gazing at the slow procession of waves invading the shore. Well before slack water, a solitary roller would build up north of the buoy, a fantastic flight of steps heaving upwards only to curl majestically in upon itself, collapsing into seafoam, like the evaporation of a mirage. Ludo could not believe that the waves were responsible for the destruction of so many ships and lives. And then the mirage would reform, the breaker arched over the horizon once again, whipping spray into the air as it carried a thunderous, seemingly crushing burden of snowy debris along its flanks. The phenomenon ceased with the ebb tide.

Ludo both loved and feared the waves. They were beauti-ful, like his mother, or the lovely pianist, who was also dressed in a halo of light, untouchable and yet so near, so alive. Ensconced in his armchair on the windy deck, he never tired of listening to the murderous surge of the Atlan-tic across the reef.

He also spent many hours walking along the beach. When the tide was out, the sand was littered with new trophies. He wore sticky ribbons of seaweed crossed over his chest to imitate alligator skin. He gathered up the sea's small change, abandoned by the surf to the beachcomber's curiosity: starfish, cuttlebones, tangles of kelp, lacerated medusas like gobs of eye-jelly, tree branches sand-blasted by the wind. He found stones worn into strange shapes, erosion of all kinds, periwinkles bleached and ground down until only their spire-tips remained, the flaccid isinglass of a dead fish, or the corrugated dome of a crab's head, crimped around the edges like a pie crust. Ludo welcomed this gaudy assortment of gifts from the sea, and strolled along the beach just as he had rummaged through the dump, as if going to market, a solitary shopper amid the sea-wrack.

Sitting on the beach in the evenings, he built bonfires of driftwood, sacrificed with regret, and gazed at the sea through the flames. As always, it was really his mother he thought about, trying somehow to win her over no matter how far away from him she had fled. He dreamed she was boarding the *Sanaga*. He himself was at the helm as Marcus Vinicius, the hero of *Quo Vadis*, slicing through the moorings with his sword to get under way. He could stay like that until dawn, with his memories and the flames for company; a roaring fire always gave Ludo the feeling that he was getting close to the truth.

He liked to challenge the incoming tide, building gigantic barricades astern of the *Sanaga*, innocent walls of sand that held the sea back for five or six minutes until they cracked, undermined at their base, and the water rushed in to claim the bed it had long scoured out for itself beneath the ship. Then he took refuge on board to watch the sandy foam lap around the rudder and propeller before flinging itself fiercely against the stern, as if all those waves had somehow sworn to cross the Atlantic to inundate this very wreck.

He found cans of paint and brushes in a cupboard and, taking advantage of the sunshine, he decorated the flanks of the *Sanaga* with big black hands radiating blood-red lightning bolts. Couélan told him admiringly that his ship was painted better than a prostitute.

When it rained, Ludo went to the Prisunic supermarket on the road to Bordeaux, outside Le Forge, where he spent hours without buying anything. He would take a shopping trolley and wind through all the aisles, selecting wines and frozen foods, women's underwear, nappies, piling everything up in his cart until it was completely full, only to abandon it when no one was looking.

Walking along the seashore one splendid afternoon at the end of March, he left the *Sanaga* so far behind that it was out of sight when he turned round. The sea was like a dream. The sand was hot beneath his bare feet. It was then that he glimpsed the wharf stretched out along the horizon, an oily smudge against a windless sky. He rubbed his eyes, now convinced that he recognized this stretch of beach, the gaps between the dunes, the curve of the shoreline, the firing range, and the narrow strip of sand at the end concealing the path he and Tatav used to take, cutting across the fields to The Hedges. When he reached the bituminized pipe, he clambered up on to it with a rush of emotion. This was his home — his whole life was here. He ran to the access-road leading away from the beach, suddenly obsessed by a single idea: to see his mother, to reassure her, to swear to her that everything was going well, that he was not dead and that he was coming back for good this time. All the words he wanted to say to touch her heart danced on his lips. He felt sick with anticipation and gestured madly as he galloped uphill towards The Hedges.

The sight of the red roof and the dazzling white walls threw him into a panic. Filthy and unshaven, he had been a vagabond for three months. What would she think, seeing him in such a state? He lay down on his stomach to crawl towards the road. His house had not changed at all. The shutters of his room were open. There was a blue car near the garage. A bare-chested young man was sunning himself in a deck chair on the terrace. Ludo could hear someone humming while taking a shower; the noise stopped. He almost shouted when Nicole came out, wrapped in a towel, leaning slightly to one side as she wrung out her dripping hair. The man casually slipped his hand under the towel without even opening his eyes. Nicole just smiled at him. Who was he? Where was Micho? What was going on? She bent over the stranger to kiss him tenderly. Ludo was beside himself, and wanted to lick the sweat off the skin of the woman he loved and hated, the mother who belonged to him alone. He stood up, determined to cross the street, open the gate and take her back. No one could stop him!

Hand in hand, Nicole and the man had just gone gaily into the house. Ludo had not moved.

Strangely relieved, he lay down on his stomach again to wait for nightfall. Why was Micho not at home? Some time during the evening the man stepped outside to close the shutters. It was almost dark, the first stars were appearing when Ludo crossed the road and slipped into the garden. He recognized the scent of wisteria, awakened by the spring weather. He glued his ear to the front door and heard the muffled noise of the television. He pressed the doorbell, keeping his finger on the button for a long time. He heard two fragile chimes sound and resound, and he panicked, like a trapped animal. There were footsteps and then the door opened. For a moment Ludo saw a big man in an undershirt frowning at him, then a silhouette appeared behind the man, he heard the words 'some kind of old tramp'—and fled like a thief back across the road into the fields.

Later he sneaked over to spend the rest of the night in his nigloo, which he found intact at the far end of the garden.

It was dawn when he returned to the ship. He spent the day lying on the floor, his hands joined as if in prayer, like a Crusader on a tomb. He was conscious only of vague impressions, hollow moments brushing past him like bubbles before vanishing. He lay there with his eyes open, listening to his heart beat, and the sea pounding beneath the stern. A drop of water fell somewhere in that mass of scrap iron, like a memory. A little boy was walking at night. A black hand was flying, stealing through the air. Someone was plaintively repeating: 'Mama says he fell all by himself,' but who, who was saying it? Nicole often came to the attic, but he did not know she was his mother. He already enjoyed seeing her. She never said anything. She was more beautiful than Nanette. He was sad, with Nanette; she always tried to make him talk, always wanted to know if he was happy, if he would remember her when he was grown up. Where do they put you when you are dead? And where was Micho? He could hear the harmonium, envisage the eight fingers running up and down the keyboard. And his real father—where was he? Was he the one he had seen at The Hedges with Nicole? Had his father come back?

He awoke that evening in a state of euphoric sadness. Looking out at the open sea, he dcided to go for a swim. It was still quite light out. He tried to forget the man he had seen the day before and no longer wanted to think that he was perhaps his father. He imagined himself swimming side by side with his mother on a hot evening, revelling in the Atlantic. They would talk to each other, as the shore faded from view and the lights of freighters began to gleam on the horizon.

Intoxicated by his dream, he had left the beach behind and came up on the reef unawares. A huge breaker crashed suddenly, treacherous, and he choked with fright. Straight ahead of him, waiting for him at the end of a vertiginous slide beneath the sea, was death: the black snout of the reef, a gulf where the oarweed swayed in a bronze-coloured trance, while up above the enormous wave thundered along like an onrushing chariot. He tried to swim away but the tide was sucking him in, and then the sea exploded, tumbling him through sheer chance beyond the swirl of the current.

He managed to return safe and sound. Standing on the shore in a state of shock, he kept staring out at the snowy riot of breakers that had almost done away with him.

At night his fear became a nightmare from which he woke in a pool of sweat. It was not the reef he had glimpsed

in the sea, it was the masked portrait: the red hair became
fins, the fingers were long tentacles writhing towards him,
and the wave was a clattering of livid bones. Eaten away
by shadows, his eyes searched the room for an evil spell;
he wondered if *they* had tracked him down, if *they* were
already there, all of them, on board; policemen, orderlies,
scrap merchants, devils, all intent on capturing him. He
got out of bed, lit his lamp, and tiptoed up on deck, where
a slight drizzle marred the silent darkness. The *Sanaga*
seemed like a meteor suspended in the phantom night, a
night on which nothing had ever existed. Ludo went below
again and tore open a paper bag to write on.

Me I'm like my father. I went far away but I'm not dead.
It's because you didn't come at Christmas. I'm a seasonal
worker now. I have a boat that's where I'm at home.
There's a village called Le Forge and if you follow the
road you come to the sea, it's around there. My boat's
called the *Sanaga*. I can even entertain you if you come.
There was a man with you in the garden the other day.
Don't know if it's my father and anyway we're not alike.
It's fine if you come that way I go back to The Hedges
with you. If you to write me it's at the café in Le Forge
where my friends are. Where's Micho? It's nice when
you have long hair.

Ludo

Chapter Eighteen

The scrap merchants arrived in a small van one April evening. Ludo was on his way back from The Hedges when he noticed them at the ship. His first reaction was to hide, but when he had got over his fright, he reasoned that medical orderlies did not usually spend their time measuring wrecks, so he came forward. A big man in a beret handed him a bouquet of flowers.

'Hi! We found this on the sand, by the boat. It's great to be a success with the girls . . .'

Ludo stared in astonishment at the faded tulips he held in his arms.

'We're the butchers,' laughed the other man, 'come to carve up your ham. They warned us in the village there was a . . . tenant on board, but that's your problem. You're not the first to get set up on a wreck, it don't bother us one bit. You can relax for another week, we just came to size up the job. It's going to be easy, too, the steel's only shot on the surface. So, see you later! And start thinking about moving all your stuff out.'

Ludo watched the van drive off and went to put the flowers in a Coca-Cola bottle filled with sea-water.

The next day he walked to Le Forge, where he had been checking regularly since posting his letter to Nicole, hoping for an answer. Once more, Bernard had nothing for him. He looked at Ludo with a strange expression.

'It's funny,' he said, 'we had the cops here this morning. Can't say we see many of those. Don't like 'em much, either. They're looking for a lunatic who escaped from an asylum. Don't have anything like that around here, we told 'em. It's funny . . .'

'Why're they looking?'

'People in these parts don't open up,' continued Bernard, 'and never to pigs. They never talk, but they're not crazy. We had the scrappers in, too. Won't be long before they slice your boat up in little pieces.'

Ludo had finally admitted that he was living on the wreck while waiting for the season to start. Bernard had informed him that they had known for a long time.

'Anyway, it'll be summer soon, you could rent a room from someone in town. I'm sure you're handy with pruning-shears.'

When he got back to the boat, Ludo found an old bouquet of flowers in his letter-box that reminded him of Lise. She was another one for giving him flowers when he was feeling low. He thought of their caresses and their love-making, but without joy, suddenly ashamed at having left her alone back there.

He added the roses to the tulips, which had dropped their last petals. Who in the neighbourhood was taking an interest in him? Who knew he was there? The ex-convict did not poach flowers.

Over the next few days he hid near the pillbox until nightfall without ever seeing anyone. When he began making his trips to the village and The Hedges again, the moth-eaten bouquets returned to grace his doorstep. One afternoon, Ludo pretended to go off into the woods, then circled back to the beach and hid behind the dune. Shortly afterwards, a little girl appeared on a bicycle. She put her bike down on the sand, took a bouquet from the basket, and went to place it at the base of the ship. She stood there for a few seconds, her hands clasped, then crossed herself, genuflected quickly, and walked back to her bike. There she found Ludo waiting for her.

'What're the flowers for?' he asked.

258

She shrugged her shoulders, as if the answer were obvious.

'Well they're for my papa!'

'Who's your papa?'

'He's dead 'cause he drank too much. My mother, said he was crazy. Now he's in a box, in the cemetery. My mother goes every day, to the cemetery. With flowers. But me, I bring them here. And also I take some from the other boxes too, that way there's more. Today's flowers, they're almost new.'

'Why do you do that?'

The little girl seemed to be thinking. 'It's my brother . . . the one that has a motor cycle. He says there's a crazy man on the boat. So if you're crazy, you're my papa.' Then, in a teasing little voice: 'That okay with you?'

'Well I don't know,' stammered Ludo, pleased and embarrassed.'What's your name?'

'Amandine. But everyone calls me Mandine. My doll's called Célestine. I've got to go or I'll get yelled at.' She straddled her bike and raced off.

She returned regularly to the beach, always with flowers stolen from graves in the neighbouring village. She chatted with Ludo but kept her distance, as if by instinct. She was on holiday, a six-year-old with a piquant, pretty little pout, a lisp that she seemed to modify at will, and eyes that glittered with so many colours and darted everywhere so quickly that they reminded Ludo of marbles. As a token of friendship, Ludo gave her a surprise: a steel-blue baby lobster caught by Couélan. Ludo cut the tendons of its claws and wrapped it prettily in paper he had bought specially in Le Forge.

Amandine was back two days later, in tears: 'Titi's dead!'

'Who's Titi?'

'My baby lobster. Already he'd stopped singing.'

'Did you eat him?'

'Oh no, never! I put him in the parrot's cage, in the

259

garage, and fed him birdseed every day, and still he died. And my mother, she yelled at me 'cause it smelled bad.'

Ludo promised her another lobster. She sulked for a few moments, digging the toe of her shoe into the sand. Then she left, still in a bad mood, announcing that he was not nice and he was not her father anymore.

Ludo spent the rest of the day scraping the wormeaten ship's longboat with his knife. Ever since the scrap dealers had been, one would have thought he was trying to make the ship like new again to persuade them to leave it alone. He oiled, scrubbed, washed. At night he imagined that the wreck was straining at its moorings, eager to be away on the tide. Sometimes he dreamed he was walking across the sea, carrying the *Sanaga* under his arm like a child's toy.

Later that afternoon he caught sight of a silhouette skirting the dunes, and thought at first it was Couélan coming to see him, but a warm, familiar feeling flooded his heart almost immediately: it was Micho. Ludo abandoned his work and rushed down to the beach to meet him. His stepfather fell into his arms.

'So it's true, it wasn't a joke!' he cried. 'You're really on this old hulk! And there was I not believing a word . . . I was sure she was just feeding me another line, I was sure you weren't really here. And you've grown, you're a man, now—just look at you!'

They walked back to the boat.

'You've come to get me? You're taking me back to the house?'

Micho stared gloomily out at the sea. 'Not that again . . . not exactly . . . no. No, I'm not taking you back to the house, I can't do anything about that. Anyway, I don't go there myself, to the house I mean. All that's finished.' He stood looking at the inside of his hat, like a beggar. 'Your mother and I, it just wasn't working out,' he continued in a shaky voice. 'I mean it was her, she wasn't working out. Nothing but lies. She even said she'd never been pregnant, she'd laughed her head off every time she thought about it.

260

Mauricette, at least, now she was straightforward. It's over, so what!'

'What's over?'

'It's all over, son, we're not together now, we're even getting divorced. I left her the house, didn't want to live there anymore. Never had anything but heartache in that house, and I never worked it out. Tatav won't lose out, he'll get the money later, and you too, actually. Here's a little something to help tide you over for the moment.'

He stuffed a wad of notes down Ludo's collar. 'I can't do any more right now. The sale hasn't gone through yet, it takes time. And then all my savings got eaten up by this damned divorce case! You'd think her parents might've made a gesture, right? Forget it! Not a sou! I might as well tell you, I haven't the heart to set myself up in business again. Anyway, I'm too old. So I'm going . . .' He cleared his throat uneasily. 'My cousin, well, she offered me a little job. I'm going to be the handyman at the Saint Paul Centre, the place where you were before. There's always things to be fixed in those big old barns. Why not, I said to her. And I didn't tell her where you were, not me! That I didn't tell her.'

'And my mother,' cut in Ludo, 'she got my letter?'

'You bet she got it. She's the one who told me you were here. Me, I didn't believe it. We thought you were dead. The cops looked everywhere for you. They searched the woods, dragged the river, the whole caboodle. But there's certainly hiding places in this damned country, and you, you really picked yourself a winner.'

Suddenly, he grabbed Ludo's left wrist. 'Me, I never thought you were batty, son, I never thought that. I always used to say to your mother and Cousin Hélène, too, he's strange, the boy, a bit dense, but batty, no! That he's not!' He looked away. 'It was after the business with the fire, you understand, that I did see they were right, but I'd never have believed it myself.'

Ludo bowed his head. 'My mother didn't come,' he said piteously.

261

'The firemen weren't sure, they talked about a short-circuit in the Christmas lights. But your mother, she was sure, and Cousin Hélène as well. The whole manger went up. There was even a chimney fire because it was all blocked up with birds' nests. They're lucky they didn't all die in their beds.'

Micho stroked the ship's flanks and sighed. 'It's not an old tub, you know, this boat. Wouldn't take much to fix it up. If I was twenty years younger, it wouldn't have worried me.'

Ludo showed him round the wreck.

'And my mother,' he implored at the end of the tour, 'when's she coming to get me?'

Micho seemed completely at a loss. 'That . . . I don't know. You never can tell with her, she'll do as she likes. She hasn't told me anything. And anyway, maybe you shouldn't have written to her. She has your address, now.'

Ludo took him back to the shore on the raft, but Micho got his trousers soaking wet anyway. He promised to come again and left without looking back.

That night Ludo dreamed a giant hand was crushing him.

The week went by. He visited The Hedges every day, but saw no one. The shutters were closed. He swung by Le Forge on his way home but Bernard was less friendly now, and kept washing glasses or agonizing over a game on the fruit machine whenever Ludo dropped in. Ludo paid for his hot milk with hundred-franc notes, forgetting his change on the table each time. It would be waiting for him in an envelope the next day, with his receipt and the correct change scrupulously marked on the outside. His pockets bulged with coins and crumpled notes that he scattered far and wide without realizing it. As for Marie-Louise, she had not changed towards him, and despite all the money he seemed to be throwing around, she never let him pay for the tinned pâté and cartons of milk he took back to the ship. 'You're a good boy,' she kept saying, 'a really good boy. I don't know what you're doing around here, but you're a good boy.' And, Ludo thought to himself, she is absolutely right. He was the best of all the good boys he had ever met.

Back at the beach, Couélan and Panurge would be waiting reproachfully for him near the *Sanaga*. 'What d'you want to go traipsing around in the village for, they're all scum, backbiters, and nothing but trouble. Shouldn't go there.'

When he checked his letter-box as usual one evening, Ludo found a message from Amandine: she was coming the next day to have her afternoon snack with him on the wreck.

When the tide comes in you don't pick up my flowers now and they float away. If this keeps up I won't bring you any more.

Mysterious initials were carefully penned across the envelope: s.w.a.k.

She arrived as announced, mischievous and delighted, wearing sky-blue Bermuda shorts and carrying her thong sandals in her hand. Ludo met her at the pillbox.

'Good afternoon,' she said, coyly. 'Are there any madeleines?'

'What are they?' he asked uneasily.

'If you don't have madeleines, I don't want to go on the boat. And it's all wet to get to it. You'll just have to carry me on your back. D'you see my stones?' She was waving around a small canvas bag. 'White ones and black ones. I picked them up on the beach. You can draw churches and people with them, and also horses, too. You know what s.w.a.k. means?'

Ludo did not know.

'Well, then I won't tell you!'

She finally decided to wade through the shallow pool to

the boat, letting out excited little cries. She looked at the opening above her head with mock horror and her arms akimbo, but Ludo gave her a leg up, and then followed her inside. Thanks to Ludo's interior decorating, the *Sanaga* breathed the cozy atmosphere of a Lilliputian home. The little girl was entranced by the saloon, which was arranged like a doll's boudoir; she clapped her hands gleefully when she saw her wilted bouquets in their Coke bottles. She seemed tickled to death, poking her nose everywhere from the store-room to the wheel-house, anxious not to miss a detail of this magical abundance. She asked Ludo questions about everything, the galley, the engine, how it worked, if it could go faster than her bicycle, if he would take her along one day to Bordeaux where her winter house was, if he was scared at night. Ludo answered as well as he could, inspired even to fib, telling stories about fabulous lands visited only in his dreams, savannas and taigas fancifully traced over the Bordeaux countryside.

'Your place is so beautiful! 'Cept for the pictures. I know how to draw horsies. Really, you're s'posed to say horses, but I still call them horsies. I'll bring my drawings to show you, if Mama lets me.'

Ludo made her some hot milk for her snack.

'I really wanted Coke, with madeleines for dunking.'

'Don't have any,' replied Ludo, somewhat miffed.

'Doesn't matter,' she smirked. 'We'll pretend the milk is Coke and the bread is madeleines. And you can be my papa. What is that noise?'

'A whistling-buoy.'

'Why's it whistling?'

'There's a reef with a sand-bar. So it whistles.'

'And your mama, she's nice?'

Blushing, Ludo mumbled that she was very nice and that she was coming to get him soon.

'Well I'm grown-up,' announced Amandine, sticking out her tongue, 'and my mama doesn't need to come and get me, I can go home all by myself. So, you still haven't guessed?'

'Guessed what?'

'My secret. s.w.a.k.—it means: Sealed With A Kiss.'

At that moment, Ludo thought he heard someone shouting and dashed up on deck.

It was the terrified mother, looking for her daughter and afraid to admit to herself that her child had disobeyed her, had been mad enough to visit 'her papa'. Her papa! The tramp on the *Sanaga*! The horrible madman who had escaped, so they said, from an asylum and was going to be taken away by the police any day now! She had found the bike on the dunes, but there was no one around, and she was horrified to see the sun going down. Her face flushed, she came towards the wreck, as if ready to kill or to die, calling for her daughter and expecting the madman on the freighter to appear and throw a bloodstained knife at her feet.

'It's my mama!' cried the little girl joyously, catching sight of her in the distance. 'Mama, Mama, I'm here! Come with me,' she told Ludo, 'we'll go to meet her. My mama is the nicest one in the world . . .'

He led her back outside. The woman ran towards them sobbing, gasping her child's name and stumbling in the sand. Amandine sped into her mother's arms, and then, her nerve breaking, the woman began to shake her head and shout 'Bastard! Bastard!' in a tearful voice, clutching her daughter to protect her from an imaginary danger. And each time he protested feebly, 'But Madame,' she screamed 'Bastard!' louder and louder, backing away with the little girl. As she left the beach she shouted at him for the last time, venting all the rage of a mother beside herself with anguish; then, staggering across the dune with Amandine, she disappeared.

Ludo remained motionless for a long time, facing the sunset, watching night spread over the sea. The heat and darkness seemed to hold some drama in suspense, a premonition of menace underscored by the lugubrious litany of the sound buoy. What harm had he done? Why

265

should anyone scream at him simply because a little girl had come to visit him? When would *they* find out where he was? When would *they* decide to come and arrest him? And what if *they* shot at the madman, what if *they* killed him just like a dog! And his eyes searched the gloomy forest where *they* were certainly hiding, all of them, with their guns. He went back to his ship, desperately wishing that he had someone to whom he could tell the story of his life.

He was wakened at dawn by the vibrating of the hull and a piercing mechanical whine: the dismemberment of the *Sanaga* had begun.

Chapter Nineteen

'I, Francis Couélan, have the honour to undersign how the tramp freighter *Sanaga* ran aground on the beach and as one might say, in my back yard. It was midnight and high tide, Your Honour, fine weather with the sea flat as the back of your hand. The next thing, I know, smack-bang in my window I see the lights of a ship, blazing away as if it was on parade. Didn't take me a minute to slip on my trousers and get my dinghy into the water, and there I was, sculling out to the idiot who'd hung himself up on the reef and hadn't even cut his engines—churning up a storm of sound back there, you should've seen it! There was bleating like crazy, a real pig-pen. And when I come alongside, there's this whole harem of sheep flinging themselves into the soup, what a racket, you couldn't even hear the buoy. I climb up a ladder. With all due respect, I'm met by a big nigger in the buff, not even underpants, with a suitcase and a wide-open umbrella just in case a star happens to come unstuck. "What the fuck's going on here?" I says to him. "Orly," he says to me. "Orly my arse!" I says. "West Orly," he says. Then he ups and jumps in the water, my nigger, with his umbrella, his suitcase, and the sheep still raining down. I make a dash for the bridge. Three officers pretending they're still on course, maybe they were even imitating the engine noise. "Gentlemen," I says, "it gives me great pleasure to welcome you to my back yard." They started jabbering away but it was all double Dutch to me. Tanked, they were! Stewed to the gills. Then the stern burst into flames, so I hotfooted it back to my dinghy—the merchant marine was all fucked up and on its own! The sheep had had it, all drowned except one asking me for help, and believe me I could understand the sheep better than the ship's skipper. That beast was calling to me, Your Honour, he was drifting out to sea, straight for the buoy, he must have thought Baby Jesus of the Sheep was talking to him. I slipped a line round him and got him back to shore. He was bleating, the buoy was bleating, so I joined in. I'll have you know I can bleat as well as any sheep when I put my mind to it! And I adopted him, Your Honour—Panurge, I call him, because of Moses when he crossed the River Jordan. He has his kennel just outside my door, right across from the one where I had my dog, the one they killed, supposedly for beating up your Alsatian. Now I've got Panurge, and he's not about to bite! He's even pals with the loony who moved into the wreck and about whom you asked me for a report. And here's my report, Your Honour. The loony is a really nice boy. He's no more loony than you, me, or Panurge. The loony don't bother nobody on the beach, and if the *Sanaga*'s old bones keep him warm then I don't see why anybody'd bother him. That's all I've got to say, and if you need it sworn on a missal, that's fine by me.'

The mayor, a small, mealy-mouthed man, shook his head.

'That'll be all, Monsieur Couélan, thank you very much. In fact, it's more than enough. We just wanted to have an idea about this boy, we don't wish him any harm. I'm counting on your discretion.'

Francis Couélan left.

Present in the mayor's office were Nicole Bossard, Hélène Rakoff, and Roger Waille, the staff psychiatrist at the Saint Paul Centre.

'Your interest must be taken into consideration,' continued the mayor, 'but there are also those of the *préfecture:* If this boy is dangerous, then we'd better arrest him immediately.'

Mademoiselle Rakoff raised her hand. 'It's not a question of "arresting" him, Your Honour, but of placing him under medical supervision once more. Ludovic is a patient, not a criminal. In any case, he's not really dangerous. The way to handle him is to treat him with kindness. Believe me, if he sees policemen, that's when he might do something foolish or even run away again, and we'd have to go through a whole song and dance to recapture him.'

The mayor sighed. 'That's very nice, kindness! But I've just learned that he fired a pistol at some young men. And then, I'd like to know exactly what's wrong with the boy. You wrote that he was a mental defective, which can mean quite a number of things. I really must have something more precise for my report.'

Mademoiselle Rakoff turned towards her neighbour. 'Here is the person to answer your questions. Doctor Waille was Ludo's psychiatrist at Saint Paul, and I asked him to accompany us so that you might hear his opinion on this point.'

The doctor began to pontificate peevishly.

'Medically speaking, Ludovic's condition is rather unusual, and somewhat difficult to categorize—the child is retarded and should be confined to an asylum, no doubt about that. In his case, it's the obliteration of the cognitive processes which is quite characteristic. In the adolescent, this deficiency is generally the catalyst for a certain degradation of the adaptive mechanisms, lexia, laterality, all of which is of course quite crippling. Ludovic has mechanized all his complexes at the wrong moment. Due to the absence of the paternal penis and the maternal breast, he was unable to mentalize them in the elaboration of a homogeneous sexuality.'

'Regarding my report, Doctor,' intervened the exasperated mayor, 'could you perhaps provide a brief medical description, two or three words?'

Doctor Waille shot him a withering look. 'In that case, write down "paranoid dysfunction," and that will suffice.'

269

'Well then, that's perfect, Doctor. And now I need to know how Mademoiselle Rakoff plans to retrieve her patient.'

'Through a cunning little stratagem,' she announced with a smile. 'The good Lord will forgive us, and dear Ludo too, I'm sure. We need only send someone out to the boat. Someone he trusts, to suggest that he come for a drive in the car. When he comes round the dunes, the orderlies will be waiting to put him in the ambulance, and that will be that.'

'From a legal standpoint, I am obliged to notify the police.'

'That's fine, only keep them out of sight. Their presence will not interfere with our plan in any way, as long as they keep their distance, and Ludovic will be back at Saint Paul by this evening.'

The mayor made a face. 'All right, let's try it. But we still have to find someone he trusts to go aboard the ship.'

When Francis Couélan arrived at the beach, he found only the scrap merchants at the ship, busy cutting its vitals into metal sheets with oxy-acetylene blowtorches.

'Got to keep at it,' the foreman told him. 'Tide's coming in. Another two hours and we'll be standing in water. The spring tide doesn't fool around!'

'What about the boy,' asked Couélan. 'Where's he?'

'Haven't a clue. Sometimes he hangs around off to one side, watching. Even though there's nothing to see. We don't pay any attention to him, we don't bother him. You never know with loonies. But as to where he is this afternoon, I couldn't say.'

The bow of the *Sanaga* had completely disappeared. A gaping hole revealed its entrails from top to bottom, cleanly dissected by the flames.

'About ten more days should do it! This one has given us a rough time. We've been sweating our brains out!'

Couélan trudged back towards the forest. He would

return later to warn Ludo. Real scum, that village! Including the mayor! Scum, all of them, suspicious characters not worth the last nail in a rotten ship's carcass.

As he reached the edge of the woods, he ran into three policemen, who asked him politely to climb inside a blue van hidden among the pines.

Ludo walked along the shore, bare-chested in the late afternoon sunlight. Ships the colour of smoke passed in the distance, moving out into the shipping lanes. Perhaps he could become a sailor. But first he wanted to see his mother again. He felt that he carried within himself a secret that, once confessed, would clear away all misunderstandings and reconcile them both at last. It was like a memory he could not quite recall. He was on his way back from The Hedges, where he had gone in the vain hope of seeing Nicole again. He was vaguely angry with Micho for having left her, for having allowed himself to be left, for having allowed this new confusion and distress to transform the future into quicksand.

He paused to suck on a tube of condensed milk he had found in his letter-box that morning, along with a packet of gingerbread and two chocolate bars tied together with sticky tape. A short note was attached:

> Please excuse me for yesterday. Amandine loves you very much.
>
> Her mama

He continued down the beach, humming that Amandine loved Ludo very much, something that no one had ever said to him before. He could see the wreck now, swimming in an opalescent haze, a half-freighter sliced down the middle that might have seemed, at a distance, to be under construction. As he drew nearer, his heart sank. The truck was manoeuvring about, the workmen were packing up. They would be there tomorrow, the next day, and the next;

then it would be all over, leaving no trace on the empty sand.

He arrived at the work site. Piranhas, gobbling up an ox. They had taken extra mouthfuls today: the stern-post and bulwarks lay pell-mell on the shingle, where a jumble of scrap metal was spread out like the remains of a kill not even vultures would touch. There was a suffocating smell of metal and burned gases from the torches. Ludo patted the heaps of junk forlornly; they gave off a dull, dead sound. The last blow was the sight of the propeller thrown on to the shore near the stern, a sad trophy of the carnage, the castration of his ship.

Once again he was alone with the Atlantic, alone with the gathering dusk, with the melancholy pleasure of an intimacy that made him one with the universe, and one with every last bolt in that ruined hulk where he had made his home since Christmas.

How many days were left, how many sunsets would he see dissolve into torpor, standing on that very spot?

Inside, nothing had changed. The masked portraits covered the walls of his room. The portrait. The woman behind the hand, the invisible woman, tattooed into the flesh of a ship destined for the blowtorch, that was his emblem, that was him. He ground his fist into the painting with all his strength. He would leave, that was definite. He would never go to a lunatic asylum. He would become a sailor. Couélan said it was easy; in Spain there was always a way to enlist. The only problem was his mother.

He stared miserably at his cabin, at the bed made up with ragged finery scavenged from the dump, the well-polished copper of the porthole, Amandine's faded bouquets, the pebbles, seashells, crabs' heads, the vestiges of so many ebb tides that he would no longer enjoy. He went up on deck in despair.

Leaning his elbows on the gunwale, he squinted at the glittering, windless sea. It was a May evening, languid and warm. The setting sun paved the horizon with sparkling rose-pink scales. He could barely hear the elusive arpeggio of the buoy, while the waves on the reef seemed to float miraculously up in the sky before breaking with a smothered roar. Ludo gazed at the misty shoreline, the sand drained of colour by the twilight, the endless ocean of pines. Consoled by the silence, he was about to return to his room when he saw someone appear on the beach over by the pillbox. Someone was coming straight towards the *Sanaga*, not strolling along, but walking as if with a clear destination in mind. Prudently backing out of sight, Ludo ran to the wheel-house to spy on the intruder.

It was a woman in a sleeveless dress, wearing dark glasses, her hair blowing in the wind. Ludo would have known that walk among a thousand, that quick, nervous stride, and the closer she came the faster his heart beat. He had thought he would see her only in his dreams, but there she was, exploding his past like a cry. Nicole, his mother. She had answered his letter and was finally coming to get him.

He lost sight of her when she reached the hull, then heard her call his name.

Beside himself with emotion, he buried his face in his hands. She must have leaned her head inside the ship; he heard her voice but could not move, the pain in his heart was too great. He tried to answer, but managed only to groan; deafened by the blood pounding in his veins, he fought to keep his balance. Now he could not hear her any more. Ludo dashed to the porthole: delicate purple streaks swept across the sky, the tide was coming in around the ship, and the empty beach was slowly fading into darkness. Where was she? Where was his mother? Sheer panic drove him out of the wheelhouse and down the ladder to his quarters.

There she was, standing in the light, idly examining the bulkheads. She stiffened at the sight of him.

'Well it's about time,' she began, trying to smile. 'I've been looking for you for a good half-hour. Anyway, hello.

273

Well, Ludovic, aren't you going to say hello to your mother?'

Her yellow summer dress with its little string belt was transparent against the light.

'I never thought I'd find myself in a place like this.'

The slanting rays of the sun touched her hair with flecks of gold, gleaming on her bare arms, her ankles, her feet in their delicate leather sandals.

'It might interest you to know that I hurt myself climbing up here, and now there's a stain on my dress, thanks a lot. Whatever put it into your head to live here? It's disgusting, and what a terrible smell! Only you would manage to do something so stupid.' She opened the door of the cabin. 'Is this your room? It's almost tidier than the one you had at The Hedges. What's that supposed to be?' She pointed at Amandine's bald and withered bouquets.

'Flowers,' answered Ludo.

'Flowers? Well they certainly don't look very happy here!'

'You've come to get me?' he asked cautiously.

She looked at him in surprise. 'Yes, how did you know? Well, don't worry about it, everything will be all right.'

'It's nice that you have long hair,' he exclaimed hoarsely after a pause.

Then he saw the look in Nicole's eyes and the illusion of sunshine faded away. It was a nasty look, harsh and disappointed, darting furtively from behind eyelids too heavy with make-up. The voice betrayed its complicity with the eyes in a thousand secret ways, drawing bitterness from the same deep well; tiny wrinkles etched the outline of her mouth through the lipstick.

'You really haven't changed,' she said. 'Even when you were in the attic you were already doing that bit with the big green eyes and the dopey look. You remember? You never let out a single peep. You used to look at me as if I was a sea-lion, and you went round and round in circles just to exasperate me. Oh never mind.'

274

She took a step towards him, moving right in front of the porthole, so that the sun shone like a fireball behind her hair. Her red hair. She was still speaking in a gloomy voice, talking about Peilhac, The Hedges, what torture it was to have a child who was not only stupid but sly, incapable of being nice to her, always causing trouble. Her mouth twisted into a sneer, but Ludo was not listening to her words, lulled as he was by the sound of her voice. He was stirred by a passionate sadness. As he looked at his mother, he sensed a secret as yet unknown to him rise to his lips, a secret he knew must be revealed there, in that fragile space where Nicole had suddenly taken the only step that had ever drawn them together.

'Why didn't you come,' he burst out, 'why didn't you come at Christmas?'

Nicole's mouth fell open. 'At Christmas? That's a good one! I had plenty of other things on my mind, believe me! But you, of course, you only thought of yourself, as usual! Listen, enough of this, I came here to speak to you, to speak to you for your own good.'

'It's true we're going to leave together you and me?' he whispered softly.

'Yes, it is, really. Just wait a minute!'

She grew more impatient with every word, looking nervously at the paintings, all those hands, all those women lined up, impossible to see clearly — it really was the work of a madman.

'Even though you ruined my life, it's time you and I made peace with each other.'

But there was no peace in her eyes, no hope, no forgiveness, despite her attempts at tenderness.

'That sullen look you had in the morning when you came to wake me up — I was always afraid you were plotting some dirty trick. You never answered questions, you were always so high-and-mighty . . . When I think that you never called me "*Mama*" . . . And you expected me to answer your letters? Forget it!'

275

Breakfast at The Hedges. The rocking-chair. Nicole in her languid, provocative poses, her black stockings, and always that poisonous little phrase: 'Say "*Mama*," Ludo . . .' It was quite true that he had never answered her.

'Even at Saint Paul Centre you managed somehow to keep spoiling everything for me,' continued Nicole. 'You never really wanted to change. You never tried. You might have been able to get well if you'd put your mind to it just a little. When I think of all that money squandered for nothing! Not to mention that horrible business with the fire, which cost us so much . . .'

'And you,' he murmured, looking at her beseechingly, 'you never kissed me, never hugged me, never touched me, you never loved me . . .'

'What are you saying, Ludovic? Please don't start all that mumbling again, and with that horrible beard I can't understand a word. You're so pig-headed! It wasn't any kind of a life having you around the house. I don't even know if you realize that I had to marry an old man because of you. I know you liked him, and he liked you, but he's old and selfish and for your information we're getting divorced. Anyway, that's not your problem. You know, Mademoiselle Rakoff is very fond of you. She was hurt when you ran away. Since she's very kind-hearted she's willing to take you back for another try. So don't make any trouble, please. And besides, I'm sure it's a relief for you. You weren't really planning to live on here like some sort of gypsy . . .'

Ludo flinched. 'Why . . .' he said, in a lost voice.

Looking deep into his eyes, Nicole had taken his hand and placed it gently on her cheek. She did her best to smile.

'Come on,' she murmured softly, 'let's forget the past, why don't we? I've suffered a lot because of you, but nothing's the same as before, I'm getting married again. We're friends from now on. Say "*Mama*" Ludo . . .'

With his hand trembling against her face, he heard himself answer faintly: '*Mama.*' A sob caught in his throat, he said it louder: '*Mama.*' She had closed her eyes. Ludo watched his hand stroke the cheeks, the lips, the forehead of the woman who had always refused him the slightest caress, the slightest token of love. The unspoken word, the unknown secret, the stifled cry unleashed blinding forces within Ludo and filled him with an agonizing euphoria. He began to shout: '*Mama, Mama,*' his voice growing ever louder, terrifying Nicole.

'Let me go, Ludo! You really are crazy, just like your father. Completely crazy!'—but he kept shouting: '*Mama,*' like a cry for help, and seemed unable to stop himself.

He had pushed Nicole, scratching and shrieking, back against the paintings on the partition. Pressing in on her, he saw his hand grip his mother's face, saw her eyes wide with horror between his fingers, her hair red with sunlight, and he chanted '*Mama, Mama,*' as he beat her head against the steel. Since she was still struggling he let his hand drop to her neck, stupefied to see unmasked before him the portrait that had tormented him since childhood. In a burst of happiness he began to squeeze, with all his strength until a tremor coursed through his body, releasing him only in orgasm.

He stared in amazement at the corpse on the floor, his mother, her eyes wide open, her dress and hair all messy and tangled. He knelt down in a breathless panic. Now *they* would surely come, to take his mother from him yet again, to take him, to lock the madman away for ever, he would never see her again. He had to hurry. Ludo took Nicole in his arms and carried her down to the engine-room, hugging her convulsively and planting little kisses in her hair. Exhausted, he kept repeating '*Mama, Mama,*' but the word was already drifting away. Still holding his mother, he staggered to the hole in the ship's side, looked down at the waves slapping against the hull, and let himself fall with her into the sea. Swimming with his right hand, he held her tightly with her long hair floating on the waves gently brushing his mouth. He mumbled words of passion and struck out towards the open water, quickly, as if hurrying to a rendezvous. A leaden stillness lay over the mirror-smooth sea. A band of mauve darkened the horizon. The buoy's red top danced to the north, its plaintive wail drowned by the dull rumble of the breakers. Ludo looked back at the shore fading into night, at the sombre line of pine trees blurring the outline of the wreck. Nicole weighed heavily on his arm. They were going to sleep in the sun's bed; life would never separate them again. But although he had escaped with her and knew that he would never go to a lunatic asylum, knew that the two of them were saved, the sadness he had eluded for a moment returned to claim him. He began to feel ill, to feel pain, in his heart and his whole body, he began to breathe heavily and shivered with fear when he glimpsed the rollers whitening the darkness ahead. 'I'm frightened,' he whispered, wrapping both arms round his mother; then he let himself sink down into the currents heading straight for the reef.